Kissed by Madness

MARCHEL DENISE

Cover illustrated by Bonnye Brown

Cover design by Sharif Wilson

ISBN: 0615849415
ISBN-13: 978-0615849416

DEDICATION

In memory of Brenda Reed Fisher.
My star in heaven.

MARCHEL DENISE

"My mother's a woman. I mean, I loved my mother to death. I ain't gonna do nothin' no more to nobody else than somebody might do to my mother, man."

Ike Turner, *Esquire Magazine*, December 2007

MARCHEL DENISE

DAY

In heaven, there is a special place for babies. It smells sweet–like talcum powder. We don't have wings and we don't have bows and arrows like they picture us in the *other* world. We still have our same tiny bodies, but we no longer see things through the eyes of those who only breathed life for a few days or months, or maybe even a year. We understand the difference between good and evil–between sinner and saint. We are the voices of the *innocent*.

Some of us were called home early. Others of us were pushed. Either way, we are now angels. When we receive our new minds and moves, some of us are told the reasons why we arrived earlier than our scheduled dates. But there is no sadness in this revelation. No memories. We were only pilgrims in *that* life. Here is true living.

In my head, I am all grown up now. I feel no pain. Only joy. I am happy. I play and laugh. I laugh and play. I can run. I can jump. I can clap my hands and turn cartwheels on the clouds without getting dizzy. I stay naked as the day I was born. I am not ashamed. If I want to, I can part the clouds and look down. I can choose to see *that* life.

Today, I look down and I'm curious as to why the grownups beneath the clouds are staring down at me. Only, it is not me they're looking at, merely my shell. But how can they know that? I watch them stare. They are all dressed in black and I wonder why? I see them cry and I wonder why? *Don't cry for me.* I want to scream to them, but nothing comes out. I'm staring down at them staring at me. I see my shell stuffed into a wooden box, ornate as it is, but still nothing but a box. Inside this box, I am dressed in a white suit with a shirt the color of the sky in front of me and a matching tie. I have on small booties. My feet surely could not feel the clouds in those shoes. Not a single curl on my head is out of place. The body I see below–it does not move. It does not skip. It cannot turn cartwheels in the clouds. It is lifeless. Yet, I am life.

I reach down to touch a piece of the fabric on the shiny white suit, but I can't feel anything. All I come up with are fistfuls of cold air. I know its cold because my fingers are turning red. I don't feel any discomfort though.

Down there, I can see about ten or so people gathered around my shell in the brown box. There are a sprinkling of other folks as well. An old man dressed in a black robe with purple stitching around the collar stands above the box that does not contain me. His skin is rough like the underside of worn shoes and his hair is missing. He is looking down at the Good Book, reciting the scriptures that I already know by heart. I make a game to see who can say the scriptures faster. I win every time. I don't have to look down at the papers of the Good Book that are rustling in the wind in his hands.

One man I notice in particular. He is blessed with natural beauty, a stout athletic body and deep hazel eyes. He never looks up from the box. His lips are quivering and he is bent over, heaving. *Daddy?* Although I was told about my earthly parents, I have never really looked at them—until now. Here, I have spiritual parents and spiritual brothers and sisters. They are all I know. In them, I know love.

Right next to the tall man, stands a slender woman. Her hair is pulled back into a bun so severe it seems to lift her eyebrows up to the top of her forehead. She shares the same eyes as the man who is now leaning his entire body onto her slight frame. His heaviness bends their bodies into a question mark. *Aunt Sasha.* I know this right away because I remember seeing her on the day I was born. She was the first person my eyes ever laid eyes on. A slightly taller woman stands to her right. She stands straight, regal-like, her back pressed against an imaginary ironing board, and in her eyes I find kindness. Although I cannot feel her blood flowing threw me, she cries like family. I want her to stop. I reach down to wipe her tears, yet they still flow. She cannot feel my touch. A man about the same height as my father—I figure this out now—has his hands stuffed inside the pockets of his all-black trousers. He is flipping change with his fingers in his pockets, and he does not want to be here. He never looks at the box. I see through his eyes.

I see my grandmother surrounded by two men on each side of her. She is weeping, but I'm not sure if it's because of me. She looks out into the distance and I know she is thinking about a past that I cannot see or feel. But I know it pains her dearly.

I see an older couple too. I feel their blood in me and I know they too are my grandparents—Vernon and Olivia Thompson. They do not cry. Maybe it is because there is no longer any love between them. How can they feel something they know nothing about? Their daughter, Netta, stands close to them. She does not have kind eyes. I can see this even though her face is partially hidden by a large pair of dark sunglasses that mock the lukewarm sun. Still, she is beautiful. But her beauty pales in comparison to my mom. Even in the dinginess of the worn black dress she wears, I see her light. She is the only person who is not looking down at the box. A wall of a man stands behind her, guarding her. She is looking up at me. She sees me and I feel a twinge of something that I have never experienced before. Something like pain. Briefly, I am able to shoulder her burdens. When I reach down to touch her face, she turns and allows me to stroke it. *Mommy!* She closes her eyes and gives way to my touch and she smiles. Only no one can see because they are too busy staring down at the box.

With my touch, I send her love. I know nothing else to give to her right now.

"Ashes to ashes. Dust to dust." The preacher man says this as he sprinkles pieces of dirt onto my shell in the box. I watch as he does this. Again, I wonder why?

I am here!

I am here!

Come join me!

It is then that I realize that I cannot explain to them, my family down below, that I have so much gloriousness inside of me all the time here, so I stop looking at them from among the clouds and I skip to find my brothers and sisters. The fluffiness still tickles my toes.

3

MARCHEL DENISE

PROLOGUE

Wayne Miner Court, 1983

"Fight! Fight! Fight!"

"Awww, man! PUNK HIM!"

Ranford "RJ" Ellis, Jr. clenched his boy-sized fists awkwardly. The chanting around him grew louder, rowdier. He and Edwin faced each other outside the Shop-N-Go corner store as the setting sun threatened to erase daylight. Summer sweat began rolling down the back of RJ's quivering knees.

When RJ opened his eyes, he saw a flash of the store with its barred windows and quarter-sized hole that had grown cracks like spider veins racing across one side of the glass entrance to the other. He also got a glimpse of the store's illuminated sign that always flashed "OPEN" even when it was closed for business. Behind that, he could see two streetlights that had been purposely busted by local hoods to help the night's darkness kidnap the innocence of boys like RJ, who was five months shy of his eleventh birthday.

They stood on the corner of Ninth Street and Woodland Avenue in Wayne Miner Court, the trampled namesake of Wayne Miner, a black soldier from Kansas City who was the last American soldier to die in World War I. RJ thought he'd be killed too as he blew out short puffs of air while holding up his arms to block Edwin's blows, which were spiraling like an out-of-control windmill.

"Come on, RJ! Man, you gonna let him push you around like that?!"

Truth be told, RJ was finding it hard to stay on his toes. He was terrified of tripping over his own shadow. His legs felt as mushy as the oatmeal he'd eaten for breakfast, or maybe that oatmeal was rising from the underside of his knotted stomach, up to his throat. Whatever it was, RJ knew his date with the concrete beneath him was imminent. His body began swaying and his head spun just as it had a few weeks ago when he and Edwin had shared their first stolen sips of malt liquor together.

"Yo, little man, you 'bout to get knocked the hell out!"

"That's enough! Break it up! I said…BREAK IT UP!"

RJ turned in the direction of the familiar gruff voice as a strong hand grabbed him by the neckline of his metallic blue t-shirt.

Edwin's father, Reverend Odom, grabbed both boys and shoved them away from the crowd and each other. The boys were like paperweights in his large hands. Reverend Odom stopped and turned in the direction of the crowd, which was now sighing and gesturing in obvious displeasure that the evening's entertainment had ended so abruptly.

"Y'all ought to be 'shamed of yourselves, every last one of you. Watchin' these two boys, these friends, knock each other senseless. Ain't you got no shame, no sense of decency? NOW GET!" he shouted. His deep baritone voice cracked through the summer air like lightning and parted the onlookers like the Red Sea. Their Moses had spoken. Through the grunts, jeers, and pouts, Reverend Odom pushed forward, never loosening his grip on the boys.

RJ's eyes glistened. Respect was hard to come by in Wayne Miner, and even harder to keep without an illegal substance or weapon of some sort in your possession. RJ knew the reverend owned the neighborhood's respect, just by the bravado in his voice. At that instant, he was in awe of the man. RJ thought about his own father, and had he been older or more mature, he would have recognized the twinge of jealousy that had formed in the pit of his stomach, a twinge that rapidly grew into a stab of all-out envy.

RJ's father, Ranford "Randy" Ellis Sr., was a brick of a burnt-toast colored man, whose very presence prompted RJ to feel that at any moment he was going to shit himself. Each morning, Randy inhaled two menthol cigarettes for breakfast and gargled it down with malt liquor. Cursing was his second language. It was never, "Bring me the milk from the refrigerator, RJ." It was, "RJ, bring me the goddamn milk from the refrigerator, and you bet not spill a motherfuckin' drop of it on the floor either." It was just his nature. Randy's language made it hard for father and son to bond.

The question of why his mother, Carmen, continued to put up with his father was too farfetched for his young mind to fathom. RJ had witnessed several of his parents' arguments, which usually turned into some form of physical altercation, only to be negated later by the squeaking of the bedsprings. The sound of his mother's soft moans emanating from the walls of the small two-bedroom apartment could be heard long into the thick of the suffocating night.

Half Puerto Rican and half Afro-Cuban, Carmen was the neighborhood MILF, even before the racy term was officially coined. She was five feet, five inches and one hundred twenty-seven pounds of caramelized spice simmering in too-short shorts or tight jeans, wild-colored halters, square-tipped fingernails painted the color of dried blood, and long saucy curls that draped to the center of her back.

Most times Carmen was as fiery as her husband, with a sharp tongue to match, but she also had a softer side. That side would still cut the meat on her son's plate – when they could afford meat – and trace her long fingernails through his unruly 'fro. The side that would visit the bedroom he shared with his sister, Sasha, and sit at the end of his bed, oftentimes with a busted lip, a black eye, or visible bruises over her entire body, as her short breaths broke through their silence with all the intensity of a brick shattering through the room's window. That side told RJ to be home before the streetlights came on, even though she knew the street thugs and dealers purposely busted the fixtures so their dirt could take place in total darkness. But seeing that side of her was about as rare as finding a witness to testify against the destroyers of the streetlights.

RJ felt Reverend Odom's hand on his shoulder. The simple weight from the touch of the reverend's fingers was like the comforting sensation of the purple taffy under his tongue. RJ recalled the cause of the earlier mayhem: one purple Now and Later candy. The swelling knot on the left side of his forehead served as a testament to his purple passion gone astray. They weren't fighting over the green candies that left RJ's tongue with a sour aftertaste, or the yellow ones he'd suck on briefly before spitting them into the palm of his hand and rolling them around until the texture of the squared-shaped taffy became gummy and stuck to his fingers. No. Edwin wanted the purple taffy. The ones RJ loved so much.

"What's the matter with you two boys?" Reverend Odom leaned down so close to RJ that he could feel the ends of the reverend's wooly, salt-and-pepper moustache touch the top of his still-sweaty forehead.

Reverend Odom didn't wait for an answer. Instead he gestured for the boys to follow him into the basement office of Mt. Ebenezer Church of Christ.

"Hmm … well, one of you answer me." Reverend Odom spun around between them as if there were five boys present instead of two. His eyebrows arched higher.

"Tell me why two friends who've practically known each other their whole lives would act like common hooligans out in the street for everyone to see?"

"Pop, I...we...," Edwin stammered. His right eye grew puffier and darker with each passing minute.

"You what, boy?"

"RJ said I took his candy..."

"You did take my candy, or else your tongue wouldn't be purple right now."

"Candy? This whole thing is over candy?" The reverend turned a stern gaze in Edwin's direction. "Son, I'm raising you to be a man – one above reproach. I'm not raising you to be a common street thug. Your mother and I expect more from you. And I expect more from you RJ," he said as RJ's forehead began to hurt more.

"Today, it's candy," he continued. "What's it going to be about tomorrow? Huh? Go on up and polish the pews."

The boys moaned in unison.

"Pick up any trash, and make sure the Bibles are straightened and evenly distributed among the rows," he commanded. "I figure by the time you're finished, it'll be dark. So Edwin, you will walk RJ home and come on back. While you're working, I expect you to put all of this nonsense behind you, and that's non-negotiable."

Their sneakers squeaked against the wood-paneled steps as RJ and Edwin ascended the narrow corridor into the small chapel, whose mere presence mocked the abundance of liquor stores, pawnshops, hooker corners, and dope houses surrounding it.

It occurred to RJ that he could just walk straight through the double doors and head home, leaving Edwin to suffer the consequences of his father's punishment. But that would be like defying God, and although he didn't know who God was, he figured it would be a bad thing to do. So RJ stayed and wiped down the pews with tattered dust cloths on the opposite side of Edwin in silence.

Occasionally, RJ would step back from the pew, rest the cloth at his side, and fix his hazel eyes on Edwin, who kept moving steadfastly from seat to seat while muttering something incoherent.

"How's your nose?" Edwin finally asked.

RJ exhaled. "It's all right. Stopped running. How's your eye?"

"Hurts like hell."

That did it. Their laughter resounded throughout the church as stained glass angels and a white Jesus looked down from high above.

"Man, I thought you weren't ever gonna stop."

"Yeah, I got some good licks in, though," Edwin boasted.

"That's why you were screaming like a little bitch," RJ teased.

"Shhh…my father."

"Oww! Don't make me laugh again." RJ winced, holding tight to his ribcage.

With their friendship cemented again, they walked their aching bodies back to RJ's building. A taller and much older boy walked ahead of them, holding a large radio with vibrating speakers and a mass of D-sized batteries atop his shoulders, making him look headless. The Curtis Blow song played so loudly it seemed to shake the foundation of every one of the seven high-rise buildings and drown out the familiar blare of police sirens, gun shots, and glass shattering.

"Man, when I get some money I'm gonna buy a box bigger than that one. Gonna have beats heard all the way in St. Louis," Edwin said.

"You know your father ain't gonna let you have no box," RJ said, while reaching down to pick up a rusty dime hidden beneath some broken glass just beside an abandoned mauve-colored Malibu Classic with three flat tires. The sticker on the dusty back window read, *TOW NOTICE Kansas City Police Department.*

Edwin stopped outside building number five, the last high-rise encircled by a scattering of town homes. They exchanged high-fives. Edwin flinched when a booming sound exploded nearby. Most sounds in Wayne Miner were reason enough to keep your guard up.

"All right man, well, I'll holler at you tomorrow," RJ said.

"Cool," Edwin said, his back already turned in the opposite direction.

Once inside the building, RJ scurried to make it past the unknown of the dark hallways to the two-bedroom apartment he shared with his mother, father, and sister.

With the elevator broken again, it was crapshoot what he'd find while taking the stairs up to the seventh floor. It was amazing to him the things he had seen in total darkness.

His heart thudded loudly inside his ears as he managed to arrive unscathed on the floor of his apartment, opening the door of the stairway.

"Motherfucka, you think I signed up for this shit? Your ass can't keep a job. You damn drunk!" The all-too familiar voice overshadowed the beating of his heart. RJ felt as if he were watching himself in slow motion as he hesitantly made his way closer to his apartment. The yelling back and forth between his parents could be heard clearly, while Michael Jackson played a couple of decibels below the shouting match.

Cause we're the party people, night and day... The lyrics seemed misplaced in the background.

"That's why I need me a real man. A man who knows how to handle his business. A man who knows how to treat a woman. Not your dumb ass!"

...Living crazy that's the only way...

"Bitch, shut. The. Fuck. Up!"

Slap! Crash! Thud!

...So, tonight better leave your nine-to-five up on the shelf...

Three of his father's homeboys scrambled from inside RJ's apartment like roaches, leaving the door wide open. The smell of marijuana, burnt bacon grease, and grain alcohol trailed behind them.

"I'm tired of this shit, Randy! Get your damn hands off me! This is the last time you will ever..."

"Ever what? What, bitch?"

The sound of more smacking, banging, and thumping could be heard from within the apartment.

...And just enjoy yourself...

The door propelled RJ inside. Sucked him inside to find Carmen holding his father's hunting rifle so tight that he could see the outlines of the veins in her hand. A half-smoked cigarette dangled from the corner of her mouth. Her face looked like a game of connect-the-dots from the blood, sweat, and swelling. His father's hands were balled into tight fists.

Boom!

RJ watched as his father charged toward her, even as his white wife-beater turned more crimson by the second. "Bitch, I'ma kill you!"

Boom!

The second impact sent Randy flying toward the back wall of the apartment. His massive body collapsed to the green shag carpet, taking a black dining room chair down with him. His right hand still held tight to a can of malt liquor. Shock filled his hardened eyes.

RJ stood unable to move. Sasha sat underneath the wooden table in the small kitchen, shaking in a puddle of her own urine.

Still holding the rifle tightly and with a blank stare, Carmen turned to face RJ. "See, RJ. I always told you niggas ain't shit."

RANFORD

RJ's body jerked suddenly. "Huuuh," he cried out from where he lay in total darkness. As he gripped the sheets tightly with his clammy hands, sweat exuded from every pore of his body. RJ's breathing was erratic. A buzz of color exploded inside his head so brightly that it mocked the darkness. *It's just a nightmare.*

Instinctively, RJ reached to turn on the bedside lamp on the nightstand. Nothing. He fumbled again. Only after his eyes had adjusted to the blackness of the room did he realize he was not in his own environment: something was off. He closed his eyes and rubbed his thumbs against his temples, then his eyes. *Where the hell am I?* Only after RJ opened his eyes the second time was he able to make out the faint outlines of various frilly houseplants everywhere. Some were big. Some small. All were overgrown.

A Siamese cat sauntered close enough for RJ to see the eerie ocean-blue of its eyes. The cat arched its back and hissed at the sound of RJ's sudden movements. *I fuckin' hate cats.* When he smelled the distinct scent of fruit-flavored candles and air freshener, he knew he had invaded a female's space, and most likely her body, too. He still didn't know which female.

A body moved beside him, shifting beneath the covers and causing a ripple effect. He turned in the direction of the tide. In the darkness, he could make out a heap of long, straight hair. A soft snore erupted from a nose and mouth he could not see or remember. As the mass of hair turned on its back, a section of the coverlet slipped from its form, revealing a silhouette of two momentous assets that made him instantly hard. It was then that he remembered.

After stepping out of the terminal at Kansas City International Airport, RJ had been standing at the baggage carousel waiting for his oversized Mulholland Brothers duffel bag. He had just returned from an extended weekend visit with his longtime friend Edwin Odom and his new wife Justine in Chicago. He eyed his Movado watch and sighed heavily with each passing second that his duffel bag didn't appear. In the one brief second he had taken his eyes off his watch, she walked past him – a vision in Apple Bottom jeans and a cream-colored sheer blouse, whose buttons screamed to let loose all they contained. Why he hadn't noticed her on the plane was a mystery. Maybe it was because she hadn't been sitting with him in first class, or maybe he'd been too busy scribbling angry comments on a certain teacher's response card about RJ's charter school. Whatever the case, he had let her slip by then, but not for long. RJ ran his hands through his low-cut wavy hair, fixed his hazel eyes on the woman, nodded in recognition, and sidled up to her. That was all it took.

Janell? Jasmine? Gina? RJ couldn't remember the mass of hair's name. Escape was the only thing on his mind as he emerged from the abyss of floral sheets and placed his feet softly on the carpeted floor. Not sure where his clothing was, he had no choice but to bend his six-foot, two-inch athletic frame on all fours and crawl until his hands eventually came across his tailored black trousers and button-down shirt. Business casual. Wherever RJ went he had to dress the part of a man going somewhere important, a man who was doing something worth a damn. Even if it was just to slam down a few drinks with an old friend.

Now where's my damn bag? As RJ slipped into his clothes the cat inched closer, wanting to protect its owner from having to wake up to unanswered questions as to why he didn't stay or say goodbye. Trying not to look into the feline's eyes, RJ swatted it away. But the cat moved in closer, baring its claws. RJ kicked it, watching it hurtle to the far end of the room with a distressed meow.

He finally spotted his luggage beside the bedroom door. He heard another tussle from beneath the covers just as he made a mad dash toward freedom.

The neon clock on the dash of RJ's black Lincoln MKS read four a.m.: just enough time for him to get to the Northland home he shared with his wife, Honor. Then he would go for his morning jog and eat his usual breakfast of three egg whites, whole grain toast with organic grape jelly, and coffee sweetened with agave nectar before heading to the Urban Achievers Academy to greet his kindergarten-through-twelfth-grade students. *My students.* The mere thought caused a faint smile to spread across RJ's face, which now sported a five o'clock shadow at this early morning hour.

He was almost three years into his appointment as superintendent of the charter school. RJ had single-handedly made sure the standardized test scores and overall grades had risen to the top of the Kansas City School District, a district plagued by lack of accreditation, underachievement, a merry-go-round of superintendents, and high dropout rates. He'd also just gotten word that, once again, all of his seniors had graduated from the college preparatory academy, many of them with honors, and were moving on to attend two-year or four-year institutions—a fact he planned to tout heavily at the board meeting to be held that evening. RJ was getting it done and every achievement, no matter how large or small, would bode well on his way to district superintendent, city councilman, mayor, and, eventually, Capitol Hill. Yes, his life would definitely be a rags to riches story. A poor kid from the streets of the now-defunct Wayne Miner, he had moved to the south side of Chicago and, after struggling to make it to the top of his class at Loyola University, had earned both bachelor's and master's degrees in education, along with a doctorate degree at Washington University. RJ felt he'd proved all the naysayers wrong, the ones who said he was too black or not black enough, too thuggish or too uppity, or too young to head a new charter school at age thirty-eight.

Yeah, and I still look good. RJ chuckled to himself as Jay Z blared from the stereo speakers and he pressed the opener to his three-car garage.

"Motha…" RJ shouted as he slammed on the brakes, bringing the car to an abrupt halt at the sight before him. The car's tires skidded loudly. His eyes took in the lifeless body of a female wearing tattered jeans and a crumbled red tank top. Its confetti straps hung loosely around her perfectly honey-kissed shoulders and the tank rode up her torso, revealing a belly piercing that dangled and sparkled in the early morning sun.

Sasha!

RJ threw himself from the car and raced to where his sister lay on the ground, her head resting on the concrete of his four-story home. Her eyelids were closed and her mouth parted slightly, showing a glint of the gold outline on one of her front teeth. As RJ moved in closer, he covered his mouth with the crook of his elbow. A potent mixture of alcohol, tobacco, and something smoky he couldn't discern filled his nose.

RJ bent down and tapped lightly on her bare shoulder. No response. He continued, each tap becoming harder until he finally just slapped her, taking pleasure in the sudden movement of her body and the shift of Sasha's head. He grabbed Sasha by her shoulders and shook her like her body was an endless store of pennies being sprung from a piggy bank.

"Sasha! Goddammit, open your eyes! Sasha!"

She slumped forward, pressing her petite frame against his large hands. Sasha coughed and cracked her eyes open. Hazel madness gazed at hazel sadness.

"What's up, bro," she mumbled in a voice only a gnat could hear. Then she reached to scratch her nose, but her hand seemed to lose its sense of direction along the way. She opted to rest it on the back of her head instead.

"My head hurts, RJ," she said, their universal code for *take care of me now just like you always do.* And that's what he did.

RJ lifted his sister's frail body into his never-miss-a-day-in-the-gym arms and carried her up the stairs to his oversized Southern-style porch. The key to the French doors led them both into the house – rich in every detail, from the brown marble flooring and alphabetized jazz collection, to the original Joysmith paintings and labeled organic-cereal containers atop the stainless steel refrigerator.

The small of her back caved against his hand as he laid Sasha down on his black leather sectional.

"So where's the wicked witch of the Midwest?" Sasha asked.

"Don't talk about my wife like that."

Sasha snickered a short, quick burst of breath before her head fell back onto the leather sofa.

"My head hurts so bad, RJ," she muttered again.

RJ covered Sasha's shivering body with one the nearby fleece throws and headed into the bathroom to find aspirin, then into the kitchen for some bottled spring water. RJ stared at his sister as he sat down beside her, aspirin and water in hand. Her eyes closed, he was reminded of the time he had taken her with him to Edwin's apartment in the midst of another one of their parents' typhoon brawls. Though it had been peaceful all day, RJ had sensed an eerie energy bouncing from room to room. The calm before the storm, a presence unknown to humans but one that dogs can sense a mile out. On that day RJ had felt *it.* He sniffed the assaulting storm approaching as sure as he'd had the arthritic knee or itching palm of a man much older.

Harm was in the air.

Sure enough, just as they'd sat down at the dinner table, Randy made an offhanded comment about the rice being overcooked, darkening the clouds.

"You think I give a shit about what you think?" Carmen had screamed, rice suddenly being thrown like arsenal from across the table.

"Woman, why you think you're screaming at me in my goddamn house?!" RJ watched as Randy had left the table in a fury that sent his chair spinning up against the wall behind him, and knocked the dinner table on its front end, sending tiny portions of rice and fried pork chops to the floor.

RJ grabbed Sasha, who couldn't have been more than three or four years old at the time, swung her body up on his hip, and carried her down the seven flights of steps, across the courtyard, and straight into Edwin's house. Edwin's father, Reverend Odom, opened the door and allowed them inside without question. Only when they were safely inside, did RJ release Sasha. He was shocked to find she'd fallen asleep in his arms during the walk over to Edwin's. Spittle dripped from her mouth onto his shoulder, but he didn't mind. Despite her slobber, he saw peace. It would be the first of many nights they would spend at his childhood friend's home.

Back then she was this boney nothing of a girl with an omnipresent unkempt ponytail. Far from that girl now, Sasha had become the small but curvaceous thirty-something woman before him, with long wild brown curls that had flicks of auburn highlights and a top that revealed the tattoo of a broken heart above her right breast. *What had she taken this time? What had she inhaled, smoked, ingested, or shot into herself?* Trying to chase away his own demons, RJ had no idea when and if this hell would let up. A wave of heaviness washed over him and he ached desperately for his morning run to ease the weight of his ills, to run from his past. He turned to head up the spiral staircase and toward the master bedroom to change into his running attire, but not before Sasha grabbed his hand, startling him.

"How do you do it, RJ?" she asked, her eyes pleading for an answer.

"Do what?"

Sasha's red-rimmed eyes grew wider. Her arms reached up from beneath the fleece cover. "All this…like it never fuckin' happened. I mean look at you. You should be just as messed up as I am, but YOU'RE NOT!"

RJ stared down at Sasha for a moment. Then he too looked around, taking in his surroundings as if for the first time. He would not have this conversation. Not now. Not ever.

"Sasha, there are no excuses in life. You're thirty-two years old. GET OVER IT! I'm going to get changed for my run. When I get back, I expect to find you gone. I don't care where the hell you go. JUST GO! And don't come back until you get your shit in order."

16

RJ's chest was heaving visibly. He decided against going upstairs to the bedroom and risking the chance of waking his wife. Instead, he opted to change into the spare running gear that he kept in the downstairs office.

"Shit," he muttered, realizing that all his toiletries were still in his bag in the trunk of his car. He couldn't even brush his teeth, and he would need his shaving kit when he returned. This thought prompted him to rub his hands across his cheeks, chasing the shadows. He grabbed a pair of his spare running shoes, a clean pair of shorts, and a grey tank from the small office closet. After throwing them across the chair, RJ sat on the edge of the desk, removed his shirt, and then slowly unbuckled his Coach belt. The weight on his chest began to crush him as the mountain of his own bottled-up emotions threatened to erupt and come to the surface. *How do you do it? How do you do it?* RJ glanced at himself in the mirror that hung on the wall, questioning the reflection staring back at him. He wanted desperately to ease the heaviness.

"Aaaaah!" he cried out. In one sweeping motion, a fraternity paperweight, a large silver-accented vase, and a few of his basketball medals shattered. Loose change scattered to all four corners of the floor as a silver change bowl was sent flying to the other end of the room, hitting the wall with a rugged thud.

"RJ, are you all right?! What's going on in there?" Sasha pounded on the outside of the bedroom door. "RJ?"

"Get the hell out of my house! NOW!"

HONOR

Honor Ellis peeked out over downtown Kansas City from her floor-to-ceiling window on the twenty-third floor of City Center Square and wondered why the sight that had enthralled her for the past four years now made her dizzy. Her stomach muscles tightened and developed butterflies the size of boulders. It had happened all of the sudden and without warning a few months ago: One day Honor looked outside and felt that at any moment she would hurl herself to the fate of the Gods below and kiss the eco-friendly hybrid car beneath her. Whenever Honor dared to glance out the window now, she feared accidentally tripping and plummeting through the glass with only the street below her to break her fall. And that wasn't all. Lately she'd become a knot of frayed nerves, jumping at the slightest of sounds. The "attacks" were beginning to claim her body and soul, threatening to crack her exterior as a strong, poised black woman, the image she had cultivated and silently promised to always uphold.

The window reflected a bigger picture of things beyond her control, things she feared would haunt her forever. So unless she had clients visiting, Honor kept the almost-sheer, mauve-colored shades tightly drawn and their remote control close by her side at all times. It was not the total escape she longed for, but it was enough to stifle her nerves and help her deal with the corporate lynching she encountered at the insurance firm on an almost daily basis.

It was the office and what it represented. Everything about it screamed mid-level, reminding her that although she possessed a bachelor's degree in political science from the University of Missouri and an MBA from Tulane University, she still did not mesh with the boys in the pinstripes—the ones with offices on the coveted twenty-sixth floor.

Even though she had the degrees and enough experience to rival the suited-up foursome, Honor was never given her due credit at the London & Schmidt Insurance Agency. Truth be told, Honor was sure all the clients who she'd personally brought into the company over the years would love to know that London was merely a figurehead now, on his deathbed with pancreatic cancer—no doubt fueled by his evilness. Schmidt was a drunk who rarely showed his face at the office anymore, opting instead to spend his days in a drunken stupor at the Northland casinos. He blew his biweekly salary on his gambling habit and frequent extravagant purchases for his girlfriend, fifteen years his junior, who forced him to pop Viagra like they were after-dinner mints.

It occurred to her then that perhaps the boys in the tailor-made suits didn't promote her to director of communications and marketing because they knew her secrets. Honor nervously ran her hands through her perfectly coifed shoulder-length bob that she kept dyed the color of midnight with slight hints of sunrise.

She stroked her French-manicured nails over her form-fitting, sleeveless black dress, which accented the athletic curves of her five-foot, six-inch body. She'd worn the dress to work in the hopes that it would lift her spirits and make her feel sexy; instead, she felt exposed. She caught a sudden chill. Getting goose bumps, she reached for her matching black sweater.

The office phone jarred Honor from her thoughts. She sighed when she saw the name flash across the caller ID, and she contemplated not answering. *Breathe. Just breathe*, she told herself.

"Honor Ellis."

"Hey, baby. How's your day going? I'd thought we'd eat out tonight…try out that new Italian restaurant around the corner you've been bugging me about."

Honor hesitated. "But I already took the salmon out last night. It'll spoil in the fridge if I don't cook it tonight."

"So let it spoil. Buy some more tomorrow. I want to take my best gal out to dinner."

"S-s-sure. Sounds good." She knew her enthusiasm did not sound the least bit sincere.

"Great. So what time shall I expect you?"

Honor glanced at the digital clock on her imitation cherry oak desk. Three twenty-five. *Shit.*

"Should be around five thirty, depending on traffic. You know how that goes." *Please God let there be a ten-car pileup on the highway after work.*

"Sounds good, baby. I'll see you then."

"Okay."

"Baby?"

"Yes."

"You know I love you, right?"

"I know. I love you, too, RJ." Honor's hand shook slightly, causing the phone to narrowly miss the cradle as she slammed it down.

Almost two hours later, Honor was sitting in her forest green Toyota Prius letting Fred Hammond's singing drown out her thoughts. She had just ventured onto Interstate 70 when her iPhone beeped a second time.

"Hey, baby."

"Hey."

"You on your way?"

Honor glanced at the clock on the dashboard. How long had she'd been in the car? Ten minutes? Barely enough time to pass gas and let the scent escape from the window.

"Yes, I am on my way," she replied slowly. "Should be there around the same time."

"Okay. Hurry up. I'm starving."

I'm scared. "I'll get there as soon as I can," she answered.

No sooner had she hit the end button her phone beeped again. She looked at the screen. *Sasha. Damn.*

"Hello, Sasha." Honor answered, instantly annoyed at the sound of Sasha's gum popping in her ear. "Sasha, can I call you back? Now's really not a good time. I'm driving home from work and…"

"What's up, sis-in-law? I was over at your crib today and seen you were MIA. You know I had to call and check on my favorite sis."

"Yeah…"

"So, girl, you got any money I can hold for a little while? I would've asked RJ, but he was in a mood this morning, all up on his high horse and stuff. Always thinkin' he betta' than everybody else jus' 'cause he…"

Honor interrupted. "Sasha! I need to…"

The sight of the suspension cables on the Front Street Bridge in front of her forced all the air from her lungs. Honor's body began to shake uncontrollably. The flashing lights of the riverboat casinos became a blur.

The phone fell from her hand as she came to a complete stop before the bridge. *Breathe. Oh God, let me breathe.* But it was too late. She had lost touch with any semblance of sanity. Fear now sat beside her in the passenger seat.

"Girl, what's up? You gonna let me hold something or what?" Sasha's voice came up from someplace beneath Honor's knees as the phone lay on the floor of the car.

A symphony of car horns began blowing for her to drive.

"Dang, girl, what's all that noise?" Sasha's loud voice still resounded from under Honor's seat. "Well, damn, you ain't gotta be all rude by ignoring me. It's just that me and Vance's lights are 'bout to get cut off tomorrow. Do you hear me?"

RANFORD

RJ's leather shoes made swooshing sounds as he paced the hardwood floors of his den, starring endlessly at the grandfather clock in the foyer ahead of him. *Tick. Tick. Tick.* Every time the monstrous-sized minute hand moved, he felt his level of adrenaline increase like tiny droplets steadfastly seeping into his bloodstream. He was a ticking time bomb.

Six twenty-five, and still no Honor. How hard was it to make it home on time, especially on an evening when RJ had planned something special for the two of them? RJ looked at the screen of his iPhone, searching again for any signs of life. One time. Two times. Six times. Twelve times. And then he lost count of how many times he'd looked down, looked up, and then hit speed-dial button number two. Still, there was no indication that his wife gave a damn that the soles of his shoes were becoming worn.

RJ's eyes settled on the poster-sized wedding portrait atop the mantle. The photo, which was taken almost five years prior, showed the couple staring deeply into each other's eyes. Honor in her flowing Vera Wang wedding gown, and him in his Cohan gray tuxedo. Even he had to admit he was just the backdrop in the photo. Honor's beauty and virtuosity outshined even him. In the second photo, RJ's muscular arms held her green-bikini-clad body close to him on the beach in St. Lucia with the sunlight and sand glistening off their tanned skin. Almost five years of memories smiled back at him, which, even now, caused a slight grin to escape from the sides of his full lips. RJ's thoughts drifted back to the night they'd met six years ago.

A full night of work still before him after a long day at the office, RJ had pulled into the parking lot of the school and backed into his reserved parking spot. Nina Simone called to him from his high-definition stereo speakers, but even her sultry voice couldn't override the splitting headache that had taken residence in his mind that day. He remembered rubbing his temples before jumping from his car. A low beep signaled to him that the lock was activated and he hurriedly walked inside, checking his watch. Six forty-five. *Damn.* He liked to arrive at least a half-hour early to board meetings. That way he could assess every board member, principal, parent, and curious community resident from his spot at the head of the auditorium.

Tonight was especially important, as his trusted colleague Alfred Washington would be introducing a new board member. Normally, he made sure he was a part of such decisions, but his everyday workload had been growing as fast as bacteria on a sponge. So he had been more than happy to let his upper school principal take the helm of the search committee to find a new member for their six-person board. Still, it worried him that he had not played a bigger role in the selection. RJ had seen the resume and he had a name: Honor Thompson. But there was little else. He surmised it was probably some old, rich, white lady who was looking for an excuse to get out of the house. One who wanted to serve her penance for having money by spending some of it on a few of the city's poor black students.

He laughed to himself as he entered the auditorium. Taking his place center stage, he was shocked to find a stunning black woman sitting to his left, with her head buried in a few pieces of paper on the table before her. The fact that she had not taken notice of him when he stepped into the room further allured him. Women always took notice when he walked into a room; it was just that way. He cleared his throat, but she didn't look up. He cleared his throat again. Still, no response. Agitation began to set in, and he sat down.

"Mr. Ellis, can I get you anything?" Mrs. Williams, a board member, asked. "Do you need me to fetch you a water?"

"No. No thanks. I'm fine," RJ answered.

His brows were on high alert, causing worry lines to spread from his forehead. RJ suddenly felt flushed. His skin became clammy and his palms itched.

"On second thought, I will take that water," he said, clearing his scratchy throat.

"Certainly," Mrs. Williams replied, smiling up at him at his place on the stage. The married-with-three-kids woman let her eyes leisurely stroll from RJ's temples to the places hidden beneath the underside of the table, stopping at the tips of his wing-tipped shoes. She licked her dark-lipsticked lips seductively. RJ noticed, but his body was not the least bit aroused. Mrs. Williams was old news. Way old. His attention was elsewhere, and she could sense it as she cut a slide glance at the attractive, younger woman at the table.

"That will be all, Mrs. Williams." RJ dismissed her with a sweeping gesture, and she scurried off, her hips swaying in a motion that was one step quicker than the rest of her curvaceous body.

Alfred stepped into the auditorium just as RJ was about to get up and introduce himself. RJ found himself surprisingly relieved.

"Alfred, how's it going, man?"

"Surviving man, the usual. Hey, have you met Honor?"

RJ hoped Alfred hadn't noticed the beads of sweat that were now forming along his forehead, threatening to evolve into an embarrassing river alongside his temples. His pulse jumped a few beats at the mention of her name.

Damn cappuccino. I knew I shouldn't have had any caffeine today.

As a rule, RJ never drank more than three cups of coffee a week, and never on consecutive days.

"RJ, where you at, bro?" Alfred snapped his fingers, the wedding band on his left hand working as an anti-hypnotic against the sight of the beauty before him.

RJ's gaze shifted to Alfred's tall, lanky frame, landing on the small ink spot on his teal-colored tie.

"Would you like for me to introduce you?"

"Yeah, man, lead the way."

The two men made their way to the opposite end of the stage, where the vision sat with her eyes still firmly glued to the papers. RJ suddenly envied the tree that had laid its life down to form the very piece of paper her hands now fondled. The sweat that had formed on RJ's forehead now threatened the center of his palms as they approached her. RJ rubbed his hands along the seams of his pants, not wanting to arouse any suspicion at his sudden feelings of awkwardness.

"Excuse me, Ms. Thompson. May we interrupt you for a minute?" Alfred asked. "I just wanted to introduce you to our school superintendent, Dr. Ranford Ellis, but around here, we just call him RJ. RJ, this is Honor Thompson. Honor is our newest board member, replacing Janyce Watkins."

Honor stood and extended her hand. For a minute, RJ was too afraid to take it. Afraid her hand was the remote that would broadcast all of his insecurities atop the stage in high-definition.

It was too much of an instant connection—the moment he finally did take her hand in his. His body tricked him, and he was running full-speed on the last mile of his daily four-mile trek: a quickening pulse, strong heart palpitations, dry mouth, heavy breathing, heaving chest, jelly legs. Euphoria. Except this runner's high was an illusion. Still, RJ had to check himself, make sure his feet were planted firmly on the floor.

"Hello, it's nice to meet you," Honor said.

She stood up from the chair, showcasing a statuesque figure worthy of its unveiling onstage. RJ fought the urge to run his fingers across her every curve and crevice. He wanted to sample the smoothness of her skin from her temples to her toes, dare himself to discover a single blemish.

I don't want to be lonely tonight. Don't let me be lonely tonight. I don't wanna ... be ... lonely. Lyrics danced inside RJ's head and threatened to explode from his mouth.

Instead he responded, "Nice to meet you as well, Ms. Thompson. I'm glad Alfred convinced you to join us here at Urban Achievers Academy."

"Well, I see you pack quite the full house," she said.

"What's that?"

With her eyes, Honor gestured out into the auditorium, which was now filled to near capacity with a sea of nameless faces. RJ had failed to notice the fullness of it all.

Why can't I get this type of turnout at football games or PTA meetings?

He surmised that the announcement of the new board member was the main reason behind the packed auditorium. He also supposed that the stars would descend from the heavens just for a glimpse of the eternal beauty before him.

To spite the direction of his thoughts he said, "Yes, we do seem to have a full house tonight, don't we? I hope that doesn't mean we'll be here all night."

Oh, please let us stay here together all night.

"So what got you interested in serving on the board here at the school?" RJ asked. *Did I even bother to read this exquisite woman's resume? Isn't she from some place in Florida or Nevada?*

"Well, I'm quite active in the volunteer arena," Honor said. "One of my activities involves working with at-risk children at the Mercy Center. So when Alfred first told me about the opportunity to sit on the board at Urban Achievers, I jumped at the chance. I actually needed little convincing."

"Well, as I said before, I'm glad you decided to join us. Please let me be the first to officially welcome you, and I hope this will be a very enlightening partnership. I'm sure a woman of your caliber can only add to all that we have accomplished and are trying to surpass at Urban Achievers."

No wedding ring. Did I just see her blush? Shy. I like that.

"Excuse me, Dr. Ellis," Mrs. Williams stood firmly in front of him, a smirk on her once-pretty face. "It's time for us to begin. We are already twenty minutes behind schedule."

"I guess the natives are getting restless," Alfred added.

"So be it. It was a pleasure meeting you, Honor."

"You too, Doctor."

"Please, call me RJ."

Not until this last statement did RJ realize that his hand still engulfed hers, and with no objection. This fact alone turned his walk into a saunter as he made his way back to his seat at the head of the table. He sat, glanced at the agenda again, and then waited for Mrs. Williams to formally call the meeting to order.

He was well aware that Honor's eyes were upon him now, and he wanted to believe it was not just because he was about to be called to the podium at any second. Why she continued to unnerve him was of no consequence. RJ was certain that Honor Thompson would soon be his, and at that moment, he was jealous of those stars, and every man in the room for having their eyes on her.

Once at the podium, those eyes consumed RJ. He cleared his throat and grabbed the bottled water that had been placed there for him. He gripped it so tight that the lid flew upward and dropped to the floor.

Water spilled onto the meeting's agenda, causing all of the words to smear and the letters to trade places on the paper, so that the "e's" became "c's," and the "u's" began to resemble "o's." If the mishap affected him, RJ seemed outwardly unfazed. He just gripped the bottle tighter and watched as large droplets spilled onto the stage and the letters began to turn into one big blur.

To this day, RJ still viewed Honor as his personal Mother Earth, and he dared anyone to defile her. However, the one thing missing that would cement their bond was a child. A child would bind them together for all eternity and make the pictures atop the mantle complete.

Besides, RJ needed a son to carry on his legacy. It was taking longer than he expected for Honor to become pregnant, although she was unaware she was even trying.

Honor's body mysteriously rejected any type of artificial hormones. It was if anything unauthentic polluted her very essence. The pill. IUD. NuvaRing. The patch. The shot. Everything synthetic gave her he most horrendous side effects, and RJ had to admit he hated the weight gain on her with the very last attempt.

When they first began dating, and after RJ had waited the obligatory month, their reliance on the "natural" methods—condoms, spermicides, the rhythm method, and the just plain count-your-blessings-I-got-my-period luck—unnerved him to no end. RJ felt he was being cheated out of prime pussy. But that was then. Now, everything worked to his advantage. It was easy to punch an unnoticeable hole in the condom or her diaphragm, and erase redraw the circles that kept track of her cycles on the small calendar located in the far corner of her lingerie drawer. He would tell her that he was using a condom and then slip it off at the height of their passion, withdrawing just enough to not waste any of his precious seed.

My wife should want to have my baby.

In his eyes, it was time for them to stop stalling and commence with his wishes. Honor would probably be upset at first about the unplanned, unexpected pregnancy, but she'd come around eventually. RJ was certain it would be a boy. How could his seed produce anything else? The only thing that would be left then to debate was if he wanted to make his son the third, to pass on a family namesake that he'd just as soon forget. Why would he subject his son to that, when his whole life, RJ had done everything to forget that he was even a dead man's junior?

RJ's pacing slowed to a complete halt when he heard the familiar hum of the three-car garage. *She's home!* His chest heaved as if he'd been punched, then the surge of adrenaline returned. He yanked open the garage door.

"You fuckin' slut! Where the hell have you been?!"

Honor stood before him, a haggard expression plastered across her otherwise flawless face. She was barely out of the car before he delivered a blow to her chest that sent her flying backward to the cement floor. Honor's head slammed against the open card door, narrowly missing the edge as the sound of the garage closing drowned out her screams.

RJ stepped beside where she lay crying and fumbled inside her car until he found her cell phone. A series of barely audible beeps rang out as he began to furiously press button after button.

Who had she been calling? How could she miss every one of my calls? Didn't she realize how worried I was? Didn't she care how upset she'd make me?

He clutched her phone so tight that the casing broke, falling like pepper from a shaker. RJ hadn't even noticed.

"Why didn't you answer your phone?!"

"I...I..."

"You ungrateful bitch! You knew I had made plans for us! You just wanted to ruin this evening for me. Too worried about that damn fish than your man. So is that what this is, huh? I mean less to you than a piece of fuckin' fish? Huh? Answer me, bitch!"

"RJ, I'm sorry. I...I..."

"Sorry? You're damn right you're sorry. Too fuckin' sorry to pick up the damn phone. Who else you been calling, Honor? Huh? Are you fuckin' someone from your office now? Is that what this is all about? Come here! Let me smell you."

"NO! RJ, stop please! STOP IT!"

Her pleas fell on deaf ears as he reached down, grabbed hold of her sling back shoes, and pried her legs apart on the cold, hard floor. In one simultaneous motion, RJ lifted her dress above her waist, pulled her lace panties to the side, and plunged inside of her with his fingers. One. Then two. He pulled out of her wetness and held his fingers up to his nose, sniffing. Then he put the same two fingers inside of his mouth, licking off her juices. Honor lay crying softly, her body shuddering against the cold floor.

"Mmm...my pussy. That's right." Standing up, he straightened the pleats on his slacks and dropped the remaining pieces of the cell phone he still carried in his other hand. As RJ stepped back into the house, his cell phone went off, Marvin Gaye's soothing voice suddenly at odds with the scene before them.

"Now get cleaned up. I'm hungry," he said, never bothering to look back.

HONOR

Death by chicken Alfredo. The whole time Honor poked sparingly at her shrimp salad, she pictured a piece of chicken lodging in the base of RJ's throat, cutting off his air supply until his skin turned a crude shade of purple. He would look at her, pleading with his eyes for help, and she would pretend she didn't see that he was gasping for his very breath.

She would drum her fingernails mindlessly across the linen tablecloth at the upscale Italian restaurant where they sat, with its recessed lighting and date-night atmosphere. RJ would then try to raise his hand to get someone's—anyone's—attention, but he would find himself too weak to do so for long. Finally, he would take his last breath and fall face first into his generous portion of poultry, noodles, and breadsticks.

Only then would Honor casually catch the attention of their waiter, ask for the check, reach for his wallet, and stride right out the door to freedom.

"Baby, where you at?"

"Huh?" Honor snapped out of her bout of wishful thinking.

"You seem a million miles away tonight." From across the table, RJ smiled before nonchantantly biting the end of a garlic-laden breadstick. It was a beautifully sinister smile.

How does he do that? Just pretend like nothing ever happened. Honor felt a tear threatening to escape the corner of her eye. She jumped up as if her life depended on finding the nearest exit. RJ reached out and grabbed her hand. Hard. Then he smiled.

"Where you going, babe?"

"Uh…I've got to run to the restroom."

"No you don't," he said slowly, pausing after each word. "Now, sit down, and let's finish enjoying this nice meal that I'm paying for."

Honor did as she was instructed. She strapped her insides to the chair and clutched the underside of the wooden seat in sheer desperation.

"Now enjoy your meal, gal." Casual banter escaped from RJ's lips while Honor blinked in astonishment, in an effort to stop the tears that still threatened to fall. *Please. Please. Please.* She willed them away.

Somewhere in the distance, Honor heard something shatter. A plate? A bowl? A glass? The sound took her back in time, and instantly she was on the street just before the Front Street Bridge. Trembling. Chest pounding.

Sweating. Afraid if she dared move forward, she would plunge into the ripples of the Missouri River awaiting her below. The crucifix that had been swinging back and forth from her rearview mirror in tune with the vibrations of the car now stood still, and although the gospel singer's soothing voice still blared from the car's speakers, Honor could not make out the song. She simply couldn't hear.

That is, until Sasha's voice seemed to boom louder from beneath her seat.

"Honor, girl, you ain't gonna talk? Well, fine. All you had to do was tell me you weren't gonna let a sistah hold a few dollars for a week or two!"

Click!

Come on, Honor. You can do this. You've done it a million times before. Just put your foot on the gas pedal. Just move!

But she couldn't. Immense fear kept her trapped considering her impending misfortune. As horns honked behind her, the other cars that were passing her hybrid stared at her as if she were a circus freak, pointing and throwing up an endless parade of middle fingers.

Your hazards. Turn your hazard lights on, Honor.

Somehow she managed to release her grip on the steering wheel and push the red triangle-shaped button on the dash. Then she clutched the steering wheel again, holding on for dear life and sanity.

Tap. Tap. Tap. Honor turned to find a couple of weather-beaten fingers drumming against her window.

How long have I been sitting here? Fear, the narcotic, had left her senseless.

It took every ounce of effort she had to push the button and watch the window descend just a crack.

"Excuse me, ma'am." The older man stood above her in an aqua coverall smeared with spots of oil, dirt, and something else she couldn't identify across the front. He smiled, revealing teeth that were badly in need of at least a year's worth of dentistry. Still, there was something genuine in his lopsided smile that lacked two teeth on the right side.

"Ma'am, my wife and I are about three cars behind you and, well, it looks like you're in some sort of trouble. Anything we can do to help you out?"

"I…I can't move. I just can't…"

30

"Did your engine conk out on you? Damn fancy electric foreign cars. No matter how new and shiny they are, they just don't make 'em like they used to."

He removed his ball cap with the matching General Motors insignia and scratched his balding head. A dozen frown lines appeared on his forehead, just above his kind, forest-green eyes.

"You think we should take you to the hospital?" he asked, concern in his every word.

"N-no. That isn't necessary."

"Tell you what, ma'am. If you would allow me, I could drive you past the bridge a ways. My wife could follow us in the truck. That's, if you feel safe with a perfect stranger riding with you in your car."

The man paused, looking behind him at the long row of cars awaiting her answer. Above, a helicopter began circling. The sound of its propellers joined in with the honks and the sound of tires screeching.

Please, God, don't let anyone get hurt because of me…because of this.

"But I tell you what, ma'am: I know it would sure get these folks home safely, if you'd agree."

So Midwestern hospitality does exist.

Words couldn't seem to escape from Honor's lips, so she simply nodded.

"Okay, let me just tell my wife, and we'll get you home safely."

A few more manic heartbeats later, the stranger was back and tapping at her window. Even in her frenzied state, Honor had to chuckle slightly at his polite gesture. The window had been rolled down more than halfway during their brief conversation earlier.

"Okay, ma'am. Laura, my wife, is gonna follow us. But I'm gonna need you to scoot over to the passenger's side. Can you do that?" he asked.

It wasn't until then that Honor noticed her hands still clutching the steering wheel and her foot parked on the brake pedal. Her hazard lights were still blinking in between the gospel melodies. "*He saw the best in me…*"

Slowly, she managed to move herself to the other side of the car and then reached to unlock the door. *What am I doing? This guy could be a serial killer or a wanted felon.* But suddenly, instinctively, Honor knew that she was safe in the presence of the sun-dried stranger.

For the next twenty minutes, Honor listened as Jesse went on about his life with his wife, three children, two dogs, and a host of other critters on their two acres of land just past Holden, Missouri. They didn't have a lot of money, he said, but they were God-fearing folks who believed if you worked hard and prayed, He would provide.

"So what's your name, ma'am? I don't think I can keep calling you that for the rest of the ride, seein' as how I'm driving your car."

"Honor."

"Honor, huh? Well, that's a very honorable name." The man smiled at his own joke, one that Honor had heard a million times.

"Family name?"

"Something like that," she replied faintly.

Honor wasn't quite willing to tell the man about her mother, father, and sister back in her hometown of Tampa. Or how she was the firstborn, the prodigal daughter, named after her father, the Honorable Vernon T. Thompson—a straight-faced man who still sat on the Hillsborough County Court bench. Her mother, Olivia, was a proud Florida A&T graduate and stay-at-home mother who nobly sat on the boards of several area charities, including a hospital, a breast cancer awareness foundation, and one school. Her younger sister, Netta, was a successful obstetrician in St. Petersburg. Every day, and in every way, they expected Honor to live up to her name. It was not by accident that she had chosen, many years ago, to attend school as far away as possible from their prying eyes, tsk-tsks, and the barrage of "we expect great things from you" speeches.

"Boy, this is a pretty fancy area you live in," Jesse commented as they passed the giant rock sculptures and man-made fountains of her gated community. "Whereabouts is your block?"

My block. "Stop!"

"Pardon me?"

"I mean…my house is just right here on the left."

They pulled into the circular driveway of a teal-colored stucco house with two mammoth stone-carved lions guarding the entrance.

Please, God, don't let these people be home. We're already the only chocolate chips in the cookie out here.

"You and your wife…you both have helped me out immensely. Here." Honor began digging inside her Prada bag. After finding her matching billfold, she began to count out the little cash she managed to keep on hand for emergencies.

Jesse pushed her hand aside, gently. "No need to pay me," he said. "I got everything I need."

"Are you sure? Your wife...she probably would like..."

"Trust me, if there's anything she wants and don't have, she ain't shy about lettin' me know. So there ain't never nothin' the wife don't have." He snickered.

Honor smiled up at the man. It was a genuine smile but it felt foreign on her face.

"Take care of yourself, Honor. I hope you feel better tomorrow."

"Thank you...for...for everything."

Honor waited until the older model blue Ford truck was out of sight before she put the car in reverse. An older woman with more silver than black strands of hair (and with a dog to match) eyed Honor curiously as she pulled out of the driveway. Honor waved and turned onto the next street heading in the opposite direction of her home. The sinking feeling in her stomach kicked her insides harder the closer she got to the reality of it all.

"Honor? Honor, baby?"

"Huh?"

"Look at me," RJ hissed from across the checkered tablecloth.

Don't do it. Don't cry.

"Now, I'ma ask you one more time what's goin' on in that beautiful little head of yours, and this time I expect an answer. You hear me?"

How does one go from bitch to beautiful in sixty seconds?

"Nothing. It's just been a long day. I'm tired, that's all." Honor looked down at her hand, suddenly realizing she was twirling her three-carat platinum diamond wedding band in a circle around her shaking finger. For the first time, she hated how the wedding and engagement bands had been soldered together, unable to pull apart.

"Listen, when we get home, I'm going to draw us a hot bath, get us a couple glasses of wine, turn on some Boney, rub your body down, and take your mind off everything."

The thought of RJ's touch suddenly made Honor nauseous.

Deer Ranford, .

It yur Mommy. I no this pen and paper cant eraze the past 26 years — the times I culdn't hold you when you needed. Times I culdn't make you chiken noodle soup when you was sick, or put a band-aid on when you hurt yourselv. Times I culdn't tuck you in at night and say I loved you. 26 years without yur mama, and all I got is this pen and pad to do my talk now.

I no son, I miss yur report cards, yur birthdays, yur first date. Yur first luv. But, son, what I learn about time since I been behind these wall is all we got is the No More, the Now, and the Not Yet. I cant change the No More, or the Not Yet. All I have is NOW! So now I telling you I'm sorry. Sorry I made you turned into a man for you was ready. I askin you to forgive me, more for you than me. I will rot in this cell, but you got life.

I no you got lots of questions. Lots of anger. Lots of hate. Let. It. Go. I pray you is with someone you luv good and strong. That you has a couple of babies, and lives free. All the pain, guilt and sorow you got botled inside, the pain that you held tight all these years, just move on, RJ, for it kills you. For it eats away at yur insides and rots yur soul.

I learn to let go. I hads to. In here, they tell me when to get up, dress, shower, watch TV, eat, pee, work, and go outside. But, inside I is free! Don't get me wrong. I regrit my actions, what got me here in the first place. Not being a good mama, and takin yur father from you. Yea, many times I wish I culd go back to the No More and just do rite. But you no what regrit is? It's a worm that sits in the pit of yur stomach biting at every thing that was posed to nurish you.

See, I came in this God for saken place with so much hate, anger, guilt and pain pulling me to pieces. Pain from yur father. He hurt me. My uncle Sallis, he hurt me. Hell, my own dam father, the very man who lay down and give me life, he hurt me. I carry that hurt burnin inside me, like a big fire ball, for so long.

Do you no what it like to live life ever day with a heart that burns so big, yur soul just melts away and yur body becums ashes? You want some one, any one to come and put you out. RJ, you were concived and borned into all that — a fire craker just waiting for someone to come along and strike a match. For that, I so deeply sorry.

Did you no that paster Odom used to visit me faithfuly every month for he got sick? That man must have walked on water next to Jesus taking you childrens in the way he did after…well, just after. Raise you as his own and giving you a good home. He good people. He never ask for a dime in turn.

He did want 1 thing.

Few years back, he came to see me, 1 o'clock, like always. He smell like cheese burgers and Old Spice. Yur father use to wear Old Spice. I hat that smell. But them onions they was stronger than my worstest memorie, specialy sense I ain't taste them in years.

I never forget that day. All I wanted was to be on the out side, taking a bite of that big ole burger. But, all I culd do was ask bout it.

"How big was it?"

"Did you ask for extra onion?"

"Did it have ketch up, musterd and pickles or jus ketch up and musterd?"

"Was it fresh or warm under a heat lamp?"

Cause you no, some times, those fast food joints be tryin to serve you old nastie burgers, thinkin they slick. Always use to make me so mad. Out there. I used to march right back up to the kounter and ask for a fresh burger or give me my cash back! Oh, specialy if I was drunk. If I was high, it didn't mater. The munchies don't make you care to much about taste no way, or any thing, sides feeding yur face.

So, I keep ask him, and ask him bout that dam burger that I culd never taste. Out of no where, he place his hand over my lip. That's when he ask for this "1 thing." "I can't give you no cochee," I say, hurt. "Not in here. Maybe a hand job." I say. You shoulda seen the look that came cross his face. If he was white, he been beat red. "No, Carmen," he says, "I'm talkin' about yur soul…I'm concirned bout yur soul."

"My soul," I say. "What the hell you talking bout Rev?"

That when he start talkin bout how he want to see me in iternity and pray for my salvachion. He say all this scriptur to me, and I wasn hearin none of it, you no?

Not rite off.

Where was God when I was getting molisted by my uncle? Where was He when I got my ass kicked ever nite by my husband? The 1 that promise to love and chirish me? What kind of God reach in to take the soul of a lil 5-year-old girl and sale it to Satan? Body and soul, I was bot and sole. I was even part of the negotiattions.

But, you no, Odom, he never stoped preachin. Hell, he preach so much, a few of the other womens started comin in the visitor room to here his preach. After a few visits, I culd not stand no more of the Word. I was geting ready to tell him to shut the hell up when he came into the visitor room with a box in his hand. He smile bout a mile wide, ran from 1 end of his big ear to the nex.

I say, "What you got there for me Rev?" You no, joking.

"Well, why don't you open it and find out," he say. He put the box in my hands. "Go head, it for you."

I jus bout hit the floor. Ain't no body ever gave yur ole mama a present before. I tried to hole back the tears cause I did want to look soft in front of them folks in the room that day. The box was so pretty, I did want to open it. I jus sat there and stare at *the gold paper and bow. There was a card on top to. It say, "For Carmen." I still got that card today.*

"Well, you jus gone stare at it until visit hour or over, or you gone open it," he say, still smile.

I tare into that box like I was you and yur sister at Christmas. You member, RJ? That lil ole Christmas tree that hang to 1 side with 6 bulbs and about 5 workin lights? I was a litle hurt when I open the box, but I did want to up set the Rev, so I try to smile. He did buy it tho, not for 1 sec. Rev Odom laugh when he see the sad look on my face. Inside the box was a Bible. Now, I never was no reader, and I new I was never gone read no dam Bible.

"Turn it over," he say.

I did and there it was on the botom, Carmen Ellis - my name in big gold letters. Felt like real gold cross my finger when I touche the leter. I keep runing my fingers over each leter. I never had nothin with my name on it be for. Nothing I own. Even the bills came in your daddy name. When I hold the Bible for the first time, it feel like I touche that heaven he always talk bout.

Odom stare at me for a long time, this big grin on his face. Still, I look at the gold.

He touche my hand than, and tell me he going and I did have to open the pages til I was ready to "perge my soul" and "open up a hole new world."

"How will I no when that is Rev," I ask?

"Well, you just no. You feel it in yur soul. You can't stay angry yur hole life, Carmen. 1 day, you gonna have to let go of all that hurt."

I never open that Bible, but I ready to perge my soul. Ready to look back at the No More, cause it may save you and yur sister from seein me as a women with a gun in my hands, to a women try to save her own life the best way she new how. May be then…may be then you can live yur Not Yet unashamed of yur mama. So we gonna have to go back to the No More, but I gotta end now. It almost time for lites out.

With love and regrit,

Mommy.

RANFORD

RJ carefully placed the vase filled with a dozen pink roses on the nightstand next to where Honor slept. Pink was Honor's favorite color: The color of her sorority. The color of her bridesmaids' dresses. The color of her birthright. He smiled down at her. She looked so peaceful, a sliver of morning's sunlight kissing the top of her forehead down to the mountains of her full lips. Instantly, an erection began to threaten the front creases of his black jogging suit. He considered delaying his morning run; Honor had always had that effect on him. He reached down to touch the dimple on her bare shoulder and was surprised when her body jerked involuntarily. The sudden movement unnerved him and he felt a familiar bile begin to rise to the top of this throat. *Doesn't she know I'll do anything in this world to protect her? That I'd walk through hell and back to save her?* He fought the urge to spit on her face and forced his erection to subside. A wave of uncertainty coursed through his body. RJ swallowed, hard. *Would she notice the flowers at first sight? Would she appreciate the gesture? Would it erase the lovers' quarrel they'd had last night?* Every couple fought. That's how he saw it. His parents fought…until…until.

RJ tightened the laces of his shoes so forcefully that the veins on his hands began to bulge, then ran down the spiral staircase and out into the street. The pavement became his escape as he chased peace with every step he took. Here was his one semblance of normalcy in the midst of chaos. He ran harder, faster, until his breath began to come in short bursts. The endorphins he craved began to explode with each passing minute.

Runners' high: the source of his survival. Running had gotten him out of poverty and into popularity at an independent college prep school. His legs had ran him into a full-ride scholarship and superstardom at Loyola University, before propelling him to the next level.

It was an instant fix whenever RJ's tennis shoes hit the pavement. The unforeseen outbursts of anger that he couldn't control: they didn't exist. He was not afraid of turning green, becoming a Hulk of a man. True abandonment was found in every stride. Peace came to rest on his shoulder, kiss him on the cheek.

So in-tune was RJ with this blissful existence that he almost tripped as he noticed a shapely pair of double D's bouncing beside him. Regina. RJ had *tapped that* more than a dozen times over the last year, but had grown bored when she started using her mouth in a different manner than he would have preferred. Regina had begun having delusions about the two of them leaving their respective spouses and running away together. RJ wanted a freak, not another wife, and that is exactly what he told her.

"Woo…slow down! Where's the fire, handsome?" Regina asked, her breath coming in short pants. Her honey-kissed skin glistened in the early morning sun.

RJ didn't respond. Instead, he picked up his pace and tried his damndest not to look down at her perky nipples standing at full attention.

"Hey, RJ…did you hear me? I'm talking to you."

He kept running, but slowed down his pace a bit. "What is it, Regina?"

"Just wondering why I haven't heard from you or seen you in a while? I miss you, baby. I miss your touch. Your kiss. Hey, remember a couple of weeks ago…the kitchen counter? The olive oil?"

He did remember, and if he didn't have a full plate on his schedule today, he'd be tempted to stop by Regina's house for a quick bite.

"Come on…RJ. Is what we had so bad? I thought things were going great. I thought we had grown closer."

"You thought wrong."

"That's it? I risked everything for you, you know. My husband. My kids. Er…everything!"

Now why is she whining? *Women.*

"I never asked you to do that."

"How can you be so damn cold, RJ?" Regina's voice was growing louder, more high pitched. "After all that we shared? The love we made?"

Regina came to an abrupt stop a few paces ahead of him, forcing him to lose momentum. He stared ahead as peace outran him. RJ came to a dead halt and turned to face the cute heart-faced woman now dangerously close to tears.

"Let's get something straight," RJ was so close now he could feel her heart breaking. "You're married. I'm married. We fucked. I never made love to you. Now…get a hold of yourself and go on back home to that square-assed husband of yours."

Her heartbreak was evident as tears began to fall from her almond-shaped eyes.

Here we go with the dramatics.

"Regina, go on home. It's over. Done with."

"You know what RJ? SCREW YOU! I don't need this shit! Okay? You think I don't know that I was just a fuck to you? I wonder how your precious wife would feel if I went over there and…"

RJ spun the curvy woman into a chokehold. One large hand firmly gripped her throat; the other held tight to her waist-length phony ponytail. To a passerby, it might look as if the two were engaged in some type of harmless horseplay. Someone would have to be pretty close to see the color draining from Regina's face.

"Bitch, if you ever come near my wife with this bullshit: I…will…kill…you," RJ said, his voice barely a whisper, but loud enough for her to comprehend every word. "Now…do we have an understanding?"

Regina nodded, her large chest heaving under the pressure of his grip.

"I didn't hear you."

"Y…yes. YES!"

"Good." RJ released Regina. She hit the ground, gasping. He looked around, all at once grateful that they were in an undeveloped part of the planned community with nothing but grass, dirt, and dozens of "For Sale" signs on vacant lots waiting to be claimed. He started jogging again.

"You crazy mother…."

RJ couldn't hear Regina anymore. He was back in the zone.

Less than an hour later, he returned home disappointed to find that Honor had already dressed and gone. He had wanted her to be in bed, waiting to show her gratitude for the roses. Figuring that she'd left early for work, he would give her an hour to call him and explain her absence. One hour.

After showering and changing into a navy Cole Haan suit, RJ climbed behind the wheel of his car and headed south to the Metropolitan Ministries Retirement Community in Midtown.

RJ carefully pulled his car into the third row of the parking lot. He left the car intentionally crooked so that no other car could pull in beside his. He grabbed the bag of food he'd purchased earlier at Rudy's Soul Food Shack and made his way through the French doors. The entire redbrick assisted-living facility was part of a bigger community renovation project, and the building itself was less than ten years old. For some reason, the age of the place had been an important factor when RJ began looking at places for his replacement father.

RJ stopped at the front desk. Ms. Julia, the manager of the assisted-living facility, smiled up at him from the stack of papers in front of her. She was wearing an oversized dress with a floral pattern that had gone horribly wrong somewhere on her robust figure. Nevertheless, RJ turned on the charm.

"Good morning, Ms. Julia. You're looking as lovely as ever."

The woman turned visibly red and ran her pudgy hands down the front end of her dress. "Morning, Mr. Ellis. How are you today?"

"I'm good. Thanks for asking. Hey, um, how's he been doing this week?" RJ asked.

Ms. Julia shook her head back and forth. Strands of her boxed strawberry-blond dye job failed to follow, landing haphazardly around her round face. The color of her hair and flushed skin seemed to be at war with the pink petals on the woman's dress, making the manger look as if she might burst at any second. Ms. Julia paused before giving her standard reply. She wanted to get a longer glimpse at RJ in his navy suit and aqua tie; she wanted to sniff his essence a minute longer, inhale the scent that was transforming the lobby of the Welcome Center into young, raw masculinity. She inhaled slowly one last time.

RJ stared down at the woman wondering what could possibly be taking her so long to respond. He rubbed his hands together at a quickening pace.

"Oh, you know...he has his good days and his bad days, Mr. Ellis. And, although there are starting to be more bad days, on his good ones he sure likes to preach up a storm, I'll tell you that much," she giggled, never taking her eyes off RJ.

RJ watched as the mass of flowered print jiggled. He smiled at Ms. Julia's response, causing her to turn a deeper shade of red. It came as no surprise that preaching remained in his blood, even as his brain grew feebler.

The man who had raised him since age eleven wouldn't have it any other way. Growing up, the "gospel" was more than words: it was a lifestyle. Every morning before he, Sasha, and Edwin would head off for school, Reverend Odom would feed them the Word at the breakfast table with a side of bacon or grits. As they sat at the dinner table later that evening, after school and chores, the Word had been a staple, right next to the macaroni and cheese, pork steak, and peas. The reverend would recite scripture while he and Edwin stuck their tongues out at each other from across the well-worn table and kick each other from underneath, stopping only when the reverend would pop his head up from the Bible. Then it was fed to them again at bedtime, along with the prayer about God taking their souls if they should die before they wake. And on Sundays…Sundays, it was an all-day feast with no breaks in the middle. There was no choice as to whether you wanted seconds or not: it was a given. RJ's smile subsided. All that spoon feeding and RJ couldn't recall one single passage of scripture.

"Well, thank you for the update, Ms. Julia. It's been a pleasure chatting with you, as always," he said.

"Oh, no problem, Mr. Ellis. The pleasure is all mine." She smiled, revealing a set of surprisingly straight, white teeth. For a minute, RJ wondered if they were real or not.

When the manager was sure RJ was out of earshot, she said again, "The pleasure was definitely all mine."

RJ left the Welcome Center and rode the elevator up to the fifth floor of the assisted-living facility. Normally he would have taken the stairs two at a time, but the altercation earlier had left him drained. He stopped at apartment 624 and tapped lightly, unsure of what to expect on the other side. The man RJ thought of as his father had been diagnosed with Alzheimer's almost four years ago. Now eighty-five years old, he was oftentimes just a shell of forgetfulness and gibberish. The disease was rapidly progressing and most days he didn't recognize RJ. His detoriation was truly a sad sight. But RJ faithfully visited the reverend once a week. It was the least he could do for the only person who had shown him that a better life was possible.

RJ knocked on the door of the apartment a few more times. When he didn't hear any footsteps, he let himself in with his key.

"Rev? Hey, Rev, you here?"

"Course, I'm here. Where else am I s'posed to be?"

The older man slowly walked from the back bedroom into the living area of the quaint apartment, decorated in the standard décor that was most likely patterned after a model apartment somewhere far enough away that no one would notice the lazy similarities.

RJ chuckled. It was nice to hear some spunk in the old man's voice and to see him up and about. Most days, the man who used to command such a presence with merely the sound of his voice sat in his easy chair with the television on mute while he stared out his window, wearing an adult diaper.

His omnipresent blood pressure monitor and walker, and myriad prescription medications for everything from acid reflux to high cholesterol, never far away. The "good book" always nearby: The only staple that hadn't changed over the years. It was as if the old man still believed that he could find the cure for what ailed him, or anyone else for that matter, on those pages.

Aging frightened the hell out of RJ. In the older man he saw his reflection, and he wanted to shatter that mirrored reminder every day. Aging had taken most of the reverend's body and twisted it so much that is resembled a worn-out sponge. Would it do the same to him? Leave him with holes in places where once there was a lean frame and, even worse, blank spaces in his mind? In this small space, RJ was constantly reminded that his youth was being soaked up.

"RJ, I want to talk to you, son. Your brother called me today," Reverend Odom said as he sat down in his beloved standard-issue recliner and placed his brown cane across the arms.

"Oh, yeah? How is Edwin?" RJ sat down beside him on the cinnamon-colored couch with matching frilly throw pillows. He grabbed one of them and tossed it to the other end.

"Doin' good. Doin' good," the reverend answered. "Making a good living for himself out there in Chicago. He said he and the family is planning a trip down soon, once they get settled in with the new baby."

"Oh, really?" That was news to RJ. Edwin rarely came back to Kansas City since moving to the Windy City almost immediately after graduating from Central Missouri over a dozen years ago. This, even after RJ had called to tell him that his father—his flesh and blood—was being moved into an assisted-living facility and dementia was taking over his mind. For the life of him, RJ couldn't fathom Edwin's lack of communication with the family. He would have given anything and everything to have, well, a father.

The two men sat silent for a while, finding everything to look at in the room but each other.

"I don't like what you've been doing. The way you've been living your life." Reverend Odom blurted out the words as if he'd blown up a balloon and needed to push the air out as fast as possible.

Is he having another mental lapse? "What the hell are you talking about, old man?" RJ answered. He stuck his chest out further and tensed his arms.

"You watch your language, boy."

RJ was wrong. The reverend's voice still breathed respect, even when barely above a whisper. "Yes, sir. I'm…I'm sorry. You're just talking gibberish again. Now, come on, I brought you the breakfast you like so much: buttermilk pancakes, home potatoes, eggs over medium, crispy bacon, and orange juice. Just the way you like it. Now, you know Ms. Julia would have my hide for this. Had to sneak this in behind her at the desk. I figure one more time can't hurt anything."

RJ scurried over to the skeleton of a kitchen and began to open the Styrofoam containers from the bag one at a time. His stomach started to growl as the sweet aromas escaped into the air. He couldn't remember if he'd eaten earlier, but he suddenly yearned for a strong Scotch instead of the food before him.

"Have you seen your sister? I haven't seen her since she came by here asking for money a few weeks ago. I told her I ain't got any. She didn't look even close to good. God knows I tried with her, you know. I really tried," Reverend Odom said. There was a pleading in his bloodshot eyes as he looked past RJ. He was not used to seeing the hint of defeat in the reverend's face. He didn't know if he was qualified to answer. *Is he even asking a question?*

"Where's Honor? She don't come around here anymore," Reverend Odom asked, a sharper edge to his voice akin to a tone that could once part the Red Sea.

The loaded question was arsenal aimed directly at RJ's chest. The force of it made him stop moving. He paused to catch his breath.

"Honor…she's been busy. You know that. She said to tell you she said 'hello,' though. Yeah…she talks about you all the time. She's going to get by here soon, real soon."

With startling agility, the reverend leaped from his chair and grabbed RJ across the shoulders with the strength of a man in his prime. The force behind the move caused the container of pancakes RJ held to fall to the floor with a soft thud, and the plastic cutlery to scatter across the floor.

Reverend Odom never loosened his grip. Instead, his knuckles dug harder into RJ's body. He spoke slowly, a tiny bit of spittle was the only thing that now separated the two men. "You think I don't see it? That I don't know? There is darkness all around you, following you. It lives in your home. A dark spirit. The Lord called to me in a dream, told me to tell you to repent, turn from your ways," the reverend was almost shouting now.

If he had any doubts before, RJ was now certain that the good reverend was not just having one of his "off" days, but was heading for a sharp decline.

"What you talkin' 'bout, Reverend? I think all the meds they givin' you in here been goin' to your head," RJ said, easily slipping back into his Wayne Minor vernacular.

"Don't you patronize me, boy. I know what you've been doin'…and ain't none of it good. Seen it clear as my own eyes, that dream was. My dreams are never wrong."

Beads of sweat began to form on the palms of RJ's hands. He wiped them on his pants. The move made his tie constrict tighter around his neck. He struggled to inhale. The smell of the breakfast food, so appealing earlier, now repelled him. RJ was trapped. An uneasy Daniel in face of the lions' den, only this time, the lions were out for blood and he had no faith to save him.

"Hey…Rev…I just remembered…I have…a conference…with one of my parents, so I gotta go. But…but, I'll be back later on…to…you know…check in on you," RJ said, backing toward the door.

"Mmmm….hmmm….," Reverend Odom said, turning to glance back outside his favorite window. "You just remember what I said, boy. 'Who can find a virtuous wife? For her worth is far above rubies. The heart of her husband safely trusts her; So he will have no lack of gain. She does him good and not evil. All the days of her life. She seeks wool and flax, And willingly works with her hands. She is like the merchant ships, She brings her food from afar. She also rises while it is yet night, And provides food for her household, And a portion for her maidservants. She considers a field and buys it; From her profits she plants a vineyard. She girds herself with strength…'"

RJ raced toward his crookedly parked car. He pressed down hard on the pedal and veered out of parking lot, almost colliding with another car in the process. Upstairs from his window, the reverend watched RJ hurry off and continued to recite the same passage of scripture. A few blocks away, RJ exhaled as his throat became less constrained. But his shoulders remained slumped, and he still felt the weight of the reverend's hands on him.

HONOR

"Congratulations, Mrs. Ellis!"

Honor stared vaguely at Dr. Williamson, her gynecologist.

"I said congratulations!"

"I'm sorry?" *What the hell is this crazy lady congratulating me about?*

"You're pregnant! By the looks of it, I'd say about six weeks along, but I won't be certain until we schedule your first sonogram. I'm so happy for you two. I know you both have been wanting a child for quite some time," Dr. Williamson looked away from Honor and began scribbling furiously on the notepad before her. Through the frames of the doctor's eyeglasses, Honor could make out a small reflection of herself on the table. A chill swept through her body. Honor felt exposed, sprawled across the examination table in a thin cotton gown, with her feet propped up the stirrups and backside bare.

Doctor Williamson continued, "You know, a lot of the infertile couples that I see don't get to witness this type of miracle, especially after they've been trying for a relatively short amount of time, like you and Mr. Ellis." The doctor's raven-colored hair kept time with her hands as she washed them in the small sink.

The doctor grabbed her latex gloves from the countertop, flipped open the bin of the matching eggshell-colored trash bin and threw them hurriedly inside. The sudden movement made a whooshing sound, just before the bin flipped closed and she removed her foot from the bottom peddle. Honor became lost in that one sound. She was watching everything she worked so hard being thrown in the trash in one swift motion.

"Infertile?" Honor asked. She could barely manage a whisper.

Doctor Williamson glanced down at Honor still on the table, legs spread. She smiled, attributing the questioning to new-mom jitters.

"Yes, your husband was here a few months ago. He mentioned that you two had been having trouble conceiving and wanted to know how you could improve your chances. Didn't he tell you?"

"Oh… I remember…he did mention something about speaking with you. I must have forgotten."

"I'm so excited for you and your husband. He seemed so anxious about the prospect of not having children. Still, he's such a polite and handsome man."

"Yes…yes…he's something, isn't he?"

Doctor Williamson walked over and patted Honor on her shoulder. Although the gesture was meant to reassure her, it caused Honor to shudder involuntarily. As the doctor pulled away, Honor noticed a hangnail and some chipped magenta nail polish on the woman's index finger. *How strange that I can notice something so simple on someone else, and I didn't even realize I was pregnant.*

"Sorry, I'm just cold," Honor explained.

I'm always so careful.

"Don't worry, Mrs. Ellis. Everything is going to be just fine. I've written you out a script for your prenatal vitamins and I'd like for you to make an appointment with Marge on your way out. Let's make it six weeks from now. As you get closer to your due date, the appointments will become more frequent," she reached for the door. "Oh, and be sure to grab your expectant mothers kit before you leave. It has a lot of good information: class information for new parents being offered at the hospital, some free samples, and a free copy of *What Happens When You're Expecting.*"

"Great," Honor willed her voice to feign excitement. The door slammed shut just as the doctor became a blurry vision before her, her feet still in the stirrups.

Honor was less than five blocks from the doctor's office in the St. Joseph's Medical Tower when she began shaking uncontrollably. She pulled over into the parking lot of a Price Shopper grocery store, and held on to the steering wheel as if it were only sustaining life force. Tears continued to cloud her vision. Through the blurriness she glimpsed the image of a striking young mother walking out of the grocery store, pushing a race-car-shaped shopping cart ahead of her. She was smiling down at a brown-haired toddler strapped in the front and making exaggerated facial and hand gestures. Honor watched as she packed up her environmentally-friendly bags, grabbed the toddler, and drove off in her red mini-van, no doubt on her way to Happiness Lane.

Honor could no longer breathe. *A baby? It can't be.* A baby would cement Honor to RJ for the rest of her life, or at least for the next eighteen years. The thought forced more air from her lungs.

How had this happened? She was always so careful to record her temperature each day to determine her peak ovulation days. On those three days, she made sure to stay as far away from RJ as possible. Not doing anything, saying anything, or wearing anything that might entice his already raging libido. Some nights, though, he forced her. *Could it have been one of those times?* One of the many times when RJ was merely masturbating inside of her, seeking a release and not caring about her satisfaction. She couldn't remember the last time he'd actually made love to her. *He is a monster, and now I am carrying his seed.* Honor tried to think back to happier times during their marriage, but they were few and far between—somewhere lodged between the screaming, the beatings, and the constant barrage of "bitch" that now seemed to be synonymous with her name. What made her take that step from the unknown to the altar all those years ago?

Honor's thoughts drifted back to the night they'd met at the school meeting. It was RJ's presence. He made her nervous, so nervous that she didn't dare look up from the papers in front of her as she'd sat at the table, even though she hadn't had a clue about what she was reading. Those damn eyes of his: They clinched the deal as soon as they'd been introduced, shook hands. How could she have possibly foreseen the future back then? Have visualized his kisses burning her very flesh? His words eating away at her psyche? His touch leaving her black and blue?

From the moment they'd met, Honor had been hooked—bitten by the love bug with no indication that it would turn venomous. Well, that wasn't entirely true. Now that she looked back over the course of their whirlwind relationship, there were signs. His moodiness, for instance. The way he'd suddenly shut down when she'd asked about his parents. RJ told her that they'd both died in a house fire when he was eleven years old. Who could survive such a tragedy unscathed? Honor could only forgive him. She prayed that he would open up to her. So immersed was she, at first, with RJ's looks, degrees, drive, and amazing lovemaking that'd she merely overlooked the flashing red warning sign. *Danger. Danger. Danger.*

Sure, Honor suspected there had been other women during their courtship, but she was certain there were none since the day they took their wedding vows. This one fact was the only thing that Honor could hang her flimsy hat on. Yes, RJ was faithful, but he was frightening. She discovered this shortly after their honeymoon, around the same time that her name changed to "Bitch." During one particular argument, over something as silly as the remote, he pushed Honor against the wall, so hard that the back of her skull ached for weeks afterward.

Another night, Honor wanted to go see a movie with her girlfriend. RJ didn't want her to go, so he picked her up and choked her by the collar of her own shirt. She called the police, and after an hour's stay in jail, during which she posted his bail, he was back home with his *"I'll never do it again"* promises. A brief court appearance and an anger management course later, Honor believed he had changed. He said all the right things. He even went to church with her, once.

RJ's nice façade didn't last long. A few months after the choking incident, RJ slapped Honor across the cheek because the bath towels had not been folded according to his military-like standards. That time, she'd had enough. Honor threw all of her belongings into two trash bags, hopped in the car, and drove the twenty-something hours straight back to Tampa.

He followed her though. Why did she think for a second that he wouldn't? She was his most prized possession. RJ appeared on the doorsteps of her parent's house in a wrinkled, pin-striped black and white suit and white tennis shoes. It was the fist time that Honor had ever seen RJ look disheveled. "Please come home," he cried, rubbing his hands back and forth across his unkempt hair. "I need you."

That was all it took to get her on Interstate 70, headed in the direction of Kansas City. Love had driven Honor somewhere south of hell.

"I can't be pregnant! I can't be pregnant!" She screamed in between labored gasps.

How different would her life be today if she'd run the other way, run away from those eyes? How different would her mother's life have been had she not married the judge? Did Olivia Thompson feel the same way about her two daughters as Honor felt about this child growing inside of her now? Trapped.

To this day, when her mother smiled, Honor saw only sadness in her eyes. Tight lines around her mouth that had developed through the years betrayed false happiness. Honor imagined a new tiny line forming each time the judge had belittled her in front of them. Another line for each occasion that he hadn't come home at night. Yet another for every instance that he did come home, and her mother was forced to stop whatever she was doing and reheat the dinners he never ate with his family. *I am reliving my mother's life.*

Beep. Beep. Beep. A horn went off somewhere in the distance of the parking lot. Honor looked around wearily. She didn't know how long she'd been sitting in the car, watching her past flash before her. Honor waited until she trusted her breathing again and the shaking subsided, then she scrolled through the directory of her cellphone, stopping at the "A's."

SASHA

"Bitch, you think I'm fuckin' playin' with your triflin' ass?! You think I'm a joke?" *Slam.* Sasha's back was up against the wall—literally. She closed her eyes as Vance's fists swam toward her face with the force and speed of a runaway windmill. The continuous motion confused her, and she moved beyond a state of shock until there was nothing, no shred of power in her words.

"No, Vance. I didn't say that." *Whack.* "I'm sorry!" *Bam.*

The never-saw-it-coming blow sent Sasha straight to the floor. Her protective instincts on high alert, Sasha curled into a fetal position and could have sworn she saw her reflection staring back at her. It was there, lying right beside her self-esteem.

Vance was kicking her now with the ragged soles of his size-13 tennis shoes, a twisted game of kickball that tossed her body to and fro. Still, Sasha tried to protect her core.

Then the game suddenly stopped. Everything went black. *Is this it? Is it finally over?* Sasha welcomed the blackness of it all. Her body crumbled under the weight of being disposable.

"Uhhhhhh," Sasha moaned, coughing up blood. She spit out one of her front teeth. She gagged and screamed as Vance poured a pitcher of cold water over her. She shivered, her body frozen on the carpet of the barren apartment they shared. *No, it's not over.*

He was still screaming at her. "Wake up, bitch! Get up and go get me my stuff, and you bet not come back here 'til you have it, neither. You hear me talkin' to you?" Vance bent down so his face was right next to hers. She could smell the rancidness of his gold-capped teeth. His unshaven face scratched her face like sharp razors.

"I said GET UP! Get yo'self cleaned up and go get my motherfuckin' stuff!"

"Ok, Vance. I'm moving as fast as I can," Sasha said, her voice chillingly childlike.

Sasha's body buckled when she tried to lift herself from the floor. She lay there, emotionally bruised and physically drained. She could feel Vance's black-as-midnight eyes still glued to her, and she could see the threat of further repercussion if she didn't get up at once from the floor.

She needed to reach toward the ceiling and make her way toward some height of dignity. Slowly she rose to her knees, and every muscle in her body screamed and cursed at her every move.

Only after standing did Sasha realize that she was gripping tightly to her own tooth. She'd like to believe that this was the first tooth that she'd ever lost from a beating, but she had lost count somewhere after the fourth time. Her once-beautiful smile was now just a jagged checkerboard pattern.

Pure adrenaline was the only thing that made Sasha limp into the bathroom of the one-bedroom apartment. She nearly tripped over a matted rug on the dark-speckled bathroom floor in the process. She picked a dirty towel off the bathroom floor and ran cold water over it, all the while trying to remember the last time she'd experienced hot water. She dropped her tooth on the cluttered counter, where it landed next to a down-to-the-quick bar of white soap and a tampon with flowered wrapping.

The coolness of the towel took away some of the pain of the bruises on her face and body. She cupped her hands to her face and let the cool water cascade over her skin like it was holy water. Sasha swished the water around in her mouth, spitting out blood-tainted bile until it was nearly clear. She could feel her right eye begin to swell. The sting was all too familiar. Her sight began to turn blurry. *That muthafucka! I gotta go through this shit – again! I'm so tired of looking in the mirror and seeing these damn bruises.*

Sasha wrung the towel out tightly until the last bit of water was released. Then she gripped it tighter with both hands. *Don't cry. Don't cry. Don't cry. Don't give him the satisfaction.* Sasha squared her shoulders, pursed her lips, rolled her eyes and forced herself to look at her reflection in the mirror. A single tear fell from her eye, which was rising with the speed of yeast. It was then that she wished she could be more like her brother, RJ. Strong and successful, with an I-don't-give-a-damn attitude that overshadowed every shred of the pitiful excuse for a childhood that they'd shared. *Screw him.*

Sasha wiped the lone tear from her heart-shaped face and stared at her sandalwood-complexion. Rage began to merge into the blurriness of it all. It hit her with the force of one of her boyfriend's blows. She gripped the small countertop for fear that she would land face first on the floor. Between the swelling, the anger, and the blurriness, it was as if she were a little girl again, looking through a paper toy: she would twirl the top half and the images would dance before her eyes, smaller then bigger. One diamond-shaped maze quickly turned into three or four. In the mirror, all Sasha could make out was a myriad of black, blue, and red.

Sasha threw the towel back down on the floor. The sink full of water was stagnate, the murky brown of a used watercolor brush. Her high cheek bones began to throb. The pain was just too much. Sasha reached inside the medicine cabinet and traced her fingers over the assortment of prescription pain killers.

Some of the bottles were prescribed to Sasha; others had Vance's name across the front. But most of them were in complete strangers' names: Rina Smalls, Donald M. Williams, Carla Milton. Sasha stopped at the bottle marked "Vicoden" and popped the cap off. *Damn.* Only two left. She swallowed each one separately, chasing them back with a handful of brown water. The pills caused a burning sensation as they slid down her in her throat, doing what they could to calm her.

Everything started to become clear to her. She nodded her head back and forth and exhaled in short, fast bursts of newfound energy. *I don't need this shit! He needs to be glad I stay around with his broke, can't-keep-a-job ass! I need a real man to take care of me. Yeah—a real man. I'm just going to walk out that damn door and not come back. He can't keep treating me like this.* Sasha squared her shoulders back in a type of tired mock-soldier stance. It was a simple gesture reserved for those who commanded bravery and respect. Her reflection knew differently, understood that her new stance betrayed her true feelings. If someone were to come inside and tap her ever so slightly on the shoulder, she would crumble. Because the reality was staring straight back at her. Vance was her life support. She needed him to breathe, to help her survive the day-to-day. Sasha needed Vance to tell her when to wake up, go the bathroom, eat, shower, walk, and sleep. Outside of their apartment, Sasha maintained a tough-girl exterior. But inside these four walls she was nothing but a puppet, and Vance pulled her every string.

Vance had been pulling them since the day she first laid eyes on him at age fourteen, about the same time that RJ and Edwin had gone off to college, leaving her all alone. Reverend Odom was there, physically. But the two empty chairs at the dinner table didn't offer lively conversations and banter. Sometimes, Sasha had to stop herself from setting plates before them at night. She hated being left alone with nothing but the *scriptures.* Sasha was no longer a little girl, and although the good reverend knew plenty about changing boys into men, he didn't haven't the slightest clue about raising a young woman—one who was developing quite rapidly into a full 36C cup and size-six jeans. Sasha was her mother's daughter, with the same bouncy curls that refused to be controlled, the flawless face that left many speechless at first glance, and the wildly curvaceous body to match. The boys, and the men too, were taking notice.

Reverend Odom's obvious inexperience with the female persuasion was no match for the watchful eyes and smooth tongues of the prowling males around him waiting to pounce on Sasha. He made sure that Sasha was in church at least every Sunday, where he could keep a watchful eye on her in the front pew, but the minute he turned away, looked down at the notes he had jotted down before him, or even when the congregation said "amen," she was gone from his sight.

He'd find her after the service, sitting in the very back pews with the boys he knew did not come from good homes. Boys who were only in church because their mothers had sent them there as a last resort. If their mothers couldn't strangle some sense into them, then maybe, just maybe, God could. Reverend Odom had even moved further from the city to avoid the likes of these boys, but still they came.

By the time Sasha had met Vance, she had graduated from the back pews to the backseats of cars and underneath the bleachers at school. Sasha discovered pretty quickly that she had a power over the opposite sex, and she learned how to use it to her advantage. A promise to let Bryan Felcher get to second base netted her a new gold chain and matching bracelet. Third base got her a trip to Bannister Mall for a new outfit. But that was as far as Bryan got.

He, like the others, became the pawn in her game of unrequited love. It was onto the next one before the first boy knew what had happened. Reverend Odom would hold his hands up in dismay, praying every day and night for a way he could reach out and save this beautiful, gum-popping, hip-swaying, large-gold-earring-wearing woman-child. He would ask her where she was getting the new outfits, the necklace with the diamond encrusted "S," the gold-hoop earrings, the red leather jacket: and Sasha would say that the items were gifts from her friends, or from her earnings from a part-time job she never worked.

One night the reverend, his eyes enflamed, searched Sasha's room looking for everything he hadn't bought her. He tossed brand new shirts, jeans, and jewelry into a trash bag and took them to the curb while Sasha screamed at him in the background. Yet the very next day, there would be new stuff, and still more the day after.

Vance was four years older than Sasha. He had a job. He had a car that wasn't his mother's. His own place. He was tall, dark, and fine, with the chiseled features of an African king. Plus, he was experienced at schooling young girls who thought they were all that. He provided the gifts, but they came at a price. It wasn't long before Vance had taken Sasha away from her school, her friends, and Reverend Odom, moving her into his place at 55th Street and Garfield. Sasha was the willing student, gladly leaving everything and everyone behind. She gave all her bases to Vance for the sheer promise of hitting a homerun at love.

For the first year or so, things were great for Sasha. She loved playing house. Fixing her man dinner every night, cleaning during the day, and watching TV until Vance came home from his job at the toy-manufacturing plant. Vance had made it clear, early on, that he did not want her to leave the house while he was away at work, and she didn't mind. Sasha was exactly where she wanted to be.

Then one balmy night, Vance brought a man named Clyde home from work. Sasha was already upset because Vance had walked in late, again. This meant that she had to reheat his dinner of fried chicken legs, peas, and boxed mashed potatoes. Sasha smelled something funny, and she sensed it too, as soon as they opened the door. The two men were laughing like two young school boys. Bypassing the meal Sasha had reheated for chips and cookies and cups of fruit punch.

After Vance had lit a funny-shaped cigarette, he invited the fuming Sasha to sit down beside them on the couch. She said no and pretended to be engrossed in Salt 'n Pepa's "Push It" blasting from the stereo.

Clyde went out to his car and came back with a fifth of bourbon, and Sasha was instructed to go into the kitchen and get them some cola so they could mix some drinks.

"Go on, gal," Vance had said, hitting her across her backside a little too hard.

"Ok, I'm going," she said, heading into the next room.

Sasha could hear them whispering as she grabbed three green plastic tumblers from the dish rack and the two-liter bottle of cola. When she returned from the kitchen with the cups and cola in hand, Vance and Clyde were seated closer on the tattered couch, rolling some tobacco into a cigarette. Or at least, she thought it was a cigarette.

"Here," Vance said. He licked the rolled white paper and handed the cigarette to her. "Smoke it."

"No, it smells funny," she said.

"I said, take a hit."

Something in his tone made her hold it to her full lips and inhale the foreign substance into her lungs. They laughed as she coughed continuously for a minute. Then Vance handed her his cup.

"Here…drink some of this now."

Sasha did as she was told. "Take the joint and inhale slowly. You got to keep it in your chest for as long as you can, and then blow it out."

A quick learner, it wasn't long before Sasha was giggling like crazy with them, drinking, inhaling, and munching on everything in sight.

"Hey, Sash, I want you to go on with Clyde in the back."

Sasha turned around, unsure of where exactly the back was. Was he asking her to show Clyde to the bathroom? She was still trying to decipher Vance's words when Clyde reached for her hand and began dragging her back into the bedroom she shared with Vance.

"Hey, hey stop…watcha' doin? Let me go! Vance, he tryin' to take me. I ain't goin' back there him." Clyde still gripped her hand.

"Go on back there and be nice to Clyde for me. He won't hurt you." The two men began laughing as Clyde pushed Sasha into the bedroom and slammed the door behind them. The sound jarred Sasha completely sober. Clyde reached to unbuckle his belt and started to take his dirty polo shirt off. Clyde was not attractive in the least and he looked way older than Vance. His stomach hung over his pants, and his two front teeth were rotting.

"Come on, girl, take them clothes off. Vance promised me a good time and I didn't pay for nothing, so come on out them drawers."

"But…but," Sasha was beyond confused.

"Vance! Vance!" she screamed into the dark room. No answer.

"Vance ain't coming. Now do what I paid you for."

Paid? Clyde tossed Sasha onto the full-sized bed like she was a paperweight. He lay his massive girth on top of her and tore off every stitch of clothing she was wearing. At first, she tried to push him off her. But it was useless. The fight went out of Sasha. She let the strange man have his way with her. His calloused hands were rough across her skin. His touch did not feel smooth like when Vance's soft hands caressed her. Clyde's breath assaulted her nose with every thrust. His small penis slid in and out of her soul. Mercifully, he hit his peak fairly quickly, groaning like a grizzly when he was done with one last mighty thrust of nothing.

Sasha exhaled loudly as he rolled from her and sat up on the bed. Without another word or glance in her direction, Clyde dressed himself and walked out of the bedroom, leaving the door wide open behind him.

"All right, man, I'll holler at you tomorrow morning," she heard Vance shout. Then the sound of screeching tires from the driveway.

A few minutes had passed before Vance made his way back to her. He flicked on the light; Sasha jumped up, pulling the covers up around her nakedness. Then he came charging for her, slapping Sasha so hard across her face that she fell from the bed and onto the hardwood floor.

"You ain't nothing but a ho, you know that? A HO!" He kicked her in her side with his bare foot and hit her again in the back. His bare fist made a loud whipping sound that echoed off her skin and consumed the walls. The bourbon, chips, and cookies began to edge up to her mouth. Sasha vomited on the floor.

"What the…?" Her retching stopped Vance in his tracks. "Clean this shit up." He left the room then, leaving Sasha to lay there in pain and her own vomit.

New "friends" began to come around more often after her first time with Clyde. It wasn't long before Vance quit working at the toy plant so he could concentrate on making more friends. In between the friends came the beatings, the miscarriages, and the making up. Because she never knew when Vance would bring one of them home, Sasha was on guard all day. She didn't like the edginess of it all. The bourbon and joints were the only things that managed to ease her anxiety and allow her to pretend to enjoy what she was doing. Through the years Sasha had graduated from marijuana and liquor, to an array of drugs that included prescription pain killers and crack cocaine. But that was the only thing that ever changed.

Sasha was so far into bondage that she no longer recognized herself as being enslaved.

Bang. Bang. The sound of Vance's fists pounding on the door caused Sasha to jerk back uncontrollably.

"What you doin' in there?! Hurry up and get your ass out here! I'm hungry," he screamed with his mouth so close to the door that Sasha swore she could smell his rancid breath through the wood. She grabbed two more pills from a nondescript bottle of pills before opening the door. Vance stood there, snarling at her. She recognized then, as though for the first time, that the years had not been kind to him. Years of thuggin', drugs, and just plain mean-spiritedness had created fine lines around his eyes. The muscles he once worked so hard to maintain were now pillows of flab. Beer had turned his six-pack into a keg, and Sasha guessed they wore about the same cup size. It was in these moments that she noticed his faults, and only in these moments. The rest of the time, Sasha only saw the man who once promised to love the hell out of her.

Sasha walked into the small bedroom and reached across the full-sized mattress on the floor for a short red skirt. She found a matching halter in a pile of clothing next to the bare mattress. Then she grabbed a pair of three-inch heels from the closet. A dab of lip gloss, some mascara and concealer over her bruised face, and she was ready. She turned back to glance at Vance before heading out the door.

"I'm going."

"Good. And bring me back something to eat, too." Vance made his way to the refrigerator, grabbing a beer from between the half-gallon of expired milk and molded cheese. He snapped the top of the can off and sat on the worn couch, staring at her in the dimness of the room. His eyes turned to the stand where the television had been before they had pawned it a few weeks ago. It had been the last piece of electronic equipment that hadn't been traded for a hit. Now it, too, was gone.

"What you waitin' for…the resurrection? I said GO!"

Sasha slammed the door behind her and headed to the corner of 31st Street and Main. Normally, she would sashay her way there with all the fierceness of a runway supermodel. She was, after all, still top dollar. Tonight, though, she walked to the corner slowly with her head down. The others took notice. Rock bottom had never seemed like something to aspire to, until now.

Hi Sasha,

I use to hold you in my arms all the time when you was a baby. I member. You didn't have to cry, I was always there. Holding you so close, runing my fingers thru your soft curls, holding yur tiny fingers. I never want to let you go. I was to afraid of what wuld happen if I did. That's the truth. One day, you must been about two at the time, I reached to pick you and you pushed me.

"No, Mama. Down!"

You was spunkie. So I had no choise but to let you go. I prayed rite then and there, that you wuld never let a man lay hands on you — ever. I hope my prayers made it to heaven and God saw fit to give you a good man. You know God and I werent on the best of speaking terms back when.

When I met yur daddy, I was yung and stupid. At first I thot Randy's jealous was cute. Thot it showed he love me. He wuld punch a guy out for even look at me. That was loyal to me. I new he wuld die for me. Oh, how wrong I was. My daddy, he tried to tell me bout Randy. But, I didnt listen to a word he say. What girl gone listen when her heart in love? My daddy was left by my moma to raise us four girls alone. I was lost in the shufle. He move us from lower east side New York to the midwest for a better life. He want to keep us from the thing I ran smack into. My daddy from the Old Kountry. His broken English get us by in New York, cause he mostly talk Spanish anyway, they laugh at him in Kansas City tho. He try to make a good life for us. He got a job on a yard crew that earn him a good living. Things cheaper in Kansas City. At nite, he drank though. Heavy. Not at home tho. Never at home. He did all his drinking at this bar round the corner, and he act like we don't no. Like we don't see him stumble home. He be so drunk he culdn't even get his key in the door or take his work boots off. most times he didnt make it to his bed. He wuld jus pass out on the couch in the liven room boots and all. A few nites he didnt even make it to the couch. We find him face down on the floor.

Look back, I think his drinking push me to Randy. Randy was only 2 year older then me but I thot he new so much more then me. He use to tell me I was beautifull. No man had ever told me that before. We marry down at the courthouse when I was 18. I had yur brother bout a year or so after. Yur father got a job at the sembly plant on the north side. I like to say things was good, but what did I no about good live?

The night we was marry was the first time Randy hit me. We had a big party in the back of my daddy's house to celebrat. I member I had on a short white miniskirt and go go boots and a matching top I had sew myself. There is a white flower behind my ear. Ever one has a good time. All My cuzins was there. My sisters. Randy's folk and are friends. We ate, drank and danced all nite.

Folk go once all the booze and food was gone. I was pickin up some paper plates from the piknic table when yur father walked over and slapp me so hard and fast cross the face I didn't no what hit me. 1 minute I standing, the next I on the ground cover in grass stains.

"You try to make me look like a fool tonite, Carmen!"

I cry then. Scream for some body to help me. Nobody came tho. Nobody came. I just lay there on the ground crying, hold my face.

"Dance with all them cats. showin yur little tail round all nite in that tight, short ass skirt. Just a cheesin' in all there faces. You mine! You hear me! Mine! You my wife!"

He swore to me that nite he'd never hit me again until the nex time. Ain't that how it always start? After the first time, he become the man I luv again. Randy stay holdin my hand or huggin me and buy me the most beautifull gold bracelet the next day after he hit me that time. To this day, I don't no where he get the cash for it. I was queen for a day. But it didnt last. Week later, he punch me in my mouth after I burn the meatloaf 1 night, and he called me them nasty names. I never hear such filth come out his mouth before. Huh, I guess I musta' picked it up from him since then. I made excuse for him that time. See, he loss his job at the plant and we had a new baby, another mouth to feed, and I had to go and burn are dinner. That's what I thot.

After that, I try really hard not to say or do any thing that set him off. I jump if yur brother cry and hush him up for he desturb Randy. Can you emagine? Who the hell can keep a baby from cryin? That's what babies do, they cry. I want my son and my husband to stop, just stop yelling at me. I can't say four sure how long I walked on egg shells round yur daddy. You shouldn't have to do that under yur own roof. It just ain't rite! Nothin I ever did was rite, ever thing was wrong. The name calling and the hitting, it only got worser. Until, 1 day I just craked! Yur daddy use to tell me many a time that he see me dead before he let me walk out that door, and I believe him. Did I ever try to leave? Once. He found me tho, hiding out at my sister's, your aunt Hilga's house. He come over drunk, bang on the door. Hilga wuldn't let him in, but Randy kicked the door in and drug me back to the house by my hair. The hole block was watching, laughing. I think that time was the worst he beat me. Love does not hurt! It took me being in jail to knowed that. Funny, huh? I had to get locked up in order to find what love be like. How it posed to feel. Love should feel like soft rose pedals and the sun beating down on yur skin, not like broken glass all across yur face.

In here, I work in the kitchin. All the girls love my cookin, cause I spice it up as best I can with what ever they got in the back. Trust me, it ain't much to work with. My father would roll over in his grave – fixin' spagheti with no fresh garlic, or eating packed tortillas. Some of the girls hug me once they finish eaten. The old-timers say the food never was this good til I got here. Sometimes, I sneak and bake a cake when 1 of the girls in my RAGE class got a birthday or if they kid gotta birthday. Some of these girls, they never even got to see they babies, hold them. I feel lucky in that way I guess. At least I get to no my kids for a while. I gotta pic on my wall of you and RJ when y'all was litle. You must have been bout five years old. RJ was probably eight. It was the dead of winter and half the folks in Wayne Miner didn't have no heat. We was sittin inside that cold apartment when I cided that if we was gonna freeze to death we might as well do it outside playin. So I bundle you 2 up, grab the camera and off we went. It was one of the best days of my life. We made a snow man had a snowball fight (I won), made snow angels and laugh and laugh. It was like the snow melt away all of the sad that day. When we done we went in, turn the oven on to get some kinda heat, and I made us some hot cocoa. Do you member that day Sasha?

You no what else make that day so special? I didn't have no bruises or scars on me. That day was one the 1 time that I can I member my face, my body, and my skin being beautifull. Do you wanna' no what RAGE stand for? Reachin Abused Girls Everywhere. So many women inside these prison walls are victims of abuse. The hurt, the shame, the guilt, it's a part of are orange clothes that we put on ever morning – only we can't take it off at nite. It's part of us. Some of these girls come in here, they've been gettin hit or molest as young as 11 months old. That's why we say Girls, because, all the time the hurt start before they old enuff to put on a training bra. The women like me who come in after their husbands beat them up one way and down the other—well that litle girl that believe in fairy tails she gone forever. Don't let that be you, Sasha. Never. Fight to protect the girl inside.

I no what I did was wrong. Hell, you to young to member that day. God no, I don't want you in no pain. I don't even want you to member me. If you did, then you would hurt each time my face came up. Don't feel none of me.

The Rev drove you up here to visit me 1 time. RJ stay home, but you, you was so glad to see me. Rev Odom said he could harly get you to go to sleep the night before, when he woke up that day you was dressed and ready to go. I have a yellow ribbon taped to my wall next to where I lay my head. It the ribbon you wore in yur hair on the day you came to visit. You were so beautifull. I just burst into tears lookin at you. How, I asked?

How could some thing so grate come from some thing so bad? When you rapped yur litle arms round me all I new was that for once, I was hole. I was a woman again. A mother who gave birth to a love that hold me so tite. In you I see a future with no metal bars and plastic spoons.

You had on this bright yellow dress that twirl when you spun round, and these baby doll socks and yellow shoes that buckle at the top. "Are you my mommy?"

Thats what you ask me.

"Yes, honey, I'm yur mama."

You draw a cute pitcher of a butterfly. It still on my wall. We laugh and talk. Boy, culd you talk! I hold you so closer to me. You smell like inocence, so good like a mix of soap and baby powder. Your long curls made me think I ran thru a field of flowers. It was a wanderful visit, until the guard call time.

"Come on mommy, it's time to go home now," you say with those big eyes lookin up at me.

"No, sweetie. mama has to stay here. So, you go on now with Rev Odom. I see you next time." I member I was trying my best not to cry in front of you. I start count to 100 back ward.

100,99,98,97.

You grab my hand.

96.95.94.

You pull me.

"Why not? You my mommy and it time for you to come home now. Why don't you wanna be with me?

"Oh, honey, I wanna be with you more than any thing in the world, but I cant go with you today."

I try hard to plane but you scream over and over again. "COME HOME NOW MOMMY!"

Rev Odom had to drag you kickin and screamin from the room.

"Mommy! Mommy! Mommy!"

The ribbon fell from yur hair and I pick it up. When I new you was away from the cold of the steel bars that I fall down and cry.

You never came back.

To this day if I close my eyes real tite and sniff yur ribbon, I can still smell flowers and innosence. I feel love when I touch the yellow.

Sasha, even if I never hold you again or this leter never see the lite of day, never find you, no you is so much more then me. No scars.

With all my love,

Mommy.

RANFORD

"Yo, Principal E. Principal Ellis. You feel what I'm sayin'?"

"W…what?"

"I said Coach Nevels threatenin' to throw me off the basketball team 'cause my average dropped below a C, but I told him I can bring it back up next semester. He can't pull me off the team."

"Um…I agree with Coach Nevels. Your grades come first. Now, get to class…"

"But Principal E, it ain't fair. I know a couple of dudes on the team be making straight C's and D's and still playin'. Just give me until next semester…"

"Excuse me, Tommy," RJ said to Tommy Bryans, one of his middle school students. RJ had barely heard a word the boy was saying to him. He could make out Tommy's short dreads and the two diamond earrings on each of his ears, but he just looked right through Tommy and headed for the sanctity of his office.

"Principal E. You just gone leave me hangin' like that?" Tommy made one final plea before RJ closed the door in his face.

Three days later and RJ still couldn't shake Reverend Odom's words at their last visit. *"There is darkness all around you, following you. It lives in your home. A dark spirit. The Lord…told me to tell you to repent, turn from your ways.*

"…I know what you've been doing…and ain't none of it good. Seen it clear as my own eyes…"

RJ slouched down in his oversized leather chair and buried his head in his hands. He reached inside the bottom left drawer for his bottle of scotch and poured the rusty-colored liquid into the solitary glass that was beside it. He downed it in one gulp, letting the drink burn his throat and clear his mind. Placing the bottle back in its hiding spot, RJ jumped up as if a fire had been lit underneath him and reached for his sports jacket.

"Wanda, I'm going out for a while. Anything comes up, direct it to Vice Principal Saunders," he barked his orders at the stout secretary who sat guard at the front desk. Wanda was a heavy, older, salt-and-pepper haired woman who had earned her loyalty simply by working past the other secretaries' expiration dates.

RJ had learned early on that even a mildly cute woman could distract him at times, and they never said no to any of his demands, even if his requests occasionally fell outside of their normal job descriptions.

"But where should I say you've gone?" Wanda asked with a hint of annoyance in her voice. The phones had been ringing off the hook all day with demanding parents who had yet to hear from their beloved principal.

"Just tell them I'll be in first thing tomorrow morning."

"Oh. Is everything all right, Principal Ellis?" Now Wanda was genuinely concerned for her chiseled-featured boss.

"Yes, I'll see you in the morning," he answered, his back already turned toward her and his gait aimed straight for the nearest escape.

He loosened his tie as he ran down the stairs to his car. The tires screeched loudly as RJ made a beeline toward home.

The twenty-minute drive had seemed longer as RJ pulled into the driveway. He opened the three-car garage and was surprised to see Honor's car inside. His first thought was that she was inside with another man, and RJ wondered if he should grab the gun he kept locked away in the tool shed before heading inside. Then he laughed to himself. *I must really be going crazy. Honor would never step out on me. I'd kill her dead.*

Still, RJ couldn't believe how hard his heart was pumping as he made his way up the stairs and into the master bedroom. A wave of relief washed over RJ as he looked down at his wife sleeping on the king-sized bed they shared—alone. The sight of her calmed his beating heart.

So RJ did not ask her, "Why are you at home, sleeping in our bed in the middle of the day?" Or, "Why didn't you tell me you were at home?" Instead he gently took off each of his black, patent leather shoes, lay down next to Honor, and listened to her steady breathing. Then he turned and put his arm around her. The palm of his hand slid across the nipple that pierced through her chiffon nightgown. The sensation replaced the waves of calm with the burning heat of the Sahara. He needed her wetness. RJ peeled his suit off and dived back into the bed naked. He turned Honor on her stomach and slid inside her in one swift motion.

"RJ, what are you doing? I don't feel good. STOP!" Honor, still dazed from her afternoon nap, rasped in between his multiple thrusts. From her position, she could not see that RJ's eyes were tightly shut. He was in a trance-like state and her pleas rose above his desire and his need to sex his way to some type of sanity. But he was in too deep. Thrusting and grinding against the resistance. With each thrust, RJ believed he was closing the disconnect that had existed between them lately. He was headed to the Promised Land, and in this land, her cries were lost in a place that was so far away.

"You are mine! Mine! Mine!" RJ screamed as he exploded inside of her. Sweat covered his body. His breathing was heavy and his mind was coming down from the frantic high he'd been in for days.

RJ rolled over onto his back and placed his muscular arms behind his head.

"That was good, huh?" It wasn't a question really, more of a statement.

No response. RJ noticed Honor's body begin to shudder beside him. He propped his head up and was surprised to see her crying. *What now?*

"Hey, what's wrong with you?"

"Nothing."

"Then why are you crying?"

"No reason."

RJ sat up and threw his feet onto the floor. A chill instantly went up his body as his toes touched the hardwood floor. He ran his hands through his evenly cut hair and sighed. Honor flinched at his slightest movement, which didn't go unnoticed.

"Why are you home in the middle of the day anyway?" RJ asked. "And why didn't you call and tell me you were home?"

"Why are you home in the middle of the day?" Honor asked through her tears.

"I asked you first," he said. RJ despised this type of elementary-school banter that sometimes transpired between them. He didn't even like speaking to his students in this manner.

"I wasn't feeling well, so I called in sick today," Honor answered. RJ wanted to see her face, but she would not turn around. Her back was a boulder between them.

"Well, what's wrong with you?"

"I'm just not feeling well. I think I'm coming down with something. Probably just a cold," she said. *I hate you. I hate you. I. Hate. You.*

Yeah, you're definitely cold. Words unspoken lay down beside Honor. RJ sensed the impenetrable presence and wanted to wring its neck.

"Why didn't you call and tell me?" RJ couldn't remember if he'd called to check on her, which was unusual because he made it a point to call her at least three times a day.

"I was too tired," Honor answered softly.

"Remember when we used to rush home during our lunch hours and right after work for our quickies?" RJ asked, trying to lighten the mood.

"I'm tired, RJ. I just want to go to sleep." Honor didn't want to remember, or entertain the possibility that there were ever any good times with this man.

"What is wrong with you?!" RJ screamed and jumped up. He couldn't fix *it*, the unspoken, and he was frustrated that *it* couldn't be fixed. He wanted a tool that would make everything all right. He needed that damn tool!

"Why won't you answer me?" RJ said. He paced back and forth beside the bed. "What the hell is wrong with you? Hell, you don't cook anymore. You barely clean. You don't screw me. So what the fuck are you good for? Why the fuck do I keep your fat, lazy ass around?!"

"I did answer you, RJ. What do you want from me?!"

"What do I want from you?" RJ's skin was on fire and every time Honor spoke another match lit inside of him.

"You should know what I want by now! I want a fuckin' wife! Not some lazy-ass heifer that can't even take her tired ass to work! Do you know how many women would love to be in your place? DO YOU? You better get your shit together before I get it together for you! Trifling-ass ho!"

Honor sat up and leaned her head against the mahogany headboard. She pulled the ivory eight-hundred-thread-count sheets up to her neck. She was crying so hard, it was hard to catch her breath. *Oh no! Not again! I'm going to die!* Honor could sense that RJ's emotional thermostat was beginning to rise. She had witnessed his hulk-like transition enough to gauge when he was about to blow. His temperament had no midpoint; it was permanently broken.

"Just leave me alone, RJ!"

"Leave you alone. Bitch, this is my house! I pay the bills here! Your little paychecks don't cover you taking a shit in this house! You hear me? DO YOU HEAR ME?!"

"Yes, I hear you, RJ."

"I make sure you have everything you need! Everything! You ungrateful bitch! All I asked in return is to be fed and fucked properly. Is that too much to ask? Is it?!"

"No, RJ," Honor said, her voice flat.

"Then why don't you do it? That's all I ask! Just fuckin' do the things I ask!" RJ leaned toward Honor, spittle dripped down his mouth as his words became more deliberate, abrupt.

"RJ, leave me alone, please!" Honor pulled the covers in closer to her shivering body. Then she screamed.

RJ pulled away from the bed, grabbed the vase sitting on the nightstand and threw it against the wall. Glass shattered, the sound resounded throughout the house. A splash of wilted pink roses lay on the floor. Then a silence so deafening it made Honor want to scream to break it.

RJ yanked his red boxers off the floor and pulled them on before heading out the bedroom door and making his way down the stairs in search of calm. He went to the bar on the far side of the den and poured himself a scotch, his hand shaking. *Doesn't she know how much I love her? Can't she see that I'm working my ass off for us?*

Minutes passed and the liquor brought with it an eerie peace. RJ was still deep in thought when the phone rang. He didn't reach to answer. He let the machine talk for him.

His deep baritone voice filled the room.

"Hello. You've reached the Ellis residence. No one is available to take your call right now, so leave your contact information and a brief message after the beep, and we'll be sure to return your call." *Beep.*

"Hi, Mrs. Ellis. This is Dr. Williamson. You forgot your attaché case the other day when you visited the office. You also forgot to pick up your expectant mothers kit from the front desk and schedule your next OB appointment. Congratulations, once again, on the good news!"

SASHA

While she was growing up, Reverend Odom often recited one particular scripture to Sasha: Something about renewing your strength and mounting up and soaring on eagles wings. Right now, with the assistance of a small rock and a glass pipe, she was that eagle soaring above the clouds. Sasha was on a phenomenal high. The cloud of smoke was her god. She worshipped anything that could take the pain away, even for a moment. Everything was beautiful when she was high, a feel-good '70s love ballad that played continuously.

She was riding in the passenger seat of Vance's rusty four-door '80s model Ford coupe, its muffler clinging to life on an old wire coat hanger. The muffler hung so low that it set off sparks at each pothole, making it look like the Fourth of July on 29th Street and Garfield Avenue.

Sasha was slouching low in the seat, an anxious Vance steering crazily beside her. He was waiting for his turn to pray to the glass pipe. Didn't matter that he was driving. He had mastered the art of steering the car with his knees while he lit up with both hands years ago.

Finally, it was Vance's turn to worship. Sasha giggled at the sight of Vance's tree trunk of a leg stuffed under the steering wheel and the car swerving from curb to curb as he choked on the glass pipe. An orchestra of car horns began to sound around them; this made Sasha laugh harder.

"Crazy bastard!" A pair of gold teeth gleamed at them from behind the dash of a dark green 1980s model Cadillac. Now they were both laughing hysterically. The white cloud of smoke began to thicken inside the car. To Sasha, it appeared that the tan cracked vinyl interior was hogging up the good stuff. Stealing it, and threatening to take it from them through the half-open windows.

"I love you, baby gal," Vance said between exhales on the glass pipe.

"I love you too, baby." Sasha watched him curiously for a minute, then began to flick the yellow lighter she held in her hands, suddenly enthralled by the flickering flame that came up after every few clicks.

She flicked the lighter's switch several more times and frowned when the flame no longer appeared. One last click and the flame sputtered slowly upright than taller. She giggled.

The vision forced her mind back to a time when was a little girl playing hopscotch along the cracked pavement in Wayne Miner. Just as she was about to land on the four, she spotted a black and brown caterpillar underfoot. When she bent down to pick it up, its furry little body tickled the palms of her hands, so much that she couldn't stop laughing. Other than the time when she pretended to be asleep while her brother carried her in his warm arms, it was one of the few joys Sasha could remember as a child.

With every breath, Sasha believed she was, at least for now, protected—cocooned in a drug-induced euphoria that only came around every tenth or twentieth hit. Yet Sasha chased the feeling, hoping to catch it every time. This glassy-eyed glee was all she had to look forward to.

"Hey, baby gal, we gone have to make a stop at the reverend's."

Just like that, the caterpillar fell from her hands.

"Baby, do we have to go to Rev's house? Maybe we can get the cash another way. I can try to hook up some extra men tonight, or we can do a jack on that corner store off Prospect again?" Sasha asked, her voice pleading.

Frown lines suddenly appeared across Vance's face. She could see his shoulders tensing on his massive six-foot-two, two-hundred-fifty-pound frame. The cracks in the car's vinyl interior began to groan as he dug deeper into his seat. That was all it took to silence her. Sasha ran her hand along her still blackened eye, a reminder of what could happen if she continued to push him to the edge. Just like Vance had mastered the skill of holding the glass pipe while he steered the car with his knees, he had a knack for backhanding Sasha while keeping one hand on the wheel.

"Ok, ok. We'll stop by the rev's."

Now it was Sasha's turn to sink deeper into the car's cracked interior. She folded her arms around chest—the closest she could come to defiance. Sasha hated to ask Reverend Odom for money. It was her least favorite thing to do, next to turning tricks with men with sweaty palms and even sweatier male parts.

It wasn't that Reverend Odom wouldn't give her any money. Most times he would, without question, graciously hand Sasha whatever amount his small social security checks would allow him to give. Since RJ took care of the reverend's living expenses, there was usually a few dollars here and there to spare. But the money always came with a price: a sermon and a guarantee that she was headed straight for the pits of hell. Yet here they were, turning the corner into the Metropolitan Ministries Retirement Community, the car leaving a trail of exhaust as it came to a stop in the spot marked "Future Residents."

"Vance, I don't…I don't wanna go up there," she mumbled. "He's always harpin' on me and sayin' I'm goin' to hell and stuff. Why don't you go up there?"

Whack. That was her answer: A punch to her chest that left her gasping for air. The love had lost its shine again.

"Go get us some motherfuckin' loot, ho. NOW!"

Sasha obliged, throwing herself from the car, leaving the door ajar.

"Hey, get back here and shut the door!" Vance called as she ran inside the apartments.

"Shut it your damn self, you bastard!" She knew she would pay for that one later. But so what? She'd have the cash and he'd be at her mercy, at least for a little while. Sasha stepped inside the grand entrance, designed to look as if people didn't come here to take their last breath. She bypassed the curious glances of the pudgy, paisley-dressed woman at the front desk. A rush of adrenaline gave Sasha a jolt as she rang the doorbell: no answer. Sasha knocked hard.

She hated that she had been made to feel like a guest and knock like this. Reverend Odom had taken back the keys to his place after several of his electronic items and other valuables began disappearing. He may have been a God-fearing man who sometimes lost his grip on reality, but he was far from stupid.

Still there was no answer at the door. Sasha rang again. The buzzer chimed a half-pulsating, half-bell sound. She knocked a bit more frantically. Lightly at first, then harder. Finally, Sasha heard signs of life from the other side. The shuffling of feet and grumbling.

"I'm coming, I'm coming. Hold your horses!" The reverend's deep baritone voice seemed to shake the door before her, or maybe that was an effect of the drugs?

Sasha's hands shook as the knob turned and she came face-to-face with the boulder of the man who had raised her.

Once, I knew a man who could move mountains, but look at him now, he ain't nothing. Just an old man.

This thought gave Sasha an instant sensation of security. The man who had taken her in as a little girl, clothed and fed her, never asking for anything in return, needed to be reduced to something less than human in her eyes so that she could feel better about herself—even if it made as much sense as a gnat emerging to conquer an eagle, she needed to hang onto it for a few seconds.

"Sasha? Is that you? Lord, have…Well, come on in, child. Don't just stand out there in the hallway looking like the lost sheep you are," Reverend Odom said. He turned to let her inside. With his cane in hand, he moved like lightning compared to the frail figure he appeared to be, despite a slight limp from hip replacement surgery a few years back.

Sasha crept in as if she were secret service, closing the vault of a door behind her. "Hey, Rev. How's it going?"

"Haven't seen you in weeks, and that's all you got?" he asked. "Well, I've been good. Where you been?"

"Ummm…Rev… I've been busy…Trying to go back to school…Sending out resumes…You know…Trying to find a job. I've been meaning to get by here, but it's hard out there, Rev." Sasha's hands fumbled in mid-air; she needed desperately to hang onto something.

Reverend Odom walked over to one of the two windows on his standard-issue eggshell-painted wall and peered through the blinds, looking at the bucket of a car below and the grungy man standing beside it, inhaling a cigarette.

"Uh-huh. You look like shit, Sasha."

This last comment threw Sasha for a loop. Not only because she'd never heard the reverend utter a curse word in her life, but, until this very moment, she couldn't remember the last time she'd given a second thought about her appearance. Sasha never cared too much about looking at herself. She ran her tongue across her yellowing teeth, laden with plague, until she got to her latest missing tooth. Her hands traveled across her unruly curls, curls that hadn't been brushed in months. Sasha touched her old faded jeans with worn holes in both knees, and fingered the tattered red sweatshirt with multi-colored stains. She glanced down at her muddy tennis shoes with no laces and ripped soles. She was a pile of dirt.

"And you stink too! When was the last time you had a shower?"

"Um…"

"Well?" Reverend Odom was still looking outside the window. Without turning around, he pointed his cane toward the open bathroom.

"Go on in there, take a shower, and brush your teeth before you say another word. There's some spare toothbrushes in the bottom drawer. In that drawer, you'll also find a stick of deodorant and some fresh, clean clothes for you to change into. Can't do nothing about your shoes now, but I'd sooner you'd walk out here with a pair of my house slippers on your feet than what you walked in here with."

"But, Reverend, I gotta go!" Sasha shouted in protest. "Vance is waiting and I got to get to this job interview and…"

Her pleading fell on old, deaf ears. "I said go get cleaned up, and throw those clothes in the trash," he said. Reverend Odom's gruff voice was not completely devoid of its parting-the-sea power after all. Although Sasha hated to admit it, his voice was also somewhat comforting. In it, there was no fleeting protectiveness. This was eternal.

Sasha peeled her clothes from her body and threw them into the trash, as instructed. *Thud.* She turned the shower on full blast, grabbed the bathtub safety rail, and sat down on the rotating shower stool. She immersed herself in the steaming hot water, letting it run down her face, into her mouth and between her toes. The water hurt as it hit the bruises on her body, but the pain reassured her that she was still alive.

The hot steam took Sasha back to her girlhood. She was twelve, in the middle of her transition into womanhood. The reverend had taken her to Penney's department store downtown, straight to the women's lingerie department. All at once, his skin flushed at the expansive array of panties and bras that surrounded him.

"Can I help you?" A thirty-something white woman with fine blond hair and aging skin approached them.

"Um…Yes…" the reverend said, clearing his throat. He looked at the braless Sasha, her nipples straining the thin cotton of the LL Cool J t-shirt she wore, and then back at the sales lady in total helplessness. Then he pushed Sasha toward the woman. Sasha gasped and jiggled.

"She needs…Fix. Her," he said in a hushed tone that could have been confused for yelling. Reverend Odom handed the saleslady his one credit card.

"Oh, I see. Yes. Yes. Come with me, please." She gave Sasha an I-feel-sorry-for-you glance and quickly put her hand across the blossoming girl's shoulders.

"Well, aren't you the lucky gal?" she tried to lighten the mood. "Not too many girls get the exclusive use of their father's credit card without a fight."

She turned to the reverend. "Don't you worry. She's in good hands. Why don't you go have yourself a cup of coffee at the restaurant across the street, or browse the men's department? She'll be all set by the time you get back."

Reverend Odom was already five steps out of the lingerie department before the pinch-faced saleslady could finish her sentence.

"Well, let's say we get you measured. Then we'll go from there."

Four bra-and-panty sets later, Sasha stood outside the department store waiting for him before he'd turned the corner. Sasha noticed Reverend Odom exhale deeply at the sight of her there, two bags discreetly tucked under her arm. It was over.

But it had only started. At thirteen, Sasha woke to find spots of blood in her panties. At first she was scared. But then she recalled the many conversations with her best friend, Debra, about "that time." *I got my period.* She relaxed then, went into the bathroom, stuffed tissue in her underwear, and waited for the reverend to return home from his new church on 63rd Street and Chestnut.

"I need you to take me to the store." That was her greeting.

"Sasha, can't it wait until tomorrow? I'm tired and I've got to prepare for the men's Bible study tomorrow night."

"No. It can't wait. I need to go now!"

"Well, why you need to go to the store so bad? I just went a few days ago, so we can't be out of too much. It's just the two of us now; we can't be out of anything. What could possibly be so important?"

"I got my period."

"Your what?" Reverend Odom examined Sasha closely, searching for a hint or some type of clue in her eyes. Then it hit him. Hard. He looked upward, expecting an answer. Sasha stared back at the reverend, her arms crossed defiantly across her chest.

"Ok, let's go then," he moved like the house was on fire. When they arrived in front of Skaggs drugstore, Reverend Odom reached for his wallet and pulled two crumpled fives from his worn black wallet.

"Here," he handed them to her carefully. "Get whatever you need, I'll be right here waiting for you."

Once inside, Sasha became lost in the feminine hygiene aisle. The different brands and types of pads astounded her. She had no idea what to pick, and what did you do with a tampon? Tears came to Sasha's eyes at the realization that this would have been a time when a mother would come in handy. She longed for one of the grinning women on the myriad boxes to instantly materialize in front of her and take her hand.

A mother could guide her. Congratulate her. Walk her through the drugstore proudly and explain everything to her with a huge smile across her face the whole time. Afterwards, they'd go out for an ice cream cone to celebrate her "becoming a woman." But her mother was not there; instead she was doing thirty-to-life behind bars. She had no one, not even a boxed woman. Sasha wiped her eyes, shrugged her shoulders, reached for the box with the woman flying a kite, and made her way to the checkout aisle, picking up a candy bar and a pack of gum before she escaped the boxes and the silly notion that she was worth having a mother.

Freshly soaped and shampooed, Sasha lavished in the aloe scent and let the water turn lukewarm, then cold. True to his word, the reverend had set aside a stash of toiletries and a fresh change of clothes for her. Sasha chose a pair of khakis that seemed to fit her small frame just right, and a teal button-down polo. Socks. *When is the last time I've worn socks?* She put a pair on her feet, painfully brushed her teeth, and wiped a tear from her face. Never looking at her reflection in the mirror. She approached Reverend Odom, who was sitting in his favorite recliner. His hands and face heavy on the top of his wooden cane. He looked up when he saw Sasha, a hint of approval in the small gesture.

"Are you hungry?" He asked. His voice sounded like a door hinge that hadn't been oiled in years.

"No."

"Course you are. Look at you: skin and bones ain't fit to make stew with."

With surprising agility, the reverend bounced from the recliner and walked into the kitchen. There was something about his matching black sweatpants and sweatshirt that reminded Sasha of his days behind the pulpit in that long black robe. A chill bit her hard on the neck, then her face and hands—all the places that were exposed. At the same time, beads of perspiration began to form on her forehead.

Sasha longed to go hide in the bathroom. There was safety there, just her and her memories. She wanted to sink back into the comfort of the lukewarm water and the steaminess of it all.

Sasha watched as Reverend Odom placed a pot on the stove in the galley kitchen and opened up a can of soup. She couldn't tell what type of soup it was from where she stood, but she could make out the noodles. From the refrigerator, he pulled out a tray of leftover ham, lettuce, cheese, and tomatoes. Sasha began to worry about Vance still waiting for her outside. She knew he was already upset, but he'd be more enraged if she returned without even a ten-spot to place in his greedy hands.

The pot of soup began to boil. Sasha's stomach began to turn at the smell. Unsure of what she was feeling at first, she realized it was growling. She was hungry.

"Well, don't just stand there. Come and get you something to eat."

Sasha was twelve years old again: she did as she was told. The food seemed to evaporate right before her eyes as she grabbed for one bite, then another, until not a drop of soup or morsel of sandwich remained. She wiped the plate with her fingers and placed them into her mouth. Reverend Odom's hand hit her hand. Gently. Even still, Sasha flinched and jumped up from the table. The chair fell fast behind her. *Bam!*

Like a moth to the flame, she was drawn to fear.

"Sit down, Sasha! What the devil has gotten into you, jumping like I just scratched you with cat's claws?" Sasha's eyes tripled in size and she looked around the apartment in a jerking motion, searching for safety.

"Calm down! You think I'm going to sit here and watch you suck on your fingers in front of me, when I got plenty of food to spare? You aren't a dog nipping at a bone. I wouldn't even do a dog like that. If you're still hungry, go on get you another sandwich and another one. Take everything I have in the cabinet. But you will not lick your fingers like a dog in my house. Do you hear me, Sasha?"

"Yes, sir."

Sasha backed into the kitchen and the countertop that still held the spread of sliced deli meat and helpings. She made herself another sandwich.

"Sasha, while you're up there, reach up there in the cabinet in front of you and grab that bottle up top, and a glass."

Had there been any traces of her earlier caterpillar-dream high, it was gone as soon as she opened the brown cabinet door and found herself grabbing a bottle of Wild Turkey.

Even in her current state, Sasha could not remember a time when she had ever seen the good reverend go near a teaspoonful of alcohol. In fact, he often referred to it as the "devil's poison" in his sermons while a young Sasha would sneak sips from Jeremy Fulton's silver flask in the back pew.

This old fool done really gone and lost his damn mind—Wild Turkey at that. This ain't no starter set neither.

Sasha placed the whiskey and a glass in front of Reverend Odom. She watched as the brown liquid swished into the bottom of the glass like a mini riptide as his unsteady hand poured more than a few drops. Sasha's already bulging eyes stretched wider. One sip. Two sips. Three sips. The reverend tossed back the whiskey and made another glass riptide. Sasha licked her lips.

"Sit down, and close your mouth," he said. "I didn't walk on water next to Jesus and I sho' didn't feed the multitudes with a loaf of bread. No sir, Jesus I am not." His voice was firmer now, edgier, almost as if the alcohol had oiled the hinges of his vocal cords. Sasha did as she was told—no, commanded—to do.

"Lord knows I always tried to do right by you kids. I tried my hardest, and I always prayed for you…until this very day. I knew I was doing the right thing, taking you all in the way I did. I couldn't let you be raised by no strangers. Even your mother's sisters didn't want you two, said they were just getting by as it was. They had no idea what family was all about. So I took you in. You understand? I took you into my home. I took over and I raised you kids the best way I knew how," he said, the squeak of his voice completely gone.

"So, you took us in out of pity…Hmmm," Sasha said, crossing her bird-like arms across her still-ample chest.

"Now, I never said I pitied you kids. Never said no such thing," he said. "It was just the Christian thing to do. I did my duty as a servant of the Lord."

"So, now we were your duty. Who were we to burden the great Reverend Odom?"

He took a long sip then, his full lips slowly breaking free from the glass. Then he slammed the glass down hard on the table.

"Stop putting words into my mouth! I never said no such thing. Loretta and I, we always wanted more kids, but God didn't see fit to bless us that way after Edwin came along. So we felt, with you and RJ, that he had finally blessed us in His own way, although it was in the cruelest manner—giving us two children with broken hearts and souls, barely big enough to make sense of all that had happened to you."

With that, the reverend paused, closed his eyes. Tight.

At first, Sasha thought he was praying to that fake God, the one that only the reverend knew.

"Your mother…Your mother…" He stopped, filled his glass again.

"What about *my* mother?" Sasha asked. Her heart felt as though it were thumping outside of her chest. An Etta James tune began to play, a serenade of "ohs" coming from somewhere from beyond where they sat. While Sasha couldn't quite make out all of the words, she knew what her pain was playing: an all-too-familiar ballad about tears that she had lived her entire life. She held tighter to her chair for fear that if she let go, she'd surely meet the floor beneath her.

"You didn't see it. How hard your mother tried to make a home for you all. But the drugs, the beatings…Well, it all took its toll 'til one day she just snapped. Before…Before it happened, I used to come around to your apartment. I would try to talk to her. Try to get her some help. I wanted her to know she had options. But I couldn't break through to her, no matter how hard I prayed. Then it was too late. I had failed her," he said, his words pouring out slower.

"In you all, I saw a chance for redemption, and Loretta got the kids she always wanted. Yeah, we had a full house, all right. God rest her soul. Then my sweet Loretta got sick. That wasn't a part of our plan. I had the church. I had people who needed me, relied on me, to guide them. So what was I to do with Edwin, RJ, and you—this sweet little girl with the face of an angel, just like her mother? I'd ask myself every day: where did I go wrong, trying to do so much right?

"You and RJ, you two were cut from a different cloth and I didn't have enough needle and thread to stitch the holes. It was patchwork at best. So I just watched you unravel right before my eyes. RJ thinks I don't know, but I know what he does. I see the demons in his eyes. The hurt all over his wife's face. I see it because I saw the same look on your mother's face every day. You all think I'm too old, too senile, not to see who you are, what you're doing. Don't you, Sasha?" he asked. He eyed Sasha for the first time since they'd sat down at the table.

"N-n-no."

"Well, I see it all. I see the bruises and marks all over you every time you come around. The wildness in your eyes. I smell the stench. It's like I'm watching your mother all over again. I know. I failed you both. Just couldn't keep you two stitched together." The reverend placed his head in his hands, which seemed to buckle under the weight of his thoughts.

"It's my fault…my fault."

A new song and Etta's voice became stuck on one word: "blind." No one seemed to notice, or maybe they just couldn't move fast enough to stop the skipping.

"What the hell you talking about, old man?" Sasha jumped up from the table. A ten-spot was not worth listening to the tirades of an old drunken fool and all of this crying over spilt milk that had spoiled years ago.

"Your mother…After Loretta died…She was so beautiful. I tried to fight the stirrings inside me…I did! I began to want her so bad. I lusted after her. I coveted her. I loved her. That's why I couldn't allow myself to get close to you, to raise you up proper, because whenever I looked at you, I saw *her*."

Crash! Sasha threw her glass against the wall; a few drops fell across her face, but she didn't notice. Surprisingly, she didn't crave a drink.

"You sick fuck! You were oogling my mother and me the whole time you were supposed to be raising me. Sick bastard! The Good Reverend Odom was nothing but a pervert. What a fucking joke!"

He didn't answer. Instead, she watched as he sank deeper into his hands, his shoulders shuddering. His brick of hands began to shake.

Sasha couldn't run to the door fast enough. Tears stung her eyes. *Is there a limit on tears? If so, I reached mine a long time ago.* Sasha still pondered this as she ran down the hall toward the steps, and saw freedom in the form of a daisy print dress ahead of her.

"Sasha? Sasha Ellis. Is that you?"

Sasha didn't recognize the voice fast approaching to her right, so focused was she on her escape.

"Well, my Lord, it is you." Sasha instantly hated the up tempo voice. When she turned, Sasha was staring at youthful, prettier version of herself. Sasha noticed a look of concern flicker across the woman's perfectly made-up face. On instinct, Sasha reached for the pocket knife she had placed in the back pocket of her hand-me-down khakis.

"Who the fuck are you?" Sasha asked.

The woman stepped back.

"Sasha! It's me, Debbie. Debra, from school," the woman said, furrows suddenly sprouting between her perfectly arched eyebrows. Sasha took in the woman's designer handbag and her business casual camel-colored attire, the giant rock on her left ring finger, smelled her designer fragrance. For the second time in one day, she ran her hands across her face, keenly aware of her appearance. The once wet curls on her head were matted now. She was trash, a crumbled-up piece of filth blowing through the hallway. It was this thought that made the stranger's face become more familiar with each second that passed.

Debra. Yes, Deb. Her best friend from fourth grade until the day she'd stopped going to school. Unlike Sasha, Debbie came from the standard-issue two-parent home with older parents who didn't drink, do drugs, or scream and fight at each other from morning to night. Debbie had nice clothes. The latest toys. Most of all, she had a type of love that warmed their small, but well-maintained, home. The one with the teal awnings that seemed to turn brighter in the rain.

Sasha had loved and hated Debbie at the same time. Deb was beautiful in a way that Sasha could never be. She had an inner glow about her, coupled with a peaceful innocence.

All of the boys on the block and at school had crushes on her, but she pushed them away. She laughed at their booty pinches and "hey, gal" comments. They were the same boys who had touched Sasha, at one time or another.

"Deb! Ummm…Hey, gal! What you…What you…doin' here?"

Sasha became keenly aware that her words were coming out a few seconds after her thoughts. The pause, she knew, left room for even more error.

"My dad. You remember my father, Earl? Well, he suffered a stroke about a month ago. He's been here ever since he was released from the hospital. Mama just couldn't take care of him on her own; she barely gets around as it is. Daddy's better, but the doctors say it's going to be a slow recovery. We're seeing progress every day though, despite what the doctors seem to think."

Like hell you are. That old man's probably a human French fry, just sitting in his room waiting to rot. Although Sasha remembered her estranged friend's father, she felt no guilt in thinking the obvious, or stating it for that matter.

"Yeah, right," Sasha said under her breath.

"What did you say?"

"I mean, really?"

"Sasha Ellis, it's so good to see you. I never knew what happened to you after… after…. I knocked on your door one day, and Reverend Odom said you'd left. Just left. Oh, Sasha, why didn't you ever try to call me or something?"

If only you knew. "I was just busy."

An awkward pause passed between the two women: the words that weren't being spoken. Debbie stared directly into Sasha's eyes, wanting some sort of clarification about her vanishing all those years ago. *Some things just shouldn't be answered.* Sasha turned away.

"Look, Sasha, please don't think I'm being intrusive, but I volunteer twice a week at the House of Hope. It's a, well…it's a home for women who have been battered. We help women recover from sexual abuse, battery, emotional and verbal abuse, and some of the habits and addictions they often incur as a result," Debbie said.

"Huh? I don't need no battered women's shelter? I'm f-fine…"

"Sasha! Sasha! Get your ass out here. You know how long I've been waiting out here for your ass?" Vance spouted Sasha in the foyer of the building and began shouting, sending the paisley-dressed manager into the safety of her corner office. Vance walked inside, his grunginess on full display. Sasha felt the heat rise from her neck to her cheeks as Debbie stood there, refusing to move. If she was disgusted by the two of them, it didn't show. In fact, she seemed oddly at peace in the situation.

"Look, I gotta go, Deb."

Debbie shocked Sasha, grabbing her into a hug so tight that she almost forgot to breathe. In the shelter of their embrace, Debbie pressed a card into the palm of Sasha's hand and whispered into her ear. "You can call any time, day or night, or you can just stop by the address on the front of the card. Group meets every Tuesday and Thursday night at 7:30. Please go. Any time."

Sasha tried to pull away, but Debbie held on. "Get help, Sasha. Please."

Sasha wanted to push her away, but at the same time she found herself burying her head deeper into Debbie's chest. She had never known comfort like this before. *When was the last time someone hugged me? Have I ever been hugged?*

Sasha was still wondering this as she slowly loosened her grip on her childhood friend and made her way over to Vance. He grabbed her arm and shoved her outside.

"You crazy bitch! Get your ass in the car! Know how long I've been out here? Do you?! And you betta have my money!" Vance was pushing Sasha into the passenger side now. Sasha turned to see if Debbie was watching them. She was. A half-smile plastered across her flawless oval face. From where she was, Sasha couldn't make out the look of concern still in her eyes. She couldn't hear that somewhere, Etta's song was still stuck on that one word.

HONOR

Something was wrong. RJ was far too kind to Honor. It threw her for a loop. Gone was the man who had stormed down the stairs in a tirade of curse words. The man who had walked back to her was smiling, whistling even. She had no idea if this new RJ, this caring, sensitive alter ego of a man, was a friend or foe. There was a complete stranger lurking about her house, and if Honor hadn't known better, she would swear he was on something *illegal*. Honor no longer felt as if she were walking around her house on eggshells; instead she was constantly checking for egg on her face. Something, or someone, had cracked in the house they shared and things remained in this fragile state for more than a week.

Each day, Honor awakened to the smell of breakfast: pancakes, turkey bacon, French toast, whole wheat toast, cinnamon and raisin bagels, freshly blended fruit smoothies, and grapefruit. RJ brought the freshly-prepared meals to Honor's bedside each morning, on a wooden serving tray that hadn't seen the light of day since it was given to them as a wedding present. When RJ spoke to her, his voice as sweet as the sugar-free syrup he poured onto her plate.

Today, he hand-fed Honor an oversized blueberry muffin and a fruit salad. If he was concerned about spilling any morsels on his impeccable navy button-up shirt, tie, and perfectly pleated suit, it didn't show. The tray was adorned with a single pink rose in a crystal vase. The sight of the food made Honor nauseous. She attempted to nibble at the muffin while RJ sat and watched her, a smile on his devilishly handsome face. Each bite he placed into her mouth seemed to suffocate Honor.

"Come on, eat up, sweetheart. I want to make sure my honey has a good breakfast before she heads off to start her day," RJ said. There were musical overtones to his voice. His words made Honor's stomach clinch tighter.

"RJ, for the last time. Thank you, but this isn't necessary. I'll just have my usual breakfast bar on the drive to work. Besides, I don't have much an appetite this morning," Honor pleaded.

"I. Said. Eat." RJ's high note turned flat.

Oh, God, I'm going to hurl right here on the goose-down comforter. Please don't let me throw up now. Why does he keep forcing me to eat? Not for the first time, Honor wondered what was behind that sheepish grin that remained permanently plastered on his face. Honor couldn't sit and wonder for long. She barely had enough time to toss the tray aside before she ran into the master bathroom, and fell onto the cold marble-colored tile. Honor held tight to the toilet as every bite she'd just eaten exploded from the pit of her stomach. She was looking at a buffet of multi-colored fruit in reverse. Not until the last dry heave did she let go of her grip. Her hands made a small suction noise as she fell back against the wall.

"Here," RJ said, handing her a face towel. "You need this."

Honor wiped her mouth, leaned against the Jacuzzi tub, placed the washcloth across her forehead, and waited for the room to stop spinning.

RJ was studying her intently.

"Must have been something I ate yesterday," she managed to murmur. *Why are you still here? Leave. Leave!*

"Well, what did you eat?"

"Umm...I don't really remember. Other than the breakfast you made me, I think I ate a salmon salad for lunch at that one café next to my job."

"Which one?" RJ asked intently.

"Umm… the Corner Cup."

"Maybe we should call them. Let the manager know that they are serving rancid food to their customers."

"That's ok. Besides I'm not even sure it was the salad, and the manager is so nice, I'd hate to cause hi– her any trouble over a maybe."

Honor knew that RJ would become incensed if he found out that Honor often chatted with Marco, the manager of the café she frequented. He did not allow her to speak to other men, even if it was just a friendly "hello." Honor had learned that rule with RJ's usual cruel instruction. Her mind flashed back to when the two were walking to the car after a rare night eating out. Honor had literally bumped into an old associate from graduate school. A male. She hadn't been able to place his name, but his face was familiar. At most, she had exchanged maybe four sentences with the nameless man. After saying goodbye, RJ had dragged Honor by her arm.

"Don't you know all any man wants to do is fuck you? And you grinning all up in that man's face, like I wasn't standing next to you. I bet your panties were getting wet just looking at that thug. Huh? Weren't they?"

"No, RJ. Stop. You're hurting my arm."

He had looked around and noticed a group of teenagers heading toward them. He left her go then, straightened his tie. Then he jumped into his car, leaving her standing in the parking lot.

"Why don't you go get a ride from the fucker whose face you was just grinning at, tramp!" he yelled out the window as he sped off, shocking the teenagers and mortifying Honor.

"Honor…" RJ removed the towel from Honor's forehead.

The motion forced Honor into the present. She had no answer.

"All right, if you say we shouldn't call the manager, then we won't."

"Huh? Oh, yes. I'll be fine."

"I just hate seeing you so sick. Maybe we should make an appointment with your doctor."

"I'm fine, RJ. Don't make a big deal out of this. Please."

With that, RJ left the bathroom. The interrogation over, Honor managed to get up from the floor and rinse her face with cold running water and brush her teeth. She avoided her reflection in the mirror. Her hand shook when she reached to turn the faucet off. RJ stood behind her, his face painted the mirror like an impressionist painting. The image burned Honor's eyes. She gasped.

"You scared me."

"Did I? I'm sorry," RJ said. He began wiping Honor's face with a dry towel that seemed to have magically appeared in his hands.

"I was thinking: You should take the day off from work since you're not feeling well. I have a teachers' workshop today, otherwise I'd stay at home with you."

Work? What day was it? Was it Tuesday? Tuesday has got to be the day.

"What day is it?"

"It's Tuesday, silly. Why do you ask?"

"Oh, I was trying to figure out if I had any important meetings today or not. I swear my memory is getting worse by the minute."

"So are you going to take my suggestion and stay home?"

"Yes, you're right. I guess I will stay home today. If I feel better by this afternoon, I may go in. But I'll call you if I change my mind."

"Stay home. Get some rest. That's an order," RJ smiled. The harmonious undertone was back in full effect.

Still, Honor knew RJ's last statement wasn't at all in jest. RJ came from behind and reached his arms around her shivering shoulders. He kissed her lightly on each shoulder, then the small of her back. The bile in her throat began to rise up again. *Tuesday.*

"Ok, well, I hate leaving you alone like this. I will call you when I get to the school to make sure you're all right and following the doctor's orders."

Drip. Drip. Drip. A few last drops of water freed themselves from the faucet. Honor watched them fall into the drain. She envied each drop that somehow managed to escape.

"Now let's get you back to bed," RJ insisted.

Honor allowed him to lead her back to the lushness of her pillows and slide the comforter around her. He picked up the tray and in two seconds had devoured the muffin that was meant for her. A few crumbs fell onto the sheets. Honor was surprised that RJ hadn't noticed the morsels fall.

"Bye," Honor called from behind as RJ made his way down the staircase. He was humming an up-tempo beat.

Honor yanked off the covers after she heard the garage door close and the soft purr of RJ's car pull out the driveway. If she hurried, she could be at the clinic before nine a.m. Hurriedly, she brushed her teeth a second time, leaving a glob of blue gel in the sink, something she ordinarily wouldn't have done. Honor showered, yanked her shoulder-length hair into a makeshift bun, put on a pair of jeans and a crimson blouse. She found a pair of non-descript black pumps in her walk-in closet and headed downstairs. The sound of her pounding heart echoed in her ears.

In the car, she punched the directions to the Rockport Women's Center in Midtown into her GPS. Honor recognized the beginnings of an attack almost from the moment the map of streets and street signs appeared on the screen. Two minutes outside of her gated community and Honor's palms became sweaty. Her legs shook and her breathing became labored. Pain left hard imprints across her chest and shoulders. *I don't need this shit today! Not today!*

"Come on, Honor! Get it together! Stop it! Stop it! Stop it!" she screamed into the car.

But, to her dismay, the symptoms grew stronger by the mile. Twenty minutes outside her destination, and Honor was forced to pull over onto the shoulder of Interstate 435. A diesel with black emissions zoomed past the spot where she sat, leaving a dust cloud of oil and black smoke. Honor smacked her fists against the steering wheel repeatedly, willing the tingling sensation to ease in her legs and her breathing to return to normal. When that didn't work, she hit each of her thighs several times, wanting to feel anything besides the uncontrollable urge to jump out of her car and into oncoming traffic. She looked out and noticed the billboard signs around her beginning to blur. *I wouldn't wish this on my worst enemy. Not even RJ.* How strange that she would think of him now. But then, he had that effect on her: always appearing when she least expected or wanted him to.

She was almost twelve minutes into the deep breathing exercises she'd read about online when her heart slowed. Still shaking, Honor was able to turn the ignition back on. She waited for the traffic to clear and jumped backed onto the freeway. *Drive Honor! Just drive! You've done this a million times before.* The shaking subsided only a little as Honor pulled into the parking lot of the women's center. She said a silent prayer for her safe arrival.

It took a couple of minutes before Honor was strong enough to get out of the car, and when she did, she held onto the driver's side door as if her life depended on it. Then she swallowed the fear and made her way up the pavement, surprised to see a silent wall of protestors barricading the four corners of the building. Some carried signs with pictures depicting embryos in various stages of development. Other signs boldly shouted harsh unspoken words.

"MURDERER!"

"IT'S A CHILD, NOT A CHOICE!"

"THANK GOD MY MOTHER KEPT ME!"

From where she stood, Honor could see a Kansas City Police squad car parked far enough in the distance to protect the First Amendment rights of the protestors. But it was close enough to stop anyone or anything that dare interfere with Roe vs. Wade. An older man reached out to hand Honor a small pamphlet. She jumped, noticing the large black Bible placed strategically under his right arm.

"Miss, please don't go in there. We are simply here to protect the rights of the unborn. We are also here to help you."

"Leave me alone!" Honor said, backing away.

"As I said, we are here to help you and your unborn child."

Honor walked faster into the automatic revolving doors. Once inside, she was surprised to see a maze of ivory-washed walls, flowered paintings, and EXIT signs–just like at any normal doctor's office. She walked over to the large counter. A petite brunette gestured for Honor to come closer. She was pretty, in a Midwestern sort of way, with the kind of looks that would become lost in the crowd on the East or West Coast.

"Hello. Welcome to the Rockport Women's Center. Is this your first time visiting us?" she asked evenly.

Honor thought the question odd, given the circumstances.

"Umm, no. No, I've never been here."

The receptionist handed honor a clipboard with a phonebook's amount of papers attached to it. "Okay, honey, well, if you'll just fill out this paperwork, front and back. Just the standard medical history forms, HIPPA agreement, and a medical waiver should you decide to change your mind later on. Just a precaution, you know. When you've finished filling these out, just bring them back up to me. Of course, you know we do require payment of all fees up front."

"Then, will I receive the...the pills?" Honor whispered.

She smiled in a beauty pageant runner-up sort of way. "Oh, sweetie, it doesn't quite work that way. Once you complete your paperwork, you will meet with one of our counselors. Then one of our doctors will see you."

"Oh, okay."

"Won't you have a seat in the lobby, please?"

"Sure. Thank you."

"You're welcome, sweetie." The receptionist turned her attention to the next woman in line.

There were a few empty seats in the lobby. Some women in the blue seats were crying, while others looked zoned out. Honor could make out the faint sound of sniffling in the far back of the room. A few men sat with their women, others were being comforted by a friend or relative. Still others, like Honor, were all alone, and probably, like her, in deep thought about the true meaning of fertility and sterility.

Honor took a seat in between a curly-red-haired teenager who kept bouncing her jean-clad leg up and down while popping her gum in an internal rhythm that was all her own, and another woman who looked to be about Honor's age, but of Latino descent. This woman simply stared straight ahead. Honor tried to concentrate on the clipboard on her lap. *Name. Address. Phone number. Date of birth. Social Security number.*

The teenager to Honor's right walked off in the direction of her name being called. "Elizabeth." That was it. No last name. Honor wondered what would happen if more than one woman named Elizabeth stood up. But she guessed that even the slightest bit of embarrassment was worth protecting one's anonymity.

Age of first menstruation.

"I want you to put those damn papers down right now, get up from that fuckin' chair, and walk the hell out that door."

"RJ?"

"Surprise!"

"How did you…What are you…"

RJ leaned in closer to Honor, so close she could feel his full lips touch her earlobe.

"I said, let's go," he whispered.

He grabbed her forearm. Hard. Honor wanted to scream. With her eyes, she pleaded with everyone, anyone to help her. But no one came to her rescue. RJ pulled her from the chair, the clipboard and papers hitting the mauve carpet with a soft thud. At the sound, the stoic Latina eyed her curiously, but said nothing. Instead, she returned to the safety of staring at the walls before her.

RJ's grip on her arm tightened as they made their way outside the brick building.

"Bless you, my sister. You have made the right choice. God will surely reward you and your unborn child."

Honor looked up at the crypt-keeper of a man for the second time that morning. *If you only knew: this is the work of the devil.*

"Bless you, too, my brother," RJ smiled at the man. "Have a great day." He pushed Honor ahead of him until they were out of earshot of the protestors.

"Get in the car. NOW!"

"But my car. I can't just leave it here, RJ."

"Car? What fuckin' car? I can't trust you with a car anymore, now can I? CAN I? Get in the car!"

Honor was frozen. The shaking started again in her legs. She thought she might urinate on herself.

"I said get in the car, bitch, before I bust your damn head open!"

The baritone in RJ's voice began to echo, penetrating the wall of pro-lifers. Their heads turned in the direction of the couple. A few of the more fearless began to walk closer toward them.

"What? What the hell ya'll Bible-thumpers gone do?" he screamed at them. "Mind your own business and get the fuck outta' here!"

See? What did I tell you? Honor wanted to cry out to them. *Help me!*

Honor noticed the patrol car inching closer. *To protect and serve, but even you can't save me now.*

"Okay, RJ. I'll get in the car." She was defeated once again.

Better a private lashing, than a public spectacle. *Slap.* She was barely into the seat when RJ swung across and slapped her face. The right side of her head met the passenger side window. The left side of her face burned instantly. Her head began to throb.

"I knew it. I knew something was up with your scandalous ass!" RJ was pointing his finger at her. His eyes became bloodshot red. Crazy red.

"I waited and I waited for you tell me you were pregnant. But you never said a damn word. One week went by, then two, almost three, and not a word out of your fine ass mouth! Now I know why! What the hell were you thinking? You think I'm just gonna let you up and kill my seed? Bitch, you out your motherfuckin' mind!" he screamed, his Wayne Miner vernacular in full effect.

"I... I..."

"What, bitch?! You what? Ain't nothing you can say that can get you outta this shit! Nothing! I outta just kill your ass right here. Let that damn cop come pick up your body! You trying to kill my damn child. My child! The child I been waiting and waiting for, and you gone try and take it from me. The one thing you know I want most in this world! The one thing! You gone just up and try to take it from me! Didn't even tell me you was pregnant! YOU DIDN'T EVEN TELL ME, YOUR HUSBAND, THAT YOU WAS PREGNANT! That's more than fucked up, Honor!"

Slap. Slap. Blood trickled down from Honor's nose as RJ sped off from the parking lot.

Honor finally screamed aloud, "Somebody help me! Help me! Please help me!" Honor became more afraid with each passing minute as RJ made his way like a maniac onto the freeway.

"Shut up! And bitch, you betta' not get any blood on my seats! You hear me?"

"Trying to kill my damn seed!" RJ kept repeating in his trance-like state.

He was screaming so much that spittle began to spill from his mouth, a few little drops landing on her. If Honor had thought she'd seen RJ at his worst, she had no idea. He didn't even seem to notice the cars around them. He was clearly in his own world, fighting his own demons, or was she his demon?

"Fuck you! Fuck you! How could you do this to me?! To us?!"

At that, Honor closed her eyes and shielded her face with her hands. Honor remained like that until they pulled into their driveway.

RJ skidded the car into the garage and dragged Honor out into the foyer. He started to raise his hand to her again; Honor lifted her arms to shield her face. He stopped short.

"Bitch, if you weren't carrying my seed right now, I would kill you! Do you understand me?! Tomorrow, you call that half-ass job of yours and you tell them you quit! And you better get comfortable in this house, 'cause your ass ain't going nowhere! NOWHERE!"

Bam! Honor hit the tiled floor crying, taking a round table and a leaf statue to the floor with her. RJ walked off. *Surely he can't keep me a prisoner in my own home?* This was her last thought before she blacked out.

RANFORD

RJ bounced down the steps of Urban Achievers on his way home after another fantastic day. This morning he was notified by the district that two of his seniors, Paul Robinson and Dwight Hilltop, were offered full-ride athletic scholarships: one to Drake, the other to the University of Nebraska. Both were scholar-athletes, so RJ had no doubt that they would do well and hold to the high standards he fully expected from all Urban Achievers graduates.

The best news of all was that he was having a baby boy! A boy!

He was more than just on top of the world: he was coasting between the planets, floating over the universe. RJ jumped into his car. Out of the corner of his eye, he spotted Mrs. Williams smiling down at him from the steps. He waved. They had been on better terms, especially since he'd bent her over his desk a few times after the last two board meetings, paddle in hand.

RJ wouldn't dare dream of touching Honor in her delicate state. Although sometimes, he had to admit, he was tempted. The sight of her ever-growing belly, the dark line down the middle to paradise. Her bigger and darker areolas, fuller breasts. Sometimes it was all he could do not to grab hold and take her, especially when he laid his head gently across her belly at night, wrapping himself up in the fullness of it all. Then a sudden movement, or a kick or two, would snap him back into his awaiting fatherhood, and his desire would fade, along with his erection.

But every man had his needs and RJ was no exception, so he would call on Mrs. Williams's ample backside to release his tensions. She was always more than happy to oblige him: easy access.

RJ was feeling so good that he thought he would stop at the store and surprise Honor with her favorite carton of cherry ice cream, and then pick up Chinese take-out. Although the doctor had given Honor a clean bill of health at her check-up this afternoon, RJ noticed darker circles under her eyes and a bit of swelling in her ankles. Most days, Honor seemed even more distracted and distant. It was becoming apparent that his wife did not share in his joy, and RJ was unsettled.

People were beginning to notice, even as Honor lay in the darkness of the doctor's office watching the ultrasound. Only her body was there as the ultrasound technician rubbed the gel on her belly and used the wand to swirl it around. RJ heard the baby's heartbeat again, and he could of have sworn their rhythms were already matching.

"Would you like to know the sex?" the toothpick-thin technician asked.

Honor didn't answer.

"Yes!" RJ bit his nails, a habit he'd kicked as a child.

"It's a boy!"

"A boy." RJ looked closer into the screen at the shapes and splotches that he couldn't quite make out. "A boy?"

"Yes, from the position right here, you can clearly see his gentalia," she swished some more. "Would you like a picture?"

"Yes. Please."

She made a little arrow right next to the unborn penis and wrote a cute saying next to it. Something like, "Hi, Mom and Dad. From your son."

I'm having a son! Tears began to make the already blurry images before him appear fainter. RJ could not believe how much love he possessed for this tiny baby forming inside of his wife. *My boy!*

While RJ grinned from ear to ear, Honor seemed less than elated.

"Mrs. Ellis, are you feeling all right?"

Silence.

"Yeah, she's fine. Just fine. Just a bit of new mommy nervousness, that's all. Isn't that right, honey?"

Honor turned to him then with a wild-eyed expression on her face that he had never seen before. It almost scared him. It was not so much the way she was looking at him, but that she was looking through him—beyond him, as if he didn't exist. He reached out to squeeze her hand, a gesture meant to make him feel more comfortable. Honor flinched at his touch. RJ hoped the technician hadn't noticed. She did.

"Are you sure you are all right, Mrs. Ellis? Should I call the doctor back inside?"

"I said she is fine," RJ said thinly. "Now, can we wrap this up so we can go?" RJ felt that any moment he would reach across the table where Honor lay and snap the technician in half.

"Ok, I guess we're done here. Let me just get you cleaned up, Mrs. Ellis."

With that, her thin arms began wiping the gel from Honor's stomach. Neither woman looked up at him again.

In time, Honor would come to understand that everything RJ was doing was for them. He needed to protect Honor from herself. He needed to protect his family. Once the baby arrived, she would see. Honor would come around as soon as she held their baby in her arms. Isn't that what all women did: bonded with their children in an unconditional superglue of love? Yes, once the baby was here, they would become a true family. RJ would give his son everything he did not have growing up. The most important being two parents who loved him and lavished on him every toy and game he wanted.

Right then, RJ promised to always be there for his son. He would take him to every Chiefs football and Royals baseball game as soon as he was old enough to understand them. There would be family vacations to Disneyworld and the Grand Canyon. Of course, there would be little league games: tee-ball, soccer, basketball, football—hell, even hockey. His son would play and excel at all of the sports, until he found his own niche. Most likely it would be track, just like his old man. But who knew? His son could wind up being a football great, going into the pros after a prosperous middle, high school, and college career. RJ would attend each and every game. Home or away, he'd cheer his son on to victory.

RJ would teach his son how to fish and they would go camping, just the two of them. And when his son came of age, RJ would be sure to tell him about girls. How they played hard to get and how they liked for men to take care of them, to dominate and control them. He would tell his son to marry someone like his mother: educated, intelligent, funny, beautiful. And to make sure she had slept with no more than five men in her lifetime because whatever number they told you, RJ would tell his son to automatically multiply that number by two. Honor had told RJ that there had been two men before him, so he knew she had slept with four. That number was manageable, for a wife. No doubt his son would be handsome and athletic. It was in his blood. Naturally, he would have his pick of the litter, just like his old man.

Boom! The image RJ had never been able to erase came to life on the black ultrasound screen. Fragments of his father's flesh splattered against the wall, a pool of blood beneath him. Then his father's face disappeared in a blink, just as fast as it had come, but long enough to make him feel like someone had doused him with a pail of ice cold water.

"See, RJ, I always told you…"

RJ covered his mouth to keep from crying out right there in the doctor's office. *Shut up! Shut up! Shut up!*

Yeah, things would be different for his boy.

His son would never go hungry. He could eat all the popcorn, chips, and cookies he wanted and drink as many sodas as he could gulp down. His stomach would never growl, or stick out in so much pain that it hurt just to take a shit. His son would never have to eat rice night after night, or oatmeal every morning. There would be meat every day, at every meal, and the sweet aroma of bacon, steaks, or lamb chops would be so commonplace in the Ellis household that when his son's boys were over they would never laugh at him. That is what RJ had worked hard for: escape from the slop Reverend Odom used to serve to them. Pork chops, pigs' feet, and chitterlings: staples of ghetto food. That mess would never touch his son's mouth.

My boy. RJ was still smiling as they drove home. At the first stoplight, RJ pulled the picture of the sonogram from his jacket pocket and touched it again. He didn't realize how wide his grin was, but he knew his cheeks were beginning to ache.

RJ ordered Honor up to bed to nap as soon they entered the house. She appeared frail, and he needed to see his wife sway those child-bearing hips in front of him once again. He walked into his study and sat at the desk, his mind still focused on Honor. Yes, eventually Honor would see that everything RJ had done was for the family. He had to protect his seed. True to his word, RJ had made sure Honor quit her job. They didn't need her little paycheck anyway. He had also hired a house manager to take over the shopping and whatever errands needed running. Contrary to his promise, RJ had returned the car back to Honor. He monitored her mileage daily and tracked it with the GPS. Oddly, though, the marker had stayed at zero for the last few weeks. And that wasn't the only thing strange about Honor's behavior either.

Lately it seemed that the floors of the house were laced with shards of glass and whenever Honor walked across them, her face was in a constant grimace. She jumped at the slightest of noises. RJ attributed his wife's being out of sorts to her fluctuating hormones. He figured she'd get better once the baby arrived. One thing concerned him though: her eyes. The dark circles were becoming more pronounced, marring her beauty, by a deeper degree each week.

Honor rarely spoke to RJ anymore, or anyone else for that matter. She pretended as if the house manager didn't exist. At first, when her sorority sisters or her other friends called, RJ would tell them she wasn't feeling well and not up to taking calls. When the calls became more frequent, RJ distracted the now-concerned callers with small talk about their children and their spouses, as if he really gave a damn. By now most of them had stopped calling, especially after RJ confiscated Honor's cell phone. A few of them, like Honor's parents, were a bit more persistent, so he allowed her to talk them for a few minutes, but he recorded all of their phone conversations. Nothing and no one could distract Honor from having a healthy baby. That had to be her sole focus. That's why he'd taken Honor's laptop as well. She didn't need constant e-mail reminders about upcoming sorority events she couldn't attend, or foolish chain letters from those nosey bitches.

RJ supposed that most women would be grateful to have a man like him. Honor didn't have to work, clean the house, or even so much as chip a nail picking up a can of green beans at the grocery store. It wasn't like RJ was holding Honor hostage. She could leave the house for doctor's appointments, and RJ made sure to take her out for a bite to eat at least once a week. Last weekend, he'd even taken her shopping for items for the nursery. But Honor hadn't seemed nearly as excited or interested in decorating the nursery as he was. After the fourth visit to the baby superstore, RJ stood torn between the Noah's ark décor or the sports theme. The cherry oak crib with the matching changing table, or the three-in-one converter bed.

Exasperated by all the selections, RJ had asked her, "Well, which one do you like?"

"Which what?"

"Which furniture do you prefer? What decorations do you like the best?"

"I don't care. Whatever you like."

"Well, you have to have some opinion."

"Can you please pick something so we can go? I'm tired," she said, looking beyond him again.

RJ didn't understand her nonchanlantness. *Isn't this what gets women all starry-eyed?* "Honor, what's wrong with you? I'm asking you about the room our child will start his life in, and you're acting like you couldn't care less." An acne-scarred twenty-something of a boy bounced over to where they stood. "Can I help you two find something?" RJ just stared at the two large, round pegs in the sales boy's earlobes.

Honor was still stuck in the beyond, her eyes focused on something next to the toddler toys and diaper aisle.

"Yes, we'll take the cherry oak converter set and all the sports theme shit. Stuff."

"Wise choice. I see you're a man of great taste. Will you be needing to have this shipped? There is a slight charge for shipping, assuming it's in stock."

"Just get it to my house."

"Anything else you'll be needing, ma'am, while you're here?" the eager boy asked Honor. She had frowned then and slumped her shoulders, like at any minute she'd fall under the weight of the question the boy had asked.

"No, we have everything for now," RJ answered. With that, he put his arm around Honor and walked toward the area marked "Cashiers." He could have just as easily been blowing a peanut through the aisles with his mouth. Honor was nothing but a shell.

SASHA

They exchanged anxious glances before strolling past two unassuming liquored-up women walking out of the Power and Light District. The neon lights from the entertainment district's bars and nightclubs cast shadows on the cement as Vance and Sasha picked up their pace and snatched their purses. The redhead, her ample cleavage accentuated by the too-tight strapless black dress, screamed at the shabbily dressed pair running ahead with her designer purse in-hand. The second partygoer, a short-haired brunette with a sleepy eye, didn't notice she was being robbed. She was bent over spewing all of her reverie onto the curb.

They ran a few more blocks past the bright lights and into a back alley. They dumped the contents of the purses onto the ground: a vial of Xanax, ultra-ribbed condoms, two fifty-dollar bills, a crumpled-up ten, a few ones, and some change. Not bad for a night's work. Vance dropped the purse he held and screamed with delight at the treasures they'd uncovered. Sasha held tight to the Coach bag she'd snatched. It might fetch a pretty penny if placed in the hands of the right druggie.

Back to Midtown now with their spoils, they found another dark alleyway, purchased a bag of marijuana and a small stockpile of jagged white rocks. In their threadbare apartment, Sasha and Vance promptly sat on the dingy sofa and disappeared inside a thick white cloud.

Night and day exchanged places again and again without either of them noticing. That is, until they smoked the last of everything. Then Sasha noticed the sunlight trying to ease its way through the makeshift curtains. She stared at the coffee table and wondered where everything had all gone. *Vance must have smoked it all. Either that or he put some in his pockets for later. Why he gotta be always hiding shit from me?*

Sasha was wrong though. Inside Vance's pockets were a few lint balls and six menthols. He stared hard at Sasha, and looked down at the same barren table. He was quiet for a long while, and in Sasha's experience, this was never a sign of good things to come.

Through the black of his burnt, crusty lips, he said, "Yo, we gonna swoop down on your brother's house."

Sasha wasn't sure she'd heard Vance correctly. She thought the drugs must've somehow affected her hearing.

"What'd you say?" she asked.

"Bitch, you heard me! I said, it's time to take down your ol' punk-ass brother's crib. Always thinking he's so high and mighty, better than everybody else, with that fine-ass wife of his, huh? Let's see how he feels once he finds his house been jacked," Vance said. His voice gritty like sandpaper as he laughed at the devious visions vying for position in his mind.

Sasha stood up, planted her feet firmly on the ground. "No, I ain't stealing from RJ! And, while we're at it, I've been thinking about going back to school." This last thought came from nowhere, but once spoken, it was as if it had been hanging in front of her for a long while.

Sasha followed this thought into the kitchen and leaned against the wall for support. Vance followed behind. *Smack!* Sasha's thoughts burst like giant water balloons over her head. A strong left hook and Sasha fell to the floor. Vance did this instinctively: a reflex as simple as a frog grabbing its prey with its tongue.

He was all over her. "Your ass is too dumb to go back to school. You too old, too. You, a crack head, in school? You done lost your damn mind. Now, when we gonna hit your brother's crib?"

From somewhere, Sasha reached and grabbed hold to a backbone. "I... I said, I ain't doin' it."

Crack! Sasha coughed up blood as Vance's boot connected with her side. Unsure of what had taken hold of her, she attempted a warrior stance. Sasha wanted to fight back! She *needed* to fight back. If this was her last day on earth, and her newfound dream never saw the light of day, then she would go down swinging!

Sasha grabbed the kitchen stool and, with all her one-handed might, she swung for his groin. It must have landed there because Vance groaned and dropped to his knees before her. The sight of Vance heaved over, looking so feeble, was all Sasha needed to drop the stool up and down hard on top of his head. Once. Twice. Three times, until the stool broke into pieces.

"Motherfucka', I hate you!" *Damn this feels good!*

Sasha turned, reached for the second stool when something like an undertow pulled her down below. He was on her then, punching so hard and fast she didn't know whether to swing back or shield her face from the incoming blows. Sasha opted for protective measures. One hand swung through the air aimlessly while the other covered her face. It was useless.

With her last bit of strength, Sasha rolled against the cabinets. She tried to pull herself up to the counter, but only succeeded in knocking over several dirty glasses, plates and fast-food wrappers that fell to the floor like weapons from heaven. Sasha reached for a piece of glass.

Bam! Bam! Bam!

"KANSAS CITY POLICE! OPEN UP!"

Bam! Bam!

Vance hopped to his knees. "Shit! Shit! Oh, shit! See what you made me do, bitch?"

Sasha spit up a few more drops of blood and what she hoped was not another tooth.

BAM!

From her vantage point at half-mast against the counter, Sasha could see four pairs of black patent-leather shoes running toward Vance.

"We got a call about a disturbance at this location. What the...?" The first pair of shoes reached her.

"Ma'am, are you all right? Do you need medical attention?" A round face frowned over her, his skin almost the same shade as the kitchen stools. Sasha was too weak to move or answer the moon-faced police officer. She just let the last breath of fight run from the apartment without so much as a goodbye.

She heard in the distance, "Well, what do we have here? Looks like you two have been throwing quite the party."

"Cuff this piece of shit!"

HONOR

Honor wasn't living anymore—she merely existed. Days and dates blended together, becoming nameless stains on the calendar. Twelve-thirty in the afternoon might as well be two-thirty in the morning; the hands of time simply stopped. Holidays morphed into one big celebration of nothingness. It took all the energy Honor could muster to brush her teeth each morning, and take a shower. Exhausted afterword, she would pull the covers back over her head and wake up just as the last rays of sunshine settled between the closed blinds in her bedroom, seeming to mirror her mood.

Somewhere, a cruel director was writing her story minus the climatic ending. This should be the scene when Honor would casually bump into her true soul mate at the grocery store, the one who would solve all her problems and save her from this non-existence. Scene one: Honor would've accidentally left her purse at home. While at the register trying to purchase a gallon of milk and a carton of eggs, he would smile at her and say, "No problem, pretty lady. Let me get this for you." He'd purchase her little items while the cashier looked on in awe. Then he'd carry Honor's bag to the car for her. They'd chat and laugh and then he'd ask her out for coffee. From there, true love and bliss would abound, the kind that only a *good* man could provide. This scene was what every woman waited, hoped, and dreamed for—the daily spoon-fed, instant oatmeal version.

But there were a couple of things wrong with Honor's storybook romance rendition. One: Honor couldn't see her feet beyond her stomach. Two: She hadn't been to the grocery store in a very, very long time. It made Honor chuckle to herself as she sat alone in her blue terrycloth robe at the kitchen table, trying to force down half a grapefruit.

Honor stared at the closed window before her. The outside, *out there*, had become her nemesis. Honor could no longer bear to look at the possibility, which is why she had insisted every window and curtain in the house remained closed. No danger could enter her home in the darkness, and neither could any silly fairytale.

At first, the outside had been somewhat of an annoyance, like the remnants of grime that somehow managed to stick to the bottom of the glasses long after the dishwasher's rinse cycle stopped. Honor blamed the panic attacks for her descent into the darkness. They'd become worse over the last few weeks, mocking Honor as she tried to open the front door. *How long has it been since I've stepped outside or breathed in fresh air? Let's see, the doctor said I'm twenty-eight weeks. How much time is that really when you're a prisoner in your own home?*

Honor walked the few feet into the front foyer. She stared at the door and willed it to open with her mind. Afraid of what would happen if it did. If she could only move forward a couple of inches, she would be able reach out and touch the doorknob. *One step. Two steps.* Honor edged closer, imaginary shackles chained around her ankles, a slave to her own insanity. She was on her third step when the kicking sensations began again in the hollow of her stomach, forcing her to stop dead in her tracks. Honor's eyes grew wide with terror and alarm. The small fluttering that delighted most mothers-to-be only served to remind Honor that RJ had taken control of her mind and body, and now his unborn child was setting up house inside her, taking possession of her soul. There was no room left for Honor. This last thought pushed Honor to open the door and let the sunlight bombard her face and the spring breeze do a jig around her hair. She stared across her driveway and marveled at how nicely last year's grass seeds were morphing into a lawn. It was enough to make her smile and laugh, if only for a fleeting second, until fear walked up and rang the doorbell. Honor tried to slow her breathing and count backwards.

Ten... nine... eight... seven...

Her palms turned moist, her legs began to tremble and give way. Right now she was about as steady as a diesel truck atop a toothpick bridge.

Six... five... four... three...

Fear suctioned the air from Honor's lungs and turned her breathing into gasps. She embroiled herself in a tug-of-war for her very breath. In one giant expense of energy, Honor flew backward and landed in the corner of the hallway, still gasping for air. She prayed the corner would eat her alive and leave behind no remains. As of this moment, Honor didn't even feel worthy enough for a morgue tag. So lost was she in the thought of her impending death, Honor didn't recognize the familiar sound of the home phone.

Ring! Ring!

She attempted to ignore the incessant ringing but the sound clamored on, demanding her full attention. RJ insisted on keeping the ringer on mute so as "not to disturb" Honor. She assumed he had forgotten to silence the outside world when he left for work. Honor knew it wasn't RJ calling, because he only used the pay-as-you-go cell phone he'd bought her for "emergencies only."

Ring! Ring!

It didn't stop. Once the machine would pick up, the phone would chant at her again. A high-pitched, intermittent laugh at the woman who couldn't pick herself up from the floor of her own house. "Please make it stop!" Honor cried out.

The phone continued to mock her.

She wanted silence. The desire spurred her to waddle to the kitchen nook and whisper "hello" between gasps for air.

"Honor... Oh... Thank God!"

"Mother?"

"Why haven't you called us? Your father and I have been worried sick out here. Just worried to death."

"I..."

"Do you know how worried we've been?"

"I'm sorry, Mother."

Olivia must have sensed the defeat in her daughter's voice. She cleared her throat. "So, how is my future grandson doing?"

How does she know that I'm having a boy? I never told her. I haven't told anyone. Oh, Mother, I want to come home. Please let me come home.

"We've been calling and calling. RJ has been a godsend, giving us updates almost every day, but I want to hear the sound of my own daughter's voice, too. I want to know how she is feeling from her *own* mouth. So, how you doing, baby? Everything okay?"

"Mother... I'm not... Something is wrong..."

"With the baby? Oh my God! I knew it! I knew it! After I hadn't heard from you. Are you two keeping some horrible secret from us? I told you not to wait until you were almost thirty-five to have a child. The babies, they come out having all kinds of problems. Well, what is it? Tell me. NOW!"

"*It* is fine, Mother. It's just that ..."

"Oh, thank God. Why would you say such a thing? Worrying me to death like that."

Honor sighed. "I'm sorry, Mother."

"So, the baby is fine. Are you feeling all right? You should have gotten over that morning sickness a while ago. Is it back problems? What is it?"

"Mother, I want to come home." The words flew from her mouth and dropped inside the phone before she could retrieve them.

Silence.

"What is this about, Honor?"

"I want to come home." There. She said it aloud again, as her tears flowed down to meet her words.

"What on earth is the matter with you, Honor? I can barely understand what you're saying."

"I said, I want to come home. Today." Honor melted onto the kitchen tile, her head rested against the coolness of the cabinets.

"Oh, I see what this is: hormones. Yeah, you're getting the pre-baby jitters," her mother chuckled. "Don't worry, honey, every woman has them right before the baby is due. Especially that first one. I remember when I was expecting you, I would cry at the drop of a dime and I was so nervous. Even after you were born, I used to check on you about every five minutes those first few days. I think I poked you awake a couple of times when you were sleeping to make sure you were still breathing. You were such a fussy baby, always fidgeting and wanting to run away. Now, Netta? I never had a single solitary problem from her when she was a baby. Of course, by then, I knew what I was doing too. You'll see. You know I plan on coming down and staying for a few weeks, after the baby gets here. So, have you thought of a name yet?

"Mother, its RJ. I-I have to get away from him."

"RJ. Oh sweetie, RJ is harmless. He's such a jewel, the way he takes care of you, allowing you to quit work so you can get your rest and prepare for motherhood. Now, he might be a little bit controlling, but he's a good man."

RJ's recent rants sliced through her mother's words, cutting her somewhere near her heart.

"Why you always throwing up?"

"Your sick ass!"

"All you do is sit around!"

"Look at you, always gotta be sick when I'm tryin' to get ready to go to work."

"I'll be glad when this pregnancy shit is over."

"Fat ass!"

"You ain't good for shit no more. Not even a nut."

"Mother. He. Hits. Me."

"Well, like I said, he *is* a little too controlling."

Controlling?! Is that what you call it, Mother?

Honor imagined herself as a child back home in Florida sitting at the formal dinning room table staring at the oven-roasted ham, asparagus, whipped potatoes and gravy, and apple pie that Olivia had prepared from scratch. Honor hated asparagus. It was rubbery and gross. She refused to eat it. That night, Olivia had insisted she and her sister be in their fanciest dresses, their hair freshly pressed and parted down the middle. Her mother looked beautiful and regal as usual, in a flattering purple dress that showed off her waves of long amber hair.

Their mother had also insisted that they sit straight up at the table and not mess up her good china or the table skirt. So that's where they sat, the three of them, straight as an arrow, until the candle centerpiece her mother had created began to drip hot wax onto the flowers beneath them and they wilted. Oliva's words began to slur when the candle dwindled down to almost nothing. The bottle of wine on the table disappeared like a sad magic act.

"Girls, go get yourselves ready for bed now," Olivia whispered. The girls walked to their rooms without touching the slices of apple pie, their backs still straight as boards in their pleated dresses.

Honor never saw the judge that night but she heard him later, shouting at her mother, telling her she was imagining things. Her mother asking, "Who is she?" The judge shouting angry parting words, the kind that break you down to nothing. All she heard afterward was the sound of her mother crying.

The sudden memory jerked Honor by the shoulders. She realized her mother could never help her. She couldn't save herself.

"Mother, I have to go. I'm not feeling too good all of a sudden. Bye."

"Well, now Honor…"

Click.

"Who were you talking to, honey?" RJ said, as he casually stepped into the kitchen. His hands were stuffed into the pockets of his black pants. His blue-flecked tie slightly loosened around his neck. Although his eyes revealed nothing, Honor noticed his chiseled jaws clinch together. Even in his brutality, he was beauty personified.

Honor was the kid caught with her hand in the phone jar. She tried to lift herself up from her position against the cabinets, but her protruding belly made even the slightest of movements more difficult. RJ reached down, grabbed her hand, helping her to her feet.

"I asked you who you were you talking to."

The trembling began again. "My mother. She called; she was worried about me."

RJ smiled. "Silly Olivia. I told her you were all right and that I just wanted you to rest. Isn't that what you told her? That you were all right?"

"Yes. That's exactly what I said to her."

"Good. Now, come on, let's get you upstairs and into bed. You look beat. The doctor said to try and stay off your feet as much as possible. Did you take your prenatals this morning?"

When did the doctor say that to me? "Yes, I took them," Honor mumbled between breaths, still trying to recuperate from having to stand up.

Honor allowed RJ to lead her into the bedroom and put her back into the king-sized bed they shared. The pillows reached out to her, accepted her head as the blankets embraced her. *Is this what it is to be grateful, Mother? Is RJ that jewel of a man you wanted me to find?* These thoughts followed Honor as she drifted off into a beaten sleep.

Deer Ranford,

For me, love was always the calm be for the storm, never enuff calm. Yur father was a storm cloud. Always threat in to go dark. When I was with him, I lived under an unbrella. But that unbrella was old, been thru to many winds, til it was nothin but broke metal. It didnt protect me from shit.

I start working with the girls of R.A.G.E. and I learn that the winds, rain, dark clouds and sun shine was a part of the cycle. That's how the violence turns-tenshion, beating and the calm. It always the calm that gets you and keeps you, cause you keep hoping and pray that it stay that way. But it dont. The rain come again. A sprinkle of bad words, a down por of slaps, a flood of kicks, and you wonder how you stray strong enuff to keep from drowning.

Yur father was the wind, the lightening and the rain. I was the snow and ice. What draw us together? I cant say for sure. But, I do no 1 of us was gone kill the other. That the only way it was gone end. When there is no sun shine, someone gots to die.

These yung girls they come to me after the same cycle cause them to steal, lie, kill, do drugs, move drugs, take the fall for drugs, when all the while all they want the calm. Those the lucky 1s, the 1s who live to tell the tail. I wasn't so lucky, RJ. Yes, I live, but look at all the folk I hurt?

It ain't right to live trying not drown, RJ. Don't live in that darkness. Listen to me, find some lite in yur life. Member that ever body has a rite to catch rays, like the songs say, "This litle lite of mine, Im gonna let it shine!" Oh, RJ, it's so true. Don't block any body's sun. Look at me, sounding like the wetherman. But I don't no how else to tell you that abuse is such an ugly cycle.

I member once, I think you bout 10, just before ... Any way, I try to get to the church, try to find out why I keep getting my ass kick all the time in a mariage that was posed to be ordaned by God him self. I didnt really no Reverend Odom back then. Sure, he wuld come round some time, but I was to stuborn, or too high to listen to him. My family was full of fake catholics so that was a dead end. I start to go to this church, this huge church. I figure with all these folk, some body wuld have answers. This 1 pastor I member him cause he seem to be truly touch by the "spirit." Hundreds of folk listen to him ever Sunday. One Sunday, I go talk to him. I walk straight up to him and I say, "Help me." That when he look at me, real funnie like and tell me to make a point ment with his secetary.

I did. 2 weeks pass for I see the pastor. He didn't no me from Adam, but I tell him bout ever thing, the drink, the drugs the abuse, mostly the abuse. I say I want out of my mariage. I want to fill safe again. He sat be hind his big ole desk and tell me bout the 3 "A's" of divorce – adultiry, abanment and abuse.

"You difinitely got 1 of the A's, but do you really want to be a single mom," he ask me? "Do you no how many single moms I see a day? Do you want that for you and yur kids?"

The pastor say each time Randy yell at me, call me out my name or hit me to picture Jesus on the cross. He say prayer can work miracle, and Randy culd change if I only pray hard enuff. I belive, so that what I did. I pray real hard and I pictur Jesus hangin on that ole ruged cross while I got the shit beat out of me. Nothing change.

Looking back, I no that pastor was dead wrong. Why he tell me to stick round and get my ass kick ever day? What kind of God wish that on any body? If I had gotten out, maybe I culd have saved us all. But, I never no now.

Son, I close that bag of guilt a long time ago. I say this to you so you can under stand that sooner or later 1 of us was gone die. Puts a hole new spin on 'til death do us part," don't it? In the storm, I find my ray of lite in you and yur sister. The only thing I did rite in this world. If you belive 1 thing, belive this—we were not call to be broken. Beatin down til we crak. No pastor in the world can tell me that now. Pick up yur cross.

With all my love,

Mommy.

RANFORD

In 1987, Kansas City used explosives to level the devil. RJ watched as the five high-rise towers known as Wayne Miner Court were demolished. He had to bear witness to the demolition—to see the mortar and bricks light up and implode in the sky—before he could say for certain that it was true: hell had fallen.

RJ had spent his whole life running as far away from Ninth Street as he could. But sometimes Ninth Street called him home. He'd drive along Interstate 70 and have an inkling, something like an itch in his palm, to take the exit ramp back down to his roots.

Today was one of those days.

A heavy-set little girl eyed him curiously as RJ sat in his car at a corner beside a row of town homes. She was jumping rope, her head full of tight braids and beads that bounced every time her feet hit the ground. He watched as the thick mane of braids hopped away and disappeared between the wide row of buildings with blue siding. Only RJ didn't see the houses; the ghosts of high towers surrounded him.

For the first time, RJ longed to go back to the days when he was a boy and "poor" was a word without merit. If his family had only rice for dinner one night, his neighbors were eating beans. If RJ went to bed with his stomach growling, he could still rest assured because he would hear the same stirrings from every child who walked with him to school the next morning. The sound of hollow stomachs was just as commonplace as the sound of the city bus's double doors opening and closing every half hour. There was an unspoken solidarity back then. The realization hit RJ that the more successful he had grown, the more alone he had become.

The good reverend had prompted RJ's latest abyss into loneliness.

Their visit hours earlier left RJ spooked. RJ hadn't seen the reverend in weeks, not since the time he'd sprinted away with scripture screaming behind him. The reverend dropped a bomb—three actually.

"Edwin's been calling a lot lately," Reverend Odom said over their usual fare of pancakes and grits. "He wants me to come live with him, Justeen, and the baby."

"Oh, really?" RJ said, nearly chocking on a strip of bacon.

"He says they got plenty of room for me, even lined up one of them home health nurses for me. Ain't that somethin'?"

"Yeah…it's something all right."

"He says I can have the whole downstairs apartment all to myself, ain't got to pay a thing."

"You don't pay anything now," RJ reminded him. "Plus, you always told me that you hate Chicago."

"I know. I do. City's too big for the Midwest, and the people all uppity like they in New York. But my son is there. My grandchild is there."

His words punched RJ in the gut.

"I see." Suddenly, the breakfast food lost its flavor. RJ set his napkin down on the table and let the silence between them take hold for a while.

"I do like that talk show lady though—that Orphan Studios."

RJ didn't feel like correcting the reverend. He knew he'd be in for an all-day debate if he tried.

"So this is what you want, huh? To go and live with Edwin?"

After all I've done for you. I'm your family, he wanted to add. Instead he bit his bottom lip.

Reverend Odom gazed upward. "Yeah, I believe it is what I want. I believe God is callin' me there."

"Well, when is Edwin talking about moving you there?"

"First of April, thereabouts."

"That's less than a month away!"

RJ spoke with Edwin only once since his last trip to Chicago and the cat-lady aftermath. Edwin had changed. RJ couldn't stomach holding a feature-length conversation with him anymore. A few months back, Edwin received "the calling" like his father. Already, he had established a church on the city's South Side with a pew-worthy congregation. "Come join me, brother," Edwin said to him the last time they'd exchanged words.

"No, thanks," RJ answered.

Since then, Edwin had left several messages for RJ. Eventually, the phone calls stopped. Now, Edwin wanted to take the reverend away from him. It was like the purple taffy all over again. *Punk.*

"Sasha came by a couple of weeks ago," Reverend Odom said, stepping right over the subject matter that had tripped up RJ.

"Really, what did she steal this time?" RJ asked, a smirk on his face.

"Nothing, but she looked a mess."

RJ hadn't seen or talked to Sasha in a while either. Not since the morning he'd found his lost little sister sitting in his driveway. "I washed my hands of that a long time ago. You know that. You can't save a person stuck in a well if they don't want to get out. Sasha made her own choices in life, just like you and I have."

"And sometimes, choices are already made for folks. I'm telling you, RJ, she looked really bad. The worst I've seen her. Girl weighs about eighty pounds soakin' wet, if that." The reverend's voice was growing louder.

"Well, what do you expect from a crack head?"

Reverend Odom's chubby cheeks grew puffy. With surprising agility, his hard working-man's hand landed across RJ's face with the force of sixty-mile-per-hour winds. "I will not have you talk about your sister like she doesn't come from the same flesh and blood as you. Bad enough you disowned your mama, now your sister!"

The reverend stared down at his hand as if at any moment it would jump from his arm. As if he didn't trust his own body.

"Don't you t-talk a-about my mother," RJ said, wanting to press his hands over his ears and scream "la, la, la" at the top of his lungs so he wouldn't have to listen. Just the mention of her assaulted him. *Who the hell does he think he is? Hitting me?* But RJ stayed put, the right side of his face smoldering red like fire.

"Listen, RJ, there's something I've been wanting to give you. Been waiting for the right time, but I figure I might as well be waiting until twelve 'til never, cause that day ain't comin' no time soon," the reverend said, still staring at his hand.

"What are you talking about? Give me what?" *Senile old man.*

RJ watched as the older man grabbed his mahogany cane, walked into his small bedroom and returned carrying something that RJ couldn't see at first glance. Then he noticed a small stack of envelopes stuck under his arm.

"Here. These are for you and Sasha. They're from your mama," Reverend Odom said. He might as well been holding a grenade in his shaking hands, although he'd spoken the words as casually as someone saying, "It looks like rain." When RJ did not reach for the letters, Reverend Odom sat them on the table before them. "It's only three. They started coming out the blue a few weeks ago. Well, maybe a month ago. How's Honor holding up with the new baby coming?"

RJ headed out. "I gotta go."

"Fine. But you will take your mama's letters with you. Now, it's not up to me what you do after that. I've done my part. You can throw them away, burn them, read them, or pass them onto your sister, if you ever decide to check in on her. I think one of them addressed to her anyway."

"I'm not taking them."

"You know those demons from the past you've been running from your whole life? They got a funny way of reappearing at all the wrong times until they beat your soul into the dirt. You've got to bury them before they bury you. Here—take 'em."

"Fine." RJ picked them up reluctantly and headed out, not even bothering to say goodbye. The letters burned his hands.

Slam. Slam. Slam. An acne-scarred boy, his skin the color of vanilla sprinkles, walked by, dribbling a worn basketball. The sound jarred RJ from his thoughts.

The demons of the past were sitting beside him, but he'd be damned if he let them bury him. RJ started the engine.

"To hell with it!"

With that, RJ pushed the power window button and threw the envelopes from the car. A quick burst of wind came from nowhere and scattered the letters along the pavement. RJ watched them scurry away, and although it went against every instinct he had, he jumped from the car and chased after the letters as they danced in the same direction as the little girl.

HONOR

The incessant ringing of the doorbell jarred Honor from her mid-day nap. Still fuzzy, she struggled down the long staircase into the foyer.

"I'm coming! I'm coming!" she screamed as she made her way to the bottom of the staircase. "Who is it?"

"Sasha."

Shit. "Um, hey, Sasha. RJ's not here. He's still at work."

"Well, can I come in and wait for him?"

"That might not be such a good idea. Can you come back when he gets home? RJ doesn't like surprises. Seeing you here unexpectedly…"

"Honor, I ain't got nowhere else to go," Sasha said from the other side of the door. "Besides, you and I both know there's no telling what kind of mood he'll be in when he gets back, whether I'm here or not."

Honor hated to admit it, but Sasha was right. Trying to predict RJ's moods was like trying to forecast the Midwest's helter-skelter weather. Against her better judgment, Honor opened the front door, then the storm door. *Click. Click.* The locks turned loudly as Honor held her breath. Her head began to pound as she looked past Sasha into the sunlight. The light mocked her and caused a shiver down Honor's spine. She wasn't the slightest bit cold, but a chill was definitely in the air.

Honor closed the door quickly after Sasha stepped inside. It was then that Honor noticed her sister-in-law's unkempt state. Her hair, normally mid-length and curly, had lost all of its luster and fullness. In its place was a matted, multicolored mess that reminded Honor of a stray shaggy dog. She was too thin, almost skeletal. Honor could make out the slight traces of Sasha's collarbone and ribs through her dingy green sleeveless t-shirt. The jeans she wore seemed three sizes too big for her small frame, leaving Honor to wonder what was being used to hold them up. A pair of tattered red flip flops failed to conceal Sasha's heavily soiled feet, and her smell was indescribable: something four steps below putrid.

Sasha's bloodshot eyes grew wider as she looked Honor up and down.

"Damn! You look like you 'bout to pop any minute now! Look at you!" she screamed, dancing excitedly around Honor. "Nobody told me I'm gonna be an auntie!"

"I'm gonna be an auntie, I'm gonna be an auntie!" Sasha chanted.

Honor couldn't help but notice several missing and cracked teeth in the front and side of Sasha's mouth as she continued on with her childlike singsong. Honor's headache was growing worse with each aching note. Someone long ago had forgotten to tell Sasha the difference between her "inside" and "outside" voice. On the phone or in person, Sasha was always amplified.

Sasha froze. She was completely out of breath from the little show she'd just put on. Her chest heaved up and down as if Honor were pushing on it and letting it go.

"So when is that thing supposed to hatch? You scared?" she asked. "I ain't neva' had a baby before, but I heard the pain of givin' birth make you wish you were dead."

"Thanks for those words of encouragement," Honor answered flatly. It hadn't escaped her that Sasha never said that she'd been pregnant before, only that there were no babies. But who was Honor to judge, knowing full well that she didn't want this baby inside her now?

Yet, here she was: all swollen and puffy, about to give birth any day. It occurred to Honor that she felt as bad on the inside as Sasha looked on the outside. She was staring into life's cruel two-way mirror. *Heaven help me.*

"Ah, you know what I mean, sis. I was just playin'. You'll do fine. I'm sure you and RJ going to all those labor classes and sh– stuff ."

Honor kept her eyes to the floor, looking for imaginary cracks. RJ had asked her on several occasions to look into childbirth classes for the two of them. Each time he asked, she had begged off with excuses ranging from "I don't feel well" to "it's too far away." Honor couldn't stomach the thought of sitting with her husband in classes led by some community birthing guru, pretending to be a normal, happy couple.

Besides, the only time Honor went *out there* anymore was when RJ took her to her prenatal visits. Honor had bypassed being on-edge. She had jumped beyond it and was wondering how she was ever going to pull herself up.

"Right. Can I get you something, Sasha? I'm about to make myself a cup of tea, would you like one?"

Sasha snickered. "Girl, you sound white as all get-out. 'A cup of tea.' Where the Kool-Aid?"

"Well, we don't have any Kool-Aid, but I'm sure there is some type of fruit juice in the refrigerator," Honor said, already heading toward the kitchen.

In her ivory terrycloth robe and matching slippers, Honor reminded Sasha of a human-sized bunny rabbit. *What is she doing home anyway in the middle of the day?* Her plans to do a quick grab-and-stash were foiled. *Why did I ring the doorbell? Stupid. Stupid.*

"Look, sis, I don't need any juice. I need some money. I need some money real bad."

As if she hadn't heard her, Honor said, "Would you like for me to make you a sandwich? We've got some turkey. Maybe I can whip up a quick pot of spaghetti. Sorry, we don't have more. It's Althea's day off."

Who the hell is Althea? "Did you hear me? I said I need some money," Sasha said, her voice still high.

Honor poured filtered water from the faucet into the stainless steel tea kettle, which matched all of the kitchen's appliances. "Yes, I heard you. I'm not stupid. Isn't that what you always come around for? Isn't that the only reason you contact us at all? I don't understand it—the two of you—how you ended up being so different. I know my sister and I aren't exactly the closest, but you two are like oil and water. I just don't get it. Sasha, look at you! You somehow manage to look worse every time I see you, the few times that I do. I don't know… Is it because you're still hurting about your parents, them dying in that house fire when y'all were little?"

"House fire. Is that what RJ told you? A fire?!" Sasha fell on the tiled floor laughing hysterically. "A fire! What the hell?" She rolled around some more, her hands clutching at her wilted sides.

Honor set the tea kettle on the flat-panel stove and turned the knob to low. "What's so funny, Sasha?" she asked.

A few minutes passed before Sasha was able to stand up and compose herself enough to speak. "My loving brother sold you a pile of bullshit from the jump, that's what's so damn funny."

"I fail to see the humor in all this," Honor said. "Actually, it's all very sad. RJ told me the whole story about how he and Edwin were out playing basketball and how he came back home to find the house on fire and rushed inside all the smoke and flames to save you."

"Like I said, he sold you a pile of bullshit. Wasn't no fire that killed our pops: it was a bullet. Our mom ain't dead; she's doing twenty-five to life at the Ohio Reformatory for Women, 'cause she the one that held the gun and pulled the trigger."

A sharp pain cut across Honor's insides. She sought safety in a nearby chair. She needed to feel grounded before she could find her voice again. "I don't believe you. You're lying."

Sasha laughed again, revealing yet another gap. "So that's how my brother got the high and mighty Honor Thompson, by selling her a bunch of lies. I knew something was up. RJ think he ballin', but he's still the same old cat from Wayne Miner, just like me, or didn't he tell you that he grew up in the hood?"

The pain hit Honor again. Harder this time. The tea kettle joined their conversation. If Honor didn't know any better, she'd swear it was whistling a sad tune.

"No." That was all Honor could find the strength to say.

In between her belly laughs, Sasha said, "It's been nice going down this little memory lane with you, but I need money, Honor, and I need it now."

"I don't have any money on me. RJ keeps it all. You'll have to wait until he gets home."

Sasha's mood turned like someone flipped a switch. "I said, gimme some goddamn money! I need it now! My man's in jail! I gotta get him out! You don't know what it's like! Give! Me! The! Motherfuckin'! Money! NOW!"

Like a human cannonball, Sasha catapulted herself into the china cabinet. Honor sat still, gripping the edges of the kitchen table as the pains grew worse. Sasha tossed plates and glasses against the wall, turning the floor into a minefield of glass. One-by-one. Two-by-two. Three-by-three. They shattered. Each one sounding louder than the first, making Honor jerk involuntarily between the pains.

"I said I need money! I need money! I need money!" A delirious chant from the now wild-eyed Sasha. *Crash!* In one giant motion, she swiped the contents from the kitchen counter, sending a rush of flour, sugar, and uncooked spaghetti flying through the air like artillery.

"Money. I need...money!"

A blazing pain left Honor clutching the table harder, then wetness. A gush of water fell from between her legs and ran down the chair onto the floor, mixing with a little bit of the flour into a type of twisted paste.

"Sasha..."

"Give me the money, Honor. I'm not playin'."

"Sasha..."

"I said…"

"SASHA! Listen to me! You have to get me to the hospital. Can you do that?"

Sasha switched to off. She looked down at the wetness, the grimace on Honor's face and said, "Yea, sure. I can do that."

Nineteen minutes later and Honor was being wheeled past the information desk of the emergency room entrance at North Hospital. One hand gripped Sasha's tightly with every contraction, which were coming now at the pace of ocean waves and the strength of a hurricane.

"Well, I guess I'm out now," Sasha said once they entered the maternity wing of the hospital.

"No. Don't leave me. Please." At this moment, Sasha was the only person Honor had in the world and she had no intention of turning her loose.

Honor's plea touched something in the pit of Sasha's fierceness. *So this is what it feels like to be needed?* And even though Sasha no longer had any feeling in her right hand from Honor's tight grip, she simply said, "Okay."

In what seemed like a few short minutes, Honor was placed into a hospital gown and stretched wide on the birthing table. A demanding nurse rushed Sasha into a pair of scrubs and mask. She stood on one side of the bed and watched as the nurse hooked Honor up to an IV and fetal monitor. *Beep-beep. Beep-beep. Beep-beep.* She never heard a heartbeat before. Sasha found the sound strangely comforting. A tie on Honor's threadbare gown came lose, revealing an engorged nipple the color of cocoa. Embarrassed, Sasha turned away.

"All right, Mrs. Ellis, we've paged Doctor Williamson. She is on her way. Luckily, she is close by because it looks like we may not have much time. This baby wants to come out now," said the long-necked nurse.

"I can't do this," Honor said.

"Yes, you can, girl. You ain't got no choice," Sasha said.

"No, I can't. It hurts!"

"Everything good is born from somebody's pain, you just gotta go through it to get to the good."

Wisdom from a crack head. But Honor listened, never letting go of her sister-in-law's frail hand.

Dr. Williamson wisped into the room, a sliver of auburn hair beyond Honor's raised legs. Another nurse appeared out of nowhere.

"All right! All right! Somebody paged me and told me it's time to have a baby. Was it you, Honor?"

Dr. Williamson turned in the direction of Sasha. "Hello, I'm Honor's obstetrician. I'll be assisting her as she brings a new life into this world."

"Sasha."

"Nice to meet you, Sasha."

"Oh, God! Get it out of me!"

"Well, no time for chit chat. The lady of the hour awaits."

"Oh, my, this baby is in a hurry to get here. You're almost fully dilated and effaced. Usually, it takes longer with the first child, but that's not the case today. Honor, I know you didn't want a natural childbirth, but that's what's going to have to happen."

"No!" Honor screamed, in between faster-approaching contractions.

"Now, Mrs. Ellis. Just breathe, everything will be all right."

Honor grasped Sasha's hand tighter. "Should I go call RJ?" Sasha asked.

"No."

"But, he may—"

"I said no, Sasha…please." Sweat dripped down Honor's eyebrows, forming a river with her tears. The nurse rushed to place a cool washcloth across her forehead. "Just stay with me."

Sasha stayed for four hours, surprising herself by soothing Honor at all the right moments, even joining in the push countdowns. *One. Two. Three. Four. Five. Come on, Honor, you got this, girl!* Modesty brushed aside, Sasha watched in the overhead mirror as the nameless Ellis baby made his entrance, and she knew, without a doubt, that she had witnessed a miracle.

Sasha found herself giddy at the sight of hazel eyes staring up at her, and the full head of dark curls on the baby's misshapen head. Honor, though, seemed less than joyous at her son's arrival. Baby Ellis had spent more time in Sasha's arms than Honor's, and if Sasha didn't know any better, she'd swear that the baby seemed more relaxed in her arms than his mother's.

RANFORD

RJ wasn't sure why he was back in Regina's bed. He left the office early, after his necktie had started to feel more like a noose with each passing hour. When his breathing became labored, he knew it was time to head home—at least was his intention when his foot pressed on the accelerator. But instead of taking a left to his house once he reached his subdivision, the car seemed to go on autopilot, heading right to Regina's house and her double D's. RJ hadn't called, texted, or emailed her to announce his arrival, but as soon as he pulled into her driveway, she was standing outside, the front door wide open.

Two hours and several positions later, RJ reached for his clothes and some type of excuse for why he was back at her house at all. "I gotta go," RJ said, one leg already in his pants.

"So soon? You just got here. Joe is having his guys' night out tonight; why don't you stay awhile? I can whip up something nice for us to eat. Pop open a bottle of wine." Her thick, long legs encircled him now, where he stood trying to dress.

"Come on, Regina. I ain't got time for all this. This was fun and all, but you know I gotta get home. I'm already late."

With that, she released him from her legs' vice grip and sat up in the king-sized plush bed, her arms crossed across her ample chest, making it appear as if, at any moment, they were going to leak open like giant water balloons.

"So I haven't seen your wife around the neighborhood lately. You sure you she still lives with you?"

RJ stopped and smiled somewhere beyond where Regina lay. "She's pregnant. Yeah, I'm having a baby boy any day now."

When his mind came back to the present, RJ was shocked to find Regina crying hysterically. *What now?*

"Listen… Um—"

"Get out!"

"Regina, what's this all about?"

"Just get out, RJ! Don't you ever darken my doorstep again. I mean it this time. Go!"

"Fuck you, then, bitch!"

"That's real mature talk coming from a simple nigga from the hood."

RJ moved in closer to the bed, hands in boxing position.

"What you gone do now, RJ. Huh? Hit me? Go ahead; I'll have the cops here so fast, before you can even cut a fart. So go 'head, do it with yo' bad self!"

"I don't need this shit. I'm outta here. Crazy bitch!"

RJ was so riled up that he'd forgotten to tuck his shirt into his pants, and he left his necktie and socks at Regina's. *Damn!* Of course he didn't realize this until his car was parked inside his own garage and he'd stepped inside the house.

"Honor! Honor! You awake?" He hoped to God she was asleep. That would give him time to throw his clothes in the hamper and take a quick shower before she even batted a pretty eyelash.

"Honor!" He headed up the stairs, searching every room. No sign of her. Suddenly he realized that he hadn't seen her car in the garage when he pulled up. RJ frantically made his way back downstairs. *Where is she? Where is she? Where is SHE?!* His train of thought stuck on the merry-go-round, RJ ran into the kitchen, stumbling over an open container of flour. He spun around and around again taking in the overturned china cabinet, the broken dishes, and the pantry door split right down the middle, hanging by just one screw. *What the hell happened in here?* He walked through his house again, looking for any sign of forced entry. His search turned up nothing. He deliberately slowed his steps.

"Honor! Honor!" A final trek downstairs to the lower level and basement, and still no Honor. He was miserably perplexed. That's when he checked the phone. No calls from home. *Where could she have gone? Who the hell was in my house?* He pressed the talk button. *Nine. One. Her overnight bag? It was gone!* He hit number three on the speed dial.

"North Hospital. How may I help you?" A voice answered, sounding as old as the hills.

"Yes, can you tell me if you have an Honor Ellis listed as a patient? She'd be in the maternity ward, maybe in the emergency room."

"Well, sir, if she's in the emergency room, we won't have a listing for her, but let me check the maternity wing. Hold on, please."

Elevator music. An elderly rendition of *Super Freak.*

"Sir, we do have an Honor Ellis. She's in room—"

RJ didn't wait for the voice to finish. He threw the phone down and headed straight for his car, leaving flour prints on the wood floors.

RJ arrived at the hospital's maternity wing, where all the babies could be viewed from behind the glass. RJ's nose pressed firmly against the window as he searched for Baby Ellis. His knees grew weak when he spotted him: second row from the front, four babies from the right. He was a sight to marvel, swaddled in the standard-issue hospital baby blankets, a blue cap atop his head, and mittens on his little hands.

All of his degrees, trophy wife, three-car garage, and successful career fell to a status of less than nothing. Here was his one shot to redeem himself. In his son, RJ could finally shake loose from the nightmares of the past and build a new vision. One look the baby, and RJ knew that it was safe to dream again. He could hang his son's little blue cap on it.

A nurse walked from behind the glass. "Excuse me, can I see my son?"

"Certainly. Can I see your wristband, please?" RJ held his arm up to show the nurse his neon orange identification wristband. He watched as she compared the name and a string of numbers printed across it to the one in her notebook. "I'll bring him to you."

RJ had to sit down before he could let the nurse place the baby in his arms. The feeling was ethereal. Never before had RJ held something so tiny in his hands. So warm.

"Hey, little guy. Hey. I'm your daddy. You going to open your eyes for your old man?" In response, Baby Ellis yawned, one barely open eye showing a flick of hazel.

"My boy."

"So have you two thought of a name for him yet?"

"Yes, Day."

"Day?"

"Day Brandon Ellis. Remember that name."

"Sounds like a fine name. I'll have the birth certificate drawn up as soon as possible."

Less than ten minutes later RJ was fuming as he charged into Honor's private room, like a crazed extension cord let loose from its socket. "Why didn't you call me?! I missed my son being born! And what the hell happened to my house?!"

Honor didn't respond.

"Hello, RJ."

He looked behind him, alarmed. "Sasha? What the hell are you doing here?"

"She's knocked out: 'sedated,' I think that's what the nurse called it. She can't hear you. You beat her, don't you?"

"What? Absolutely not!"

"Then tell me why she didn't want you here with her. Why she was holding onto my hand instead of yours? Why you busted in here yelling like gang busters? All my life I've been standing in the shadow of a fool. You ain't nothing. I always thought you were so much better than me, but you ain't nothing. You cut from the same cloth, standing there with her blood on your hands, just like our daddy. Just like Vance. The two of you should have Daddy reserve seats for you next to him in hell. Telling Honor both our parents dead when you know damn well mama rottin' up in prison for killing our daddy." She laughed. "All this time... All this motherfuckin' time."

Sasha stood against the far wall, blowing cigarette smoke outside the open window, despite the obvious "NO SMOKING" signs posted before her. "Yes, sir. It all became clear as mud. Didn't even have to ask her shit. I could smell the fear the second I walked in your house. I always knew something was up with you."

"You busted crack head. What did you tell my wife?"

"The truth? And I may have a drug addiction, but at least I'm not a monster who feels so low about himself that he gotta take it out on a woman. It wasn't 'til today, when I seen my little nephew being born, that it all started making sense to me. Men like you, like Vance? Ya'll are afraid of us because we have so much power. We fight. We love. We cry. We struggle. We get hit on, and sometimes we hit, but under all that fight and struggle is a strength that you can never feel or have. The strength to keep going. The strength to push for hours and give birth to a new life. That's power! Instead of tapping into the source, men like you try to squash it out of us. So you see, I'm a hell of a lot better than you can ever hope to be."

"So what, you Socrates now, all philosophical and shit? You didn't even finish high school. Give me a break. I don't hit on my wife!"

"Maybe not, but you doing somethin' bad to her. I don't have to have a diploma to know that. You come in hear yelling at her, instead of thanking

120

her for just giving birth to your son. Seems a little strange to me."

It wasn't until that moment that RJ noticed Sasha's disheveled appearance. What was it Reverend Odom said? *She looked a mess.* That was an understatement. To look a hot mess would be a step up from where she was at now.

"You're delusional. How long has it been since your last hit? You need help, Sasha."

"If that ain' the pot calling the kettle black." Sasha hadn't moved from the windowsill, the cigarette dwindling closer to her fingertips. RJ wondered if his sister would even feel anything if the cigarette burned clear to the quick of her ragged fingernails.

"Look, I'm trying to offer you some help, dammit! If Vance is beating on you, then why don't you leave him? I can put you up somewhere. Get you clean."

Sasha exhaled slowly, releasing a cloud of smoke that seemed tangled in a strange slow dance with her voice before it vanished completely. "Why doesn't Honor leave you? I don't need—"

"Say anything more about Honor and I'll punch your damn teeth in, the few you have left." Only the red EXIT sign above him stopped RJ from doing just that. He realized he was in a public place.

"Go ahead, big brother. You can't do no worse to me than what's already been done. I know you won't though, because I'll scream so loud that everyone in this damn hospital will come running. What would everyone think then about the great Principal Ranford Ellis? Think what would happen if folks found out that this city's black second coming ain't nothing but a big ole punk."

"Shut up! You think I'm just going to let a crack head bitch sit up in the hospital room that I'm paying for and judge me? You really are crazy."

"Is that all you got? Come on, big bro. You know you got to dig a helluva lot deeper to get under my skin. You ain't even scratched the surface. You know what else? This crack head: she's your sister. Yeah, we got the same flesh and blood, which means we more the same than different. Hell, we even look alike. I'm just more out there with how fucked up we truly are. I ain't ashamed to say I come from the projects. Hell, still there. But, you… You more fucked up than I'll ever be because you try to hide it, and who's paying the price? Your wife? Does she even know about all those hoes you run around with all over town, or didn't you think I knew? You ain't slick, and if she wasn't laying there after having my nephew, I'd spill all your motherfuckin' beans on the floor. Can you hear them fallin', RJ? Drop. Drop. Drop. Dro-o-o-o-p."

Sasha flung the cigarette butt out the window and headed for the EXIT sign, leaving RJ standing there his mouth wide open and Honor, eyes tightly closed, listening to her every word.

SASHA

Sasha didn't leave the hospital. She roamed the hospital floors grateful for the shelter, wondering if their landlord had finally decided to act on the ever-present eviction notice taped to the front door of their apartment. With Vance in jail for his latest offense and a slew of bench warrants, there was no need to return home anyway.

On her third trip past the cafeteria, Sasha began to feel the familiar pains of hunger. She entered and walked straight to the conveyer belt where family members of loved ones, most of them too anxious to eat, had placed their trays filled with uneaten food. Sasha grabbed a tray and mindlessly began shoving half-eaten portions of chicken fried steak, mashed potatoes, and applesauce. She noticed a Barbie look-alike in green scrubs eyeing her suspiciously. It was then that Sasha realized she was eating with her hands and licking her fingers. A savage among overpriced gift shop trinkets and the dignified ill. Sasha rolled her eyes at Barbie and got up from the table.

Sasha became faint midway into her fourth lap around the hospital. When the dizziness failed to subside, she sat down in the nearest waiting area, ignoring the strange glances from the hospital staff and visitors. Didn't matter. Sasha was used to being the main attraction wherever she went, a traveling freak show. *What to do?*

In her haze, Sasha knew she was at the end of her rope. She wanted to let go. To turn that rope into a noose and hang the last bit of existence. She fumbled around in her pockets and fished out a frayed business card. She'd been carrying it around like a security blanket since the day she had bumped into her old friend at the senior home. Call it a supernatural nudge or a dying woman's last burst of hope, whatever it was, it forced Sasha up off her feet and to the phone between two standard-issue hospital tables and a lone chair.

She dialed.

"Operator, I'd like to place a collect call." Sasha gave her name and the number; her hands shook so much it was hard to cradle the phone next to her ear.

"House of Hope, Angie speaking."

"Hello, I have a collect call from Sasha Ellis. Will you accept the charges?"

"Yes! Put her through, please."

"Thank you for choosing Mobile Bell." Sasha heard a series of clicks and then shuffling in the background, as if someone were playing a game of hot potato with the phone. Was she it? Then silence and a familiar voice on the other end.

"Sasha, I've had you on my heart since the day I bumped into you. That wasn't a coincidence. That was divine intervention. I was meant to be visiting Daddy that day, and I've been praying for you to call me every day since. I know I shouldn't have done this—they could kick me off the board if they knew—but I've reserved a bed for you. Has your name written all over it. Beds here are hard to come by, so that was no easy feat, especially when they saw no one laying there. But I knew. I knew. Thank you, Jesus."

Sasha thought about hanging up on her childhood friend, afraid she'd have to listen to another sinner sermon from a holy roller. But something like peace made her pull the phone in closer. No one had ever been happy to hear her voice. No one had ever wanted her.

"A bed?"

"Yes, just for you. Well, you'll have a roommate."

"A roommate. I don't ..."

"Sasha, hold on. Let me put you on with one of our intake coordinators. They will take good care of you, and I will be with you every step of the way. Oh, it's such a beautiful day."

Sasha smiled. It was her second genuine smile of the day. The first was when she had been privy to a miracle: witnessed an action that was so powerful, it left her speechless. Her nephew had fought hard for a chance at life. Honor was equally as impressive, pushing with her all her might to ensure his opportunity. Being witness to a miracle had changed her in some way. She saw life as a gift now, one she had never fully unwrapped and had been about to throw away. Yes, she'd been dealt a lousy hand, but that didn't mean she couldn't find a fresh deck of playing cards. What was this strange sensation—something like optimism? Or was it simply a chance to stick it to Vance, RJ, Reverend Odom, and every man who'd ever hurt her?

"House of Hope, this is Carrie. At this very moment, are you in danger?"

"No," Sasha answered.

"Has your life been threatened?"

"Y-yes, many times."

"You understand that once you come to stay with us, you cannot, under any circumstances, contact anyone or tell them where you are?"

"Word?!"

"I'm sorry?"

"I mean… Yes."

"We take your safety and the safety of the other women and children here seriously. Please understand that even one phone call could jeopardize not only your life, but that of everyone in the whole house."

"I understand."

"You also understand that, if you decide to come here, not only will you be cut off from those around you, but you will be assigned daily chores or duties, you will adhere to the rules of the House of Hope, attend regular meetings and receive job or GED training, if needed."

Sasha was becoming jittery. She wasn't too keen about sitting around with a bunch of women in some koom-ba-ya meeting or cleaning up other people's messes. Still, what other choice did she have? Although her hope was growing, options were hard to come by.

"Yeah, I understand."

"Do you have children?"

"No."

"Are you a substance abuser?"

"Why is that important?"

"We need to know what areas you struggle with so that we can assist you in every way possible. Women who are in domestic violence situations, well, let's just say it takes its toll."

"Yeah."

"Yes, what?"

"I am a…whatever you called it."

"I see, and what substances are you addicted to?"

Sasha hesitated, suddenly wanting to wrap herself up in a warm hospital blanket. "Crack. Weed. Prescription pain killers. I think that's all."

"What about alcohol? Do you drink?"

"Yeah." Sasha watched nervously as a silver-haired woman inched her way into the waiting room. She reminded Sasha of a blue question mark, with straight slender legs and a hunched-over back—navy polyester pants and a sky-blue sweatshirt that read *Grandmas Are The Closest Thing To Heaven* across her sagging breasts. She moved slowly, as if the journey to the nearby chair was too painful to make.

"How often do you drink?"

"How often?"

"Do you drink daily, once a month, once a year, only socially?"

"Shit, daily, if I can."

"I see. At House of Hope we have a zero tolerance policy. No drugs, alcohol, or derogatory language. Violating one or all of these policies could result in full expulsion from the program. Do you understand?"

"Yeah. I mean, yes, I understand."

"Residents with substance abuse issues will attend daily rehabilitation sessions at our sister facility until such time is deemed appropriate that they have successfully completed the program. They also will undergo breathalyzers and urine testing at our discretion. Failure to pass either the urine testing or breathalyzer will result in your expulsion from the house and the program. Is all of this clear?"

Am I signing up for boot camp? "Yeah, I guess so."

"You're about to embark on a life-changing journey, one that you have to more than guess at. Our director, staff, and volunteers put a lot of time and effort into House of Hope and we can't lose everything on a whim."

"I said, I'm ready!" Sasha was becoming annoyed by the voice on the other end of the line. Her calmness threatened to leave her and run inside one of the patient rooms.

"That's the confidence we are looking for. Fight for it and hold onto it. You're about to do battle with yourself and everything you thought you knew existed."

"Lady, I've been fighting my whole life."

"Good. Where are you calling from?"

"North Hospital."

"Are you injured?"

"Only my spirit."

A chuckle escaped from the voice on the other end. "Good girl. Glad you still manage to have a sense of humor. I need you to get a pen and a piece of paper." Sasha ripped a small scrap of paper from the local section of the *Kansas City Times* and grabbed a pen with the hospital logo imprinted on one of its sides.

"Okay, I'm ready."

"From North Hospital, I need you take the number twenty-five bus.

Only the twenty-five. You're going to make two transfers. Get off at the Zona Rosa Shopping Center; transfer to the sixty-four. Take the sixty-four to Front Street, then you'll need to get on the bus headed to the 18th and Vine District. Someone will be waiting for you when you arrive. I need you to follow these instructions to the letter and remember, tell no one where you are going."

Sasha scribbled fast, her hand shaking. "Wait… I don't have any money for the bus."

"No need. When you get on the first bus, tell the driver that you would like a piece of chocolate."

"A piece of chocolate?"

"Yes, he'll let you on and hand you your transfers. Oh, and make sure you sit at the back of each bus on the right hand side."

A burst of nervous energy erupted somewhere deep inside Sasha, threatening to mar her newfound self-confidence. The sad spy game was already demanding too much of her concentration. Her time.

"Did you write down my instructions?"

"Yes. I wrote them down." *Then I threw them in the trash*, Sasha wanted to add.

"Good. I applaud your courage. Not many women get this far and sadly many are killed by their abusers, never knowing that help is out here. When you get on that bus, keep in mind that the steps you're taking are ones that many other women did not have the chance to take. Had they done so, maybe they would have lived…although we realize we can't save every woman. This is a step toward a new life, and the climb is sometimes painful, but I promise you happiness is at the top."

Why did she have to say that? "I'm ready," Sasha said. *Am I ready?*

"Good luck." *Click.*

Sasha wasn't aware that she still held the phone against her ear until the faint dial tone turned into a series of menacing beeps. It was then that the question mark woman noticed she wasn't alone and turned toward Sasha. *Was that a frown?* Resisting the urge to go straighten the elderly woman out, Sasha set the phone gently back on its cradle. She grabbed the piece of torn paper from the trash can and headed toward the revolving doors.

Almost two hours and three bus transfers later, Sasha stood on the corner of 18th and Vine, her body shivering, even though the night's temperature was well above the sixty-degree mark. Just like the voice had said, the invisible piece of chocolate had gotten her this far, but she was at a loss as to what to do next. A shorter woman walked up to where Sasha stood, staring blindly ahead. The first thing that caught Sasha's attention was the heavy main of blond dreads that hung down her back, a pink breast cancer awareness bandana wrapped around her forehead.

Sasha had never seen a white person with dreads before. The woman had a round face and almond-shaped green eyes that were so close they almost seemed to touch each other. Her long and narrow nose led the way to an almost non-existent pair of lips. She wore a pair of hip-hugging jeans that accented her curves and flared at the bottom, revealing a pair of black Crocs that matched her black top with a large multi-colored peace sign. There was a faint scar line that traveled from her chin to her left ear. Sasha didn't have to be a mind-reader to know there was a story behind that line. Every scar on Sasha's battered and bruised body could tell a sad story all its own.

"Would you like a piece of chocolate?"

What's with all the damn chocolates? I need a hit, not a piece of fuckin' chocolate.

"Yes," Sasha said, hesitantly, surprised by the answer that escaped her severely burned lips.

Sasha jerked when the woman with the blond dreads softly pulled her by the arm. She wanted to pull each one of her twists out then. *Why'd she gotta touch me?*

"Do not draw unnecessary attention to yourself, or to me," she said. "Now, I'm going to hug you like we're old friends, and if you expect this to work, you will return the hug. At the count of three. One… Two… Three."

The stranger flung her arms around Sasha, and Sasha awkwardly returned the gesture. "Oh my God, girl, it's been ages. I'm so glad you could make it out here. Let's go get a drink and celebrate."

Her arm still around Sasha, they moved at a fast pace to a nondescript maroon sedan.

"Get in," she said.

"Are we really going to get a drink?" That was all Sasha could think to ask, not caring in the least that she was in an unmarked car with a strange woman.

"Hell naw! They don't allow that crap at the house. Girl, you must really be feenin'—you shakin' so hard the passenger seat is rattling. Don't worry: when we get to the house, they gone take good care of you. I'm Anina."

"Sasha." Sasha looked down at her hands. She really was shaking.

"Hey, you mind cracking your window? No offense, but you'd be passed over as an extra in a douche commercial right now."

Sasha hit the button. The night breeze felt good on her face. Her body still racked with a terrible case of uncontrollable movement and dizziness.

"When's the last time you had a hit?" Anina asked matter-of-factly.

"Look, I'm not no dope fiend. I can stop whenever I want so don't you sit there and look down on me."

"Woo. Slow down. I never called you a dope fiend, but I recognize the shakes when I see 'em. You might say I've been around the block a few times too many myself. By the looks of you, I'd say your drug of choice is crack, which you hit several times a day…maybe a little weed and prescription meds thrown in for good measure, and your last hit was this morning."

"How did you…?"

Anina laughed, revealing a row of yellowing teeth that were surprisingly straight. "I guessed. But like I said, I ain't no stranger to things. Plus, I was raised by two diehard hippies… Well, when they would have me. Most times, I was a ward of the state, in and out of foster homes, forced into the streets at eighteen. Trust me, we wouldn't be sitting here today if we both weren't singing the same blues. White, black, it don't matter when life deals you a lousy hand. You just gotta wake up every day and pray that today ain't the day you fold. You know what I mean? Myself, I been clean for five years, since the day I got to the house. Yeah, I was something else. My old man used to beat the crap out of me every hour, on the hour. You could set your watch by it. I found immunity in staying high, but that ain't no way to live."

Anina reached into her jean pocket with her free hand and took out an almost-full pack of menthols. She lit one with ease as they drove deeper into the city.

"Want a cigarette?"

Sasha didn't answer. She just reached for the pack, lit the menthol, and inhaled with all her might, imagining it was something, anything stronger.

"Where exactly are we going?" Sasha asked. The cigarette was helping to clear her head, only slightly.

"All you need to know that is that we're going someplace safe."

"What's up with all the secrets? You all act like I'm joining the CIA or something."

Anina laughed again. She had girlish giggle that held the promise of kettle corn and cotton candy. "Maybe not the CIA, but by the time everything is over, you will think you've been through training hell. I did a stint in the military too. I think they might have been easier on me there than they were at the house."

A stab of fear pierced through Sasha's chest. Her expression showed it all.

"Hey, don't worry. You're in good hands. They're good people and everything is voluntary. If you want to give up, you can walk right out the door at any time. You'll like Ms. Jones: she created the House of Hope and, for some reason, sticks around. She don't take no shit either for an old lady. One time I watched her chase this girl's old man off the porch with a pistol in her hands. Later, she told us all the pistol ain't never loaded. But you couldn't tell it when she dared that man to lay a hand on one of her girls again. She's something else all right." That girlish giggle again.

The sedan came to stop in front of a tri-level yellow house with green painted awnings on both sides. A white swing was on one side of the oversized cement porch, and bushes adorned the entrance to the porch's four steps. Gigantic trees covered the house from front to back, shielding it from the urban decay around it. The house's clean-cut country appeal was somewhat out-of-place among the rows of city homes in various stages of disrepair.

"Well, we're here," Anina said, as if Sasha hadn't already figured that out. All at once, Sasha was too weak to lift herself up from the passenger seat, and when she was finally able to stand, she felt light-headed from the struggle.

"I need to sit down," Sasha reached for the grass beneath her.

"Oh, no, you can't be out there too long. Hold on." Sasha sat down anyway.

Anina used all of her stout five-foot-two frame to lift Sasha from the ground and push her toward the porch. The door swung open and a familiar face approached them.

"Deb?"

"She's here, Ms. Jones!" Debra shouted, never once taking her eyes from Sasha's.

"Hello, Sasha. I am so glad to see you."

"We gotta live one," Anina said.

"I can tell. Ms. Jones, I think she could go straight to Winchester. What do you think?"

A tall stoic woman walked outside, wiping her hands on a dishtowel. She had a long narrow jaw line that matched her neck, and she was slender, save for her small patch of belly fat that served as testament to her giving birth to six children. Her fine straight brown hair was cut into a sleek style that tapered almost to her ears, where a pair of butterfly earrings dangled. She was dressed in a business-casual tan blouse and brown pants that seemed too fancy to be anywhere close to a dishrag.

"Oh, dear. I think you're right. Get her to Winchester."

"I'll stay with her," Debra said.

"Fine. We will see you in a few days, Sasha." Ms. Jones said, still wiping her hands.

A few days? Sasha was too feeble to ask where she was being taken as both women slipped her into the back seat and drove a few blocks west of the house.

Debra made a quick call on her cell phone. "Dr. Schreirer, please. ... Hello? ... Yes, Doctor, this is the woman I spoke to you about. ... Thank you so much. We will be there in a few minutes. ... Yes. ... I'm not sure. ... I realize that. ... I do, thank you."

Sasha could hear bits of Debra's hurried conversation.

"Where are you taking me?"

Anina answered. "Rehab, girl. 'They tried to make me go to rehab I said no, no, no...'" More of that giggle.

"Anina," Debra said. Her voice was beyond firm.

"Sorry. I'm just trying to lighten the mood. So Sasha, why didn't you tell me that you was Debra's old friend? She's been waiting forever for you to get here. We told her you weren't never gone come, but she never gave up. You gotta good friend here."

Sasha said nothing, not even when they stopped and both women stood on either side of her and helped her inside the clinic next to the University of Kansas Hospital.

"I'll wait in the car," Anina said after they entered. It was as if the sight of the clinic spooked her.

"Come on, Sasha." Debra said.

They sat down on an empty row of black chairs; Sasha was still shivering, Debra's arms wrapped tightly around her. They molded into each other and moved together like a gelatin mound.

The place was menacingly dark and surprisingly silent. A short, portly man, more salt-and-pepper beard than anything, walked over to them. "Hello, Sasha. I'm Dr. Schreirer," he said. "You are at the Winchester Clinic, an outpatient facility for drug rehabilitation. Do you understand why you're here?"

Sasha nodded.

"Now, we cannot treat you unless you're ready to admit that you have a problem. You have to want to get better for yourself. I can't do it for you, and neither can Debra or Ms. Jones. It all falls on you. Do you understand?"

Again, Sasha nodded. "Help me," Sasha managed to mutter.

The doctor turned to Debra. "Do you know what she's been taking?"

"From what I understand, cocaine, pain killers, and marijuana."

"Ok, Sasha. Your body is craving the drugs now. But what you're experiencing is only a taste of what's to come. We are a methadone clinic, although we have suboxone available. These drugs will assist you by limiting the cravings, and by making the withdrawal process a bit more bearable. There is a slight risk that they themselves could become habit-forming, but we monitor—"

"No!"

"I'm sorry?"

"No drugs!"

"I wouldn't suggest that. With your small frame, and what appears to be a long history of drug abuse, the risks could be too great."

"No more drugs!"

"You don't understand the risks of going cold turkey. Yes, it seems heroic and all, but the reality is you're not a superhero. You need help. You need to be made as comfortable as possible through this process. You could die from withdrawals. Someone will have to be with you at all times—all times."

"I'll stay with her."

"I still don't think this is a good idea. But I will give you a week, at the most, without medication. I will need to see her here daily. She must complete the program."

"She will, Doctor. You have my word."

"Debra, have you ever done this before? Do you even know what you're about to go through as a caretaker? The next forty-eight to seventy-two hours are crucial. Her life is in your hands. Do you want that?"

"With all due respect, Doctor. Her life was in my hands the day I bumped into her a few weeks ago at the senior center. I just needed her to get to me."

"Very well, then. I'll stop by the house periodically to check in on her. Until then, you must make sure she gets plenty of fluids, even if she doesn't keep them down for long. She may grow hostile toward you one minute, and then fall into a deep depression a minute later. The only thing you can do is watch her."

"There is one other thing I can do."

"What is that?"

"Pray."

PART II

"I publicly express my deepest regret and accept full responsibility."
Chris Brown, July 20, 2009

HONOR

RJ's moods were becoming easier to predict. He was permanently stuck on "gloomy with a slight chance of torrential terror." No longer a human incubator, Honor was of no more use to RJ, except that she be *kept*, and that she take care of Day. Day was RJ's sunshine: the only thing that could bring a smile to his handsome face when he was at home. Every morning and evening, Day was the first person RJ greeted. He looked past Honor to get to wherever Day was, regardless if the baby was napping or nursing. "Daddy's home!" became synonymous with "Daddy and Day time," unless Day needed changing, feeding, or bathing. Then RJ would pass him to Honor like a minor league quarterback gripping a slippery football. Inaudible time outs that left Honor exhausted.

When Day turned twelve weeks old, RJ reached for Honor, pulling her nightgown above her breasts. She shuddered, actually grateful for his attention. That is, until RJ plunged inside her with all the gentleness of a grizzly bear, hitting her perennial area, still sore from stitches. When she cried out, he pinched her raw nipple until it bled. "Shut up, you'll wake the baby," was his only response. Then he groaned and rolled over. Honor turned on her side and let the tears fall at the sound of his snoring. *He didn't even take the time to fully undress me.* Honor wondered how it was possible to lay down with a woman, your wife, and never really touch her.

Honor was violated to a point of becoming inhuman, even in her own eyes. RJ had let the cleaning lady and house manager go as soon as she returned from the hospital with their three-day-old son in her arms. After going upstairs to put Day down in his nursery, Honor walked into the bedroom they shared. She sat down on the bed and noticed a peculiar musky scent that was not her own. Immediately she began to change the sheets. Was she imagining things? The words Sasha had spoken in the hospital room echoed in Honor's mind for the millionenth time. *Does she even know about all those hoes you run around with all over town?* RJ looked at her oddly when he came upstairs and saw Honor changing the linens, but he said nothing except, "I'm hungry. What are you cooking for dinner?"

He rarely hit her anymore. Instead, his words began to deliver the blows of a heavyweight champ. "Why you still so fat?" This, just two weeks after giving birth.

"When you gonna start cleaning yourself up, taking better care of yourself?" This after Day had spit up all over her for the second time that evening.

"You stink," he said after she had just finished changing one of Day's diapers.

"Why is the house always so damn dirty? Lazy bitch, what the hell do you do all day?" he said, several times when Honor was just beginning to get Day on a schedule so he would no longer confuse day from night, or need two-hour feedings throughout the night.

So distraught was Honor by her six-week checkup, that she broke down in tears before Dr. Williams could even examine her. "Oh, sweetie, you're just suffering from a case of post-partum depression. A lot of women go through this, some more than others."

After clearing her for exercise and intercourse, the doctor sent Honor home with a prescription for Zoloft. "Crazy pills," RJ would hiss at her each time he would watch her swallow one. "What, you crazy now?"

Honor never answered her husband, although her heart would pound somewhere outside of her chest, and she'd wipe sweaty palms on her quivering legs. Worse than the daily arsenal of insults was the sickening need to try harder to please him. The thought that RJ would forever walk away and leave Honor alone with their baby terrified her. More than anything, Honor did not want to be left all alone with Day.

Motherhood eluded her.

Only the robotic side of Honor existed to clean, cook, bathe, walk, bounce, burp, wipe, feed, change, nurse, and wash. But during those quiet moments, when she was rocking Day to sleep, she might as well have been holding a sack of potatoes. One of them was becoming lifeless, and, most days, she couldn't figure out if it was her or the baby.

Honor was not excited by the things even mothers three or four times over treasured: the first smile; that tiny finger laced around its mother's; the smell of freshly bathed skin lathered down in baby oil and talcum powder; the new outfit too adorable to pass up; the feeling of holding something only God could create. Although she prayed daily for this magical maternal bond to occur, the only tie they shared disappeared when the umbilical cord dried and fell off. The love was severed, if it ever existed at all. Day stayed awkward in Honor's arms, and he seemed to sense her uneasiness, always squirming.

"Mom, when are you coming to Kansas City?" Honor asked her mother several times over stilted phone conversations.

"Soon, baby, I'll be there real soon. Just waiting on the right time. You know your father. The man's so spoiled. Wouldn't eat if I didn't set his plate down in front of him every night."

The right time had yet to come, and Honor could use a familiar face around her. The faces in her own home failed to comfort her. She only saw isolation and a sad solitude. Still without a cell phone, Honor wondered many days how she had managed to let RJ alienate her from sorority sisters and all of her friends in just a few short months. If she could, she would summon enough courage to simply walk out the door and never return. Would she take her son? She couldn't say for sure. The one thing Honor knew for certain was that if she took Day, RJ would kill her.

Honor stood over a sleeping Day's crib and searched again for that fictional feeling of oneness. Would it come today? Honor hoped that the sight of Day napping would soften her heart, even a little. She watched as he lay peacefully on his back in his sky-blue onesie, a small gurgle escaping from his mouth with every exhale, his pacifier close by his side—his small hands resting above his soft curly hair. Fear was all she had. Fear that, at any second, Day's eyes would pop open along with his mouth, and her peaceful afternoon would be no longer. She questioned whether it was selfishness or trying to save what little sanity she had left.

Honor cursed under her breath as the doorbell rang. She tiptoed out of Day's room and quietly shut the door behind her, before heading for the door, wondering who would be at her house at this time in the afternoon? Hardly anyone had come by the house since the day Sasha had created a drug-induced tirade in her kitchen. Sometimes Honor still managed to cut her finger or her foot on a piece of glass left behind in the melee. Strangely, the resulting blood managed to comfort Honor. It made her feel as if she still held Sasha's hand, tightly. More than Sasha's hand, Honor wanted desperately to grasp hold of an unforeseen strength she'd recognized. The feeling was like an electric current, pulsating over the drugs and all the pain. Maybe she was back? Maybe her mother had finally made good on her promise of an extended visit?

Without thought, Honor opened the door. Immediately, the day's brightness began to hurt her eyes and promise a verging migraine. Regina stood on her front porch, her hands behind her back, DD cups on full display in a form-fitting black sports tank. Her matching stretch pants accentuated the v-shape between her hips. Even though she appeared to be gearing up for some type of exercise, her cheeks were blushed rosy and false eyelashes flickered beneath her perfectly arched eyebrows.

Honor fumbled with her ponytail, which was not was not nearly as polished as the woman's highlighted hair before her. She suddenly felt exposed standing in her black MU t-shirt and black and yellow flannel pajama bottoms, her still-protruding belly on full alert. In the presence of this woman, this stranger, Honor was undone.

"Can I help you?" Honor asked. With one hand she continued trying to smooth down her unkempt ponytail.

"You must be Honor? I can see why RJ speaks so highly of you. I'm Regina." The woman extended her hand; her freshly French-manicured nails drew Honor's eyes to her own chipped and chewed-up nail beds. Honor was reluctant to shake her hand, but she did so because politeness was the Southern way. Olivia raised her daughter to be a lady. The hand that gripped Honor's chilled her palm like a fistful of ice cubes.

"Hello. It's nice to meet you. Should I know you from somewhere?"

"Oh, sorry. I live about a block or so from here, up the hill a ways. I jog past your house about five times a week."

The woman, this Regina, had said a mouthful while saying nothing at all, and it came too easy for her, the same way it would a sleazy politician. The woman before her did not look even vaguely familiar to Honor.

"What can I do for you, Mrs. ...?"

"Regina. Please call me Regina. Don't seem neighborly with all those unnecessary prefixes." She smiled at Honor. If Honor hadn't known better, she'd swear the sunlight was reflecting off the whiteness of the woman's veneered teeth.

"Well, how can I help you...Regina?"

"It's a little embarrassing to discuss out here on the front porch, dear. Can I come inside?"

"I'm sorry, how did you say you know my husband?"

"I didn't. We really need to talk...woman to woman."

"And why would we need to do that?" Honor crossed her arms in a mock confidence that threatened to melt away at any minute. Her legs began the familiar jig of anxiety under the sunlight.

"RJ left this at my house yesterday." Like Kali, the Hindu goddesses with many arms, a smartphone appeared in one of the woman's hands that she pulled from behind her.

"Why do you have RJ's phone?" Internal ice turned to stone as Honor spoke.

"Come on, girl. We're both adults. Honestly, how do you believe I came upon his cell? Oh, let's see, maybe I stumbled over it during my evening jog yesterday, or it must have flown out of his hand yesterday and landed smack dab in my bed along with your husband."

"You chesty bitch! How dare you come to my house with this trash? That's not even his phone!"

"Call him. Go ahead. Dial the number," Regina smirked. Her teeth did not look as heavenly to Honor anymore. Honor ran to the phone on the sofa table in the living room. Her bare feet made slapping noises across the hardwood floors as she scurried back and forth. Speed dial number two and the phone in Regina's hand hummed a Marvin Gaye tune: "*Heard it through the grapevine. How much longer will you be mine? Oh …*"

Bam! The cell phone hit the floor, taking Honor along for the ride.

"Why are you doing this?! You bitch!" Honor pushed the door close. Regina's Nike-clad foot created an instant wedge.

"Surely you must know something is up with RJ? That man is too damn fine for his own good. He deserves to get what he's been dishing out to me for months. Don't believe me? Come by my house around four o'clock today. Twenty-one thirteen Bawling Oak Drive. It's Tuesday. RJ always pays me a visit at four on Tuesdays. I can set my watch by the time he's going to bust a nut."

"Get out!"

With that, the foot disappeared, leaving Honor and the cell phone on the floor amidst the devastation: a four-G sonic boom. Honor sat, in a fetal position, not even bothering to will herself from shaking. She didn't dare move until she heard Day awake from his nap with a loud cry.

At three forty-five Honor had Day dressed in a navy sailor outfit and strapped into his ill-used stroller, bottle in hand.

They stood by her nemesis: the front door.

Honor thought of the people who had come through that door, dropping hurt and despair everywhere as if they were removing their shoes. More than that, she thought of everything it had come to represent: her loneliness, isolation, her fear, and her inability to open it and climb outside into a life of normalcy. *What are you doing? This is insane. You know that woman was lying to you. She's not worth having to open this door.*

As if sensing his mother's unease, Day began to squirm about and sniffle. *One. Two. Three. Now!* He giggled as the warm sunlight tickled him. Honor stepped outside, afraid if she turned around, she'd run back inside. *For what? Certainly not for safety.* Honor knew she was no longer safe anywhere, not even in her own bed.

Honor swallowed hard, ignored the sweat forming on her forearms and pushed her jelly-filled legs forward. An unforeseen force was pulling her closer to Bawling Oak Drive, something stronger than fear. An elderly couple walked hand-in-hand past Honor and Day on the opposite side of the street. They both wore warm-up suits and, though they spoke no words, the comfort in their silence told volumes. The type of love story that only wrinkled skin, weathered storms, and many years of lovemaking could tell without having to utter one syllable. They waved from across the street, and Honor returned the gesture. She envied their oneness, their matching strides. Honor wasn't too far up the incline when she spotted RJ's black Lincoln parked in the driveway of an autumn-leaf painted stucco house with patchwork grass and little curb appeal.

Day, still tucked away in his stroller, cooed and made better friends with the daylight. Her first inclination was to knock when she approached the house. Instead, Honor found herself twisting the doorknob open, not surprised in the least to find the door unlocked. She decided to keep the door open so she could keep one eye on Day, without having to go through the trouble of unstrapping and unsettling his contentment.

Her heart went arrhythmic as she stepped inside, noticing the modestly decorated interior, the white leather sectional and matching glass tables. As she approached the stairs leading toward the bedrooms, a soft moan caused her to stumble. Honor sat on the second step, listening as the moans grew louder, becoming near screams that might turn the neighbors jealous. What does one do in this situation, she wondered? She could jump up, run into the bedroom where the screams were emitting from, and then...then what?

"Oh, RJ!"

She could grab a sharp knife from the kitchen, walk upstairs calmly, and stab them to death, putting a sour end to their mid-day tryst.

"Oh...Oh...Yes! That's my spot!"

She could search for a blunt object, race upstairs, and bludgeon them until the sheets were saturated and they lay motionless in their own blood.

"Make me come! Make me come!"

Honor chose neither of the options she'd imagined. With her heart pressed wildly against her chest, she sank into the heaviness of it all—and it was all too much. So she backed outside, carefully shutting the door behind her. Then she walked, spotting the same elderly couple making their way back up the hill, still holding hands.

Honor returned home surprised to find the house just as she had left it, down to the half-eaten bowl of breakfast oats on the counter. A laundry basket she'd meant to bring down earlier still waited for her at the top of the stairs; the wedding photos over the mantle, along with Day's newborn picture, in matching solid gold frames. Everything was exactly as it should be, yet nothing was the same. Honor no longer had the hat of fidelity to hold onto, so why wasn't everything around her shattered in pieces? It would almost be easier for Honor to accept RJ's indiscretion if something was out of place, if plates were everywhere and her feet were walking on flour again.

Day's cry let her know that dinnertime was near. She hadn't realized she'd been gone for over an hour. She placed the stroller back in the garage and walked Day over to his bouncy seat, placing a *I Love My Daddy* bib around him. From the cabinet, Honor took out a box of infant cereal, mixed it with formula and warmed it in the microwave for fifteen seconds. She'd forgotten it was in there until the microwave's intermittent reminder beeps snapped her from her fog. The beep sent Honor into autopilot and she fed a fidgety Day until he turned away, the bowl more than half empty. Taking him from his bouncer, a more content Day gurgled and spit up a bit of cereal that bypassed his bib and landed on his sailor suit.

With his hazel eyes, the ones he inherited from his father, Day stared at Honor as if it were the only thing he would rather do in the world as they headed upstairs to the bathroom. Honor turned the bathwater to warm and sat Day's baby bath into the tub. She undressed him, throwing his soiled diaper into the nearby diaper pail. RJ insisted that a diaper pail be in every room in the house because he couldn't stand the smell of his son's urine or feces. A few days ago, RJ had hit her because he found a diaper in the trashcan. Now she was careful that every diaper be disposed of in its proper place, just as she was careful that the house be spotless and dinner warming on the stove when RJ arrived home from work.

Even when he "worked" late, Honor made sure a plate was warmed up for him, scotch straight-up on the right side of his dinner plate. *Dinner?* Day was in the tub now, kicking his feet generously and grabbing at the rubber duck that swam within an inch of his tiny circumcised penis. *I don't have dinner ready! What can I throw together in just fifteen minutes?* She could boil some okra and place a couple of KC strips on the gas grill. Maybe grill a couple of chicken breasts, toss it into a salad, and add some garlic toast? *Garlic? Do I have any fresh garlic? I can't remember if I have any garlic. There should still be a little left. If not, maybe I have some garlic powder. Can't use garlic salt – RJ's blood pressure. Why didn't I pick some up when RJ took me to the grocery store last weekend? I made a list. Didn't I make a list? Did I use the last of it when I made the lasagna? How could I have forgotten to get garlic?*

As Honor's mind raced on a garlic windmill, the water continued to flow and the vapor clouds grew heavier. Day's legs stopped moving and the water stilled, save for a small air bubble that chased its way up to the top of the tub and burst.

SASHA

Sasha stared at herself in the mirror, afraid the reflection before her would vanish if she turned away. She looked...healthy. Dare she say, even pretty? She smiled, deep and wide enough to overwhelm her high cheekbones, causing them to ache. She didn't care. There was beauty in that pain and extensive dental work. Twice-a-month visits to Community One Dental Center had resulted in two partial bridges, a root canal, several fillings, whitening, a fluoride treatment and, of course, cleanings. All free of charge. When Debra had first taken her inside the clinic, she'd been embarrassed, unable to remember the last time she'd owned a toothbrush.

Next was a trip to Planned Parenthood, where she received a free gynecological exam that revealed Chlamydia, genital warts, and pelvic inflammatory disease. The antibiotics she was given also aided in curing the infection in her gums. Weekly weigh-ins at the rehabilitation clinic proved that she was putting on a healthy amount of weight, and Sasha admired her newfound curves in a pair of hip-hugging jeans with a pink short-sleeved sweater and matching scarf.

No longer was she a toothpick in the wind, just waiting for one strong gust to blow her over. She stood taller, walked steadier, and dared the wind to push her. Her hair reflected this new healthy image. Her soft, saucy curls were back, almost to her shoulders. She was the spitting image of Carmen almost twenty years ago.

But more than the external transformation were the changes that had taken place inside of her since she'd came to the house. Battered and bruised on the outside, shattered on the inside, Sasha was one thread away from unraveling at seams that were already threadbare. But here she stood, smiling. Smiling! And it felt so good.

For the first time in her life, Sasha was at peace, and this peace belonged to her. This peace was her birthright. The counselors and weekly group sessions had taught her that. She knew now that she had a right to smile, to laugh, a right to give love and be loved in return. It had taken Sasha several weeks to grasp hold of the concept that love healed. It didn't leave you covered in bruises and scars that cut much deeper the skin.

Sasha learned that the drugs only served to numb the pain of so-called love, like ibuprofen for a headache or arthritis cream for a backache—a temporary fix at best. The only remedy for a bruised soul was old-fashioned, ceaseless hard work, digging deep to the core and tears.

A knock at the door interrupted her thoughts.

"Sasha, it's time. Are you ready?"

"Yes. Yes, I believe I am."

Debra stepped insider the door, a grin across her face as well.

"You got everything?" Debra asked.

"Yes. Not like I have much of anything, really."

"Oh, will you stop, Sasha? You know you are rich beyond your wildest dreams."

"Thanks to you," Sasha said.

"Stop, now. Don't get me crying already. This is all about you. You made this happen all on your own. I merely pushed. Moving on… How was class last night?"

"Which one? It seems like I go to so many! One for drug rehab. One for overcoming abuse. One for my GED. One for life transformation. Classes, classes, and more classes on top of classes," Sasha sighed. "But I wouldn't have it any other way."

Debra grew silent. Her eyes moved over Sasha, a look that permeated approval and contentment. In front of her stood her beautiful friend, the one who could turn any boy's head with a flip of her hair, or the wink of her eye. The inner and outer beauty she once envied. It radiated now, and dared the sun and stars to step aside.

Debra moved closer to Sasha until both their faces fit into the full-sized mirror before them. "I am so proud of you. You know that, don't you?" Debra said, embracing Sasha.

"I couldn't have done this without you. You know that?"

"Yes, you could have. Don't say that. Let me have this time to tell you how very proud you have made me—all of us at the house. Joan tells me almost every day how much you do here, whether it's scrubbing the kitchen floors or sweeping the porch. How sometimes she doesn't even have to ask, you just do. How you've taken the two new tenants under your wing…"

Sasha's eyes began to mist. "Can we go now?"

"Yeah, yeah. Let's blow this popsicle stand! It's such a nice day. What do you think about walking to the clinic?"

"I think you read my mind."

The house was strangely quiet. Sasha didn't know that most of the tenants and volunteers were at the clinic, waiting for them to celebrate her graduation from the rehab program. Sasha, too, was quiet as they began the few blocks to the graduation ceremony.

"So how do you feel?" Debra asked. She looked casually chic in a pair of khaki capris and a multi-colored top that accented her long straight hair, sun-kissed with auburn highlights.

A red Dodge Charger with dark tinted windows drove past the women. The bass of the car's music bounced the quietness of the block. A few whistles came from the car as it sped away. The women joined hands and laughed in a gesture reminiscent of their school years together long ago. Their girlish laughter resounded in the clinic where the waiting room was packed with women from the house, Sasha's GED class, her therapists, and the clinic's other outpatients she'd grown close to during her many sessions.

"SURPRISE!"

A congratulations banner lined the back of the room, and a white sheet cake was on the table in the center of the room. Stevie Wonder blared from the radio. A few of the nurses had already formed a *Soul Train* line in the center of the waiting room. Debra joined them, breaking out in a classic robot move that got the room roaring with laughter.

Sasha spotted Monice and rushed to hug her. Monice had come to the Winchester Clinic just hours before Sasha. As a result, they were often paired together during group therapy sessions and the like. Theirs was not a fast-forming friendship. The first few days, they each sat in their own stew, popping their gum and rolling their eyes at each other. Until one particular session when Dr. Schreirer, fed up with their mum-mouth routines, threw down his notepad in clear frustration.

"Dammit, I'm trying to help the two of you!" His face had turned beet red. "You are both addicts and you're going to stay addicts for the rest of your lives! That's never going to change! But you've got to let someone in. If not me, someone else who is going to work with you and give you the tools to face these addictions head-on. To be there for you when the cravings hit and you'd both sooner sell your bodies than resist the temptation. You've got to be able to lean on someone! Now for Christ's sake, will one of you tell me why the hell you're so damn mad at the world that you'd rather destroy yourself than grab it by the balls?"

Sasha was the first to loosen her arms an inch or so. "When I was little, I saw my mama shoot my father right between the eyes." That was all she said, and it was enough.

"So what? Least you had parents. I ain't never known mine. Some old man found me in a bag in Union Station when I was a baby, and I was kicked around from foster home to foster home 'til I turned eighteen. So cry me a river, bitch," Monice said. It was then that Sasha noticed how light and airy her voice was. How it didn't match Monice's tough exterior, deep ebony skin, and short afro cut. It was as if Monice had gotten the vocal cords of a twenty-something yoga instructor by mistake.

Dr. Schreirer intervened. "Are you two going to sit here and one-up each other on misery? If that's the case, we'll be here all night and, frankly, I'm doing this pro bono, so I have no intentions on staying over an hour."

"Dr. Schreirer…"

"Yes, Sasha?"

"What's pro bono?"

That did it. The two women looked at each other and laughed themselves silly for the rest of the session, much to the doctor's chagrin. From then on, a relationship marinated between them slowly, but still solid.

"Girl, can you believe we've come this far?" Monice asked, tears already running down her Egyptian-chiseled cheekbones.

"No, girl. Sometimes I have to pinch myself just to remind me that this is all real. When I look back on how far I've come—we've come—it just blows my mind. I was so scared…"

"Huh! You were scared? I was about to pee on myself the first time I walked in the door," Monice said. They laughed and shared another hug.

"You're my hero. You know that, don't you?"

"Me? Why? You back on that stuff?" Sasha chided.

"Stop playin'. I'm being for real. You did somethin' I never was able to do," Monice said, and her smile faded slightly. "You went cold turkey. Not even an aspirin when I know those withdrawal pains must have been tearing you apart. Me? I'll probably be on methadone or suboxone for the rest of my life. You inspire me so much."

"Hey, it doesn't matter how we got here. The point is, we're here and we ain't ever going back, and you know I always will need the nicotine!"

"Amen to that." They toasted with their plastic champagne flutes, filled to the brim with sparkling apple cider.

"Hey, you two. Aren't we all supposed to be celebrating here?" Debra said, jumping between them. "Monice, do you mind if I borrow Sasha for a minute?"

"No, not all. I see a piece of cake that has my name written all over it."

"Save me a piece!" Sasha yelled behind her as Debra prodded her into a private corner.

"I've been waiting to give you this all day," Debra said, handing Sasha a plain white envelope. Sasha turned it over: Missouri Board of Education. *My results! Oh, Lord! What if I didn't pass? I'll just take the refresher courses again. I'll pass next time. But I want to pass this time!*

"Well, go ahead. Open it!" Debra's hands were shaking.

Sasha ripped open the envelope, scraps of white paper flying on the floor, landing beside the glitter and balloons.

"I PASSED! I PASSED!" Sasha jumped up and down like an eager puppy vying for its bone.

"Everybody, I passed the GED exam! I got my GED!"

A thunder of applause shook the walls of the Winchester Clinic.

Sasha reached out and hugged Debra tightly, needing her support to keep from falling to the floor. Was this all a dream? Both women were crying as they pulled apart from each other.

"I can't tell you again how proud I am of you, Sasha."

"And I can't keep telling you had it not been for you…"

"And?"

"And the grace of God, none of this would be happening right now. I didn't believe in angels until God sent me you, Deb. I truly mean that."

Sasha didn't tell Debra that there were many times during her heavy withdrawals that she had envisioned her as just that, with an iridescent halo, a flowing white gown, and wings to match. Other times she was the devil, dressed in a red cat suit with a tail as a pitchfork. Those times she had shivered even though the volunteers had put a blanket, coverlet, and comforter on her while she lay on her twin bed, bathed in sweat. Snippets came back to Sasha of being fed ice chips, only to vomit them up into the trash pail she kept beside the bed at all times. Dry heaving until she could take no more. The minutes she cried. The seconds she prayed. The hours she cursed at Debra. Through it all, Debra had never left her side. She took the good with the bad and she clung to Sasha as if it were her own life at stake.

"Come on, Sasha. You can do it. Just one more day."

"No, I can't. I can't do this anymore. I need something. Give me something."

"I can't do that, Sasha."

"Fuck you then, bitch! I don't need you. I don't need this shit. I don't need these damn people. Fuck all ya'll. What ya'll know about me? I need a hit! Damn you!"

At Sasha's first of many outbursts, Debra, ever the calm one, said flatly, "I will not be talked to like that. You will treat me with respect. I'm here to help you, Sasha, not be badmouthed, and I will not let you talk bad about the other women in this house either. Are we clear?"

"I'm sorry. Please don't leave me! Don't leave me!" Sasha would break down then, as she did for several days.

One morning the fog lifted and Sasha turned over in her twin bed feeling hungry. Debra was there. Laying on the twin bed next to her in the cramped room, fully dressed in a short cedar-colored skirt and loose-fitting blouse with flowers outlined in gold. Her pumps still on her feet. Her hair fanning the pillow.

"Deb... Deb, wake up," Sasha said from her bed. Her head in her still hands.

Then louder, "Deb!"

"Huh? What is it? Oh, God! How long was I asleep?!" Debra jumped as if bitten by a million bedbugs at once.

Sasha giggled. "Calm down. I was just saying good morning."

Debra's soft brown eyes grew wide. "Good morning. How do you feel?"

"Like I'm climbing out of hell. I can't remember everything I've been through, but I think the worst part is behind me now."

Debra smiled then.

"Can I ask you something?"

"Sure, anything." Debra stretched and yawned.

"Why did you stick around for this long? What's it been..?"

"Eleven days."

"Eleven days. Have you been home at all? Is your family mad?"

"Well, I haven't been by your side every minute of the day. I left to shower, change, pray with my family, went to work some days, and was back in time for the night shift."

"You did all that for me? Why?" Sasha asked, clearly dumbfounded.

"Because I love you," Debra stated matter-of-factly, an *isn't it obvious* tone in her voice.

"You love me. Why?"

"Because God loves you, and you and I are a manifestation of God's love."

Sasha furrowed her brows, not quite understanding.

"God is love and we are his children. I love you as a child of God. I love you as my friend."

"You do?" It was childish question, really.

Debra sat down next to Sasha, wrapping herself around her, the broken butterfly finally free from its cocoon. "Yes, I do love you."

With that, Sasha sat up and allowed herself to be held in her friend's warmth. To be loved amid the tears.

Now, teary-eyed again, Sasha wondered what she had done to deserve a room full of people celebrating her and her accomplishments, with no drugs or alcohol in sight. Still laughing. Still having a good time.

"What's on your mind?" Debra asked.

"Debra, you've done so much for me and I hate to ask you for one more thing, but I need a favor."

"Anything, you name it."

"Can you take me to see my mother?"

RANFORD

A sliver of blue cloth caught RJ's attention as he stepped outside of Regina's house. For a second he thought it was a balloon that had burst and come to rest on his lover's doorstep. But when he leaned over he was surprised to find himself touching a baby bootie, a navy sailboat imprinted on its side. The discovery rendered him motionless for a few counts. He scratched his head.

"Naw, couldn't be," he said aloud. Then he whistled to his car, still parked boldly in Regina's driveway in the early evening, mocking the neighbors, daring them to glance sideways or breathe a word. For some unknown reason, RJ threw the blue sock into the car as he climbed inside, turning his Sirius radio to sports talk. Two smoky-voiced commentators debated their respective March Madness brackets. He'd have to call Alfred when he got home to remind him to pick up their Big Twelve tickets at the Sprint Arena. He loved this time of year. It reminded him of his famed high school and college days. The days when he could run track and play basketball for hours without being painfully punished by his body the next day. The sin of growing older.

RJ's thoughts turned to Regina as his hand tapped the garage remote. He smiled. She seemed to have had a special need to please him earlier. He remembered her smiling up at him, before bending to her knees and sucking him to something close to heaven. She had screamed louder, which had intensified RJ's desire, and he was thinking that if she kept performing in that manner, he just might return after all. That was the last though he had before opening the door and walking into total darkness: Regina.

"Honor!" he cried into the pitch-blackness. No answer. The familiar scents of roast beef and potatoes, or of lamb chops and grilled onions, did not fill the house as usual.

"Honor! You here?" *Of course, she's here. Where else would she be?*

RJ called a third time, his voice coming down like a hammer. "Honor!" Still nothing.

An unnerving sensation flooded RJ as he flicked on the light closest to the steps that led to the bedrooms. Upstairs, too, was dark. He thought about going into the bedroom and grabbing his gun before diving further into the darkness. He neared the highest step and saw a beam of light showing from underneath the guest bathroom. It called him closer. RJ's stomach battled for position in his throat as he pushed open the door. What he saw at that instant made him fall to his knees.

Honor sat on the floor near the edge of the garden tub, her arms wrapped around her legs. Her hands pressed together in a twisted prayer-like pose. She was singing a song softly to herself, a song RJ didn't recognize.

"I won't be afraid.

"I will declare your glory.

"I'll say yes. My soul says yes."

A record player without a nickel taped to its needle, Honor's voice sounded scratched, repeating the same words over and over again.

"Oh, God! Honor! Honor! What have you done?"

RJ stepped over his wife. He needed a closer look to make sure that what he saw was real. His son's motionless body, floating atop his small baby bath in a cold lake of talcum scents, just waiting. Day's hazel eyes were wide open, his cheeks unusually puffy. "Day," he said, his voice almost a whisper.

"Day, Daddy's home." *Shhhhh. Daddy's home.*

In one swift motion, RJ pulled Day's tiny naked body from the water, slippery from the soap that permeated his nostrils with the smell of flowers. Baby smells. *Don't do this! Please, don't do this!*

"Day!" RJ screamed. His large hands were at the small of his son's back, and he willed his fingers to coat his son's body with warmth. He was so cold, and the coldness heated RJ's chest, something deeper than heartburn. RJ shook Day gently. He pinched his small nose and breathed into his mouth. *One. Two. Three. Four. Five. Should I press on his chest?* RJ breathed into Day's mouth again. The force of his breath left him gasping for his own air. Day remained a doll in his hands. His chest did not move. His eyes refused to blink.

"No...no...no...NO!" RJ cradled the boy's head in his hands and held him closer to his chest as he paced the hallways upstairs and sprinted down the stairs. He ran outdoors and the sky began to cry with him: softly at first, then harder. He walked in circles around his home, then dropped once again to his knees in the middle of the street.

"Somebody help me, please!"

Upstairs, Honor sang on. "I'll say yes. My soul says yes."

They placed a white sheet of surrender over Day's head and sent him on to heaven. The place where babies fly around together and come back to the other life as angels. RJ had to turn away when the paramedics placed his son onto a gurney too large for his body and closed the doors behind them. RJ's soul went with them, and in his mind he was running as fast as he could, with all his might, behind the ambulance to bring Day back home. Had the overbearing police officer let go of his arm, RJ would have chased the ambulance as it drove into the distance. He would have chased it to get his soul back and bring it home.

The neighborhood eyes that he had always mocked before were all over him now, staring through their windows or standing on the street watching RJ unfold. They looked at him, many never even knowing that there had been a son who once lived at 3256 Chesterfield Lane. In that sea of eyes, RJ found one all-too-familiar face as Regina pushed through the crowd, her husband's twelve-pack belly not far behind. With his eyes, RJ dared Regina to move one more inch toward him. While the neighbors were being intrusive, her presence was invasive—she had crossed the line.

"Mr. Ellis. I'm Officer Collins. I'm sorry for the loss of your son, such an unfortunate accident." Accusation was behind every syllable of the word *accident*, as the wall of an officer spoke. He imagined the officer's meaty fingers were already typing up a report, slamming heavy on the "a" and hard on the "t."

"Do you mind telling me what time you got home today?"

"What?"

"The time, sir. When did you arrive home?"

"I...I'm not sure...ummm...the usual time. A quarter to six, I guess."

The sirens on the ambulance stopped flashing, as if the lights required too much energy to transport a baby no longer of this world. Slowly, it veered forward.

"Where are they taking my son?"

"To the mor— I'm sure the coroner will want to do a thorough autopsy."

"Autopsy? You mean they're going to cut Day open? What kind of sense does that make? He's just a baby...a...baby."

"Well, Mr.… Mr. uh… Ellis. Given the nature of the scene, an autopsy would be our best possible measure to get to the bottom of what exactly happened."

RJ looked up from where he still sat on the curb, not able to trust that his legs would hold him up. "Don't let them cut open my son."

"Getting back to today's event. You said you arrived home about five forty-five. You sure about that time? You didn't make any stops after work?"

"No."

"Notice anything unusual when you came home? Anything out of the ordinary?" The wall was no longer looking down at RJ, his attention focused solely on the pen and notepad in his hand. His scribble reminded RJ of a bad true-crime movie he had seen a few months back. A low-budget flick that starred the stereotypical clueless father, a savior of a police officer, and the ever-popular chase-through-house-even-though-the-front-door-is-wide-open ending. *Why was I watching that stupid movie anyway? Oh, yeah, couldn't sleep.*

RJ murmured. "The lights."

"I'm sorry?"

"The lights. Everything was so dark."

"So all the lights inside of your home had not been turned on, or were turned off. Is that correct?"

"Yes."

"Anything else?"

"My dinner was not on the table." This last statement made him feeble and he put his head back down his hands. His body shook with a fresh batch of sobs.

"Trust me. I understand this is hard for you Mr. … uh… Ellis. But the more you can tell me, and the faster, the sooner I can move on here."

Move on?

"So, you come home. The lights are out and there's no dinner. Do you typically have dinner as soon as you get home?"

"Yes, I do."

"And, your wife… Mrs. Ellis. She cooks dinner for you?"

No, a dinner fairy comes and sprinkles it on the table. Presto. "Yeah, man. She makes my dinner every night."

"Lucky man. Some of us don't have it so good, know what I mean?"

RJ put his head back down.

"Um, let's see. Your wife, she seem okay to you lately?"

The question lit up the old jukebox of RJ's mind. Michael Jackson started singing.

Living crazy, that's the only way.

"Now, son, can you tell me what you witnessed when you walked inside the apartment?"

"Approximately what time did you get home?"

"Was your sister with you?"

"Was your mother or father upset?"

So tonight gotta leave that nine to five up on the shelf.

"Did you see your mother shoot your father?"

And just enjoy yourselves. Life ain't so bad at all.

RJ blinked. That one blink made Honor's straight ponytail appear as a mass of bloodstained curls. It was not Honor's short fingernails, bitten down to the quick, that were in handcuffs; instead they were long, bright red nails behind her back. The past and the present divided into a two-faced mask. *Mommy!*

He was that little boy again, back in Wayne Miner, watching his mother being driven away in the back of a squad car. No goodbyes. Nothing but flashing sirens and the words "Police Department," big and bold, and, above it in smaller letters, "Kansas City." Holding tight to his sister's hand.

No goodbyes. The police car becoming smaller and fainter while RJ sat on the curb in his wet clothes, looking on in disbelief.

SASHA

Debra and Sasha drove four hours to Ohio, listening to gospel music the entire way. Debra said gospel music helped her survive some rough times in life and that the songs kept her sane when she was going "through." Sasha wondered if it was the same way now, as Debra grew silent during some songs and belted out others, her beautiful falsetto daring the birds to take notice. What Debra thought during those quiet parts, Sasha couldn't say for sure. What she did know was that Debra's father still sipped his food from a straw and his recovery progress was at a standstill. *All of this opening your heart crap, is it really worth the pain?* Even though Sasha had taken her heart off the hanger, most days it lay there at the bottom of the closet, buried under layers of wash-n-wear skeletons.

When they were not listening quietly to the gospel or playing I Spy, the women were preparing for Sasha's upcoming interview at World Boutique, an upscale consignment shop in the Brookside area. Sasha hoped to be a shop clerk at the boutique, organizing items as they came into the store, tagging them, and working on displays.

If she interviewed well and accepted the position, it would be a while before Sasha would be allowed to handle money or run the boutique alone: that part was made quite clear. The owner, Eleanor Caswell, a fierce and feisty seventy-year-old, was a generous benefactor of the House of Hope, and she had taken many of the residents under her wing. Only Ms. Jones and Eleanor knew that her devotion to the house and its residents was more than a passing whim or a charity write-off. Eleanor was one of the first women to ever lay her head on one of the home's beds.

Sasha had met Eleanor at one of House of Hope's charity fundraisers. Sasha was in charge of making sure that the guests' cups of water and sweet tea stayed full for the duration of the sit-down dinner. During the final course of the night, as Sasha served the chocolate cake layered in mousse and raspberries, Eleanor dropped her spoon.

"Young lady, can you run and get me another spoon?" Eleanor asked, the offending spoon pinched between two fingers as though she were holding a dead rat.

"You dropped it. Get a new one yourself or, better yet, just spit on it and wipe it off with your napkin." It was late. Sasha was tired of serving rich white folks.

Ms. Jones's face puckered as if she had just swallowed a mountain of lemons. She clasped both her hands to her chest in exasperation. "Sasha, apologize to Mrs. Caswell!"

Eleanor reached for Ms. Jones' hands. "No, let her be. I like this girl. She got *chutzpa*. Send her to the shop next week."

"Sasha, you really should apologize to Ms. Caswell. For heaven's sake, she just offered you a chance to come interview to work at her boutique," Ms. Jones said. She seemed to not know what to do with her hands. She clutched a white linen napkin as if it would grow legs and run off at any second.

"All right," Sasha said, unsure of what had just transpired between the three of them, but knowing it something major.

Eleanor stared Sasha directly in her eyes. "Apology accepted." She held her wrinkled hand out for Sasha to shake. Sasha took it willingly, although she never really apologized. Eleanor smiled at Sasha.

In the car, Debra was teaching her how to talk properly, or "white" as Sasha called it.

"Don't say 'ain't,'" Debra said at the start of their trip, as the car veered onto the Interstate 70 onramp.

"Watch your double negatives," she said as they passed by a semi-truck.

"Double what?"

"You know, like 'not never.'"

Sasha nodded, trying to commit the reminder to memory.

"Stay away from slang altogether," she said while pumping gas somewhere in the cornfields of Kansas.

A traveling etiquette class with a Lexus emblem. Sasha was taking notes. Not because she was unsure of how to conduct herself anymore, but to ward off all thoughts of where they were headed. Each mile marker mocked her decision. FOOD HERE signs and billboards became taunts.

"I don't even remember what my mother looks like," Sasha said, somewhere between Town and Next Town. "I try to picture her, but I lost that picture in my mind a long time ago."

"So today you'll create a new picture."

"It's not that easy. I don't remember that day. I don't remember the day my mother killed my daddy. Who doesn't remember that? She smelled like green apples, but everything else about her in my head? It's like a body with no face. She's invisible."

"So you'll take a new picture. You'll make the mental picture you want to remember. Look at it as a chance to create a new canvas," Debra turned off the gospel.

They were in front of the prison. *Heaven help me.*

There were no more mile markers, just barbed wire and fences as far as the eye could see. A giant fortress of bricks, a hamster cage holding all of society's animals.

A burly uniformed guard stopped them at the entrance to the cage, looking down at them from his spinning wheel. "Name?" he shouted.

Debra answered, "Debra Baxter and Sasha Ellis."

"For?"

"Carmen Ellis."

This got somewhat of a reaction from the guard. He lifted his head and glanced at them a few seconds longer than his normal gaze, eyebrows raised.

"Carmen, huh?" He looked back down at his clipboard. "IDs," he said, a little less than a shout this time.

While Debra fumbled for her wallet inside her designer purse, Sasha proudly handed the guard her new Missouri identification card, courtesy of Ms. Jones and a trip downtown to the Missouri Department of Motor Vehicles. Sasha's face smiled back at her, solid evidence that she existed.

"Ok, pull on up and follow the signs to the visitor's entrance."

A craving, a yearning stronger than she had ever experienced, knocked the wind from Sasha's chest. She knew that right now she'd jam her palm into a piece of barbed wire if it would guarantee her a hit. Still, the car moved deeper into the cage's maze, closer to that new picture of her mom.

A few more identification checks and buzzing doors later, and Sasha found herself smack in the center of the visitor's holding area. The room was made to look homey with two paisley couches and matching throw pillows, round cafeteria tables and chairs within inches of each other. Still, there was a drabness in the air and a mild mildew smell, as if the walls had soaked up every tear ever cried here.

Two guards who looked like henchmen were positioned at opposite corners of the room. It was early in the two-hour visiting period, and the room was barely half full. In one corner, a pale-skinned woman who looked to be about the same age as Sasha sat at a table with two pigtailed twins with blue eyes as big and round as the moon. She held on to them so tightly that it seemed those big eyes would pop out from the squeeze. On the other side, a younger brown-skinned woman, one who looked too young to be sitting in the visiting room of a women's prison, sat with a lighter complexioned young man with a gold-teethed half smile. He whispered in her ear and the girl laughed. When his hand went to touch her breast, the guard tapped him on the shoulder and shook his head, never noticing that his other hand was already doing things to the woman underneath the table that made both her legs quiver. Then there was a stoic short-haired woman, skin like onyx, that sat by herself, turning to look at the clock every other minute.

Sasha grabbed a chair in the center of the room and waited. For a minute, she thought about sparking up a conversation with the short-haired woman. What's the right way to ask a stranger, *"Are you my mother?"*

Another buzzer, and Sasha stiffened as she watched a woman saunter in, her hands planted firmly on her hips. A woman whose ageless beauty could not be contained or constricted in a form-fitting, powder-blue jumpsuit. Long curly hair, tied high atop her head by a single ribbon, and hazel colored eyes with flecks of gold in them. For the second time in less than fifteen minutes, Sasha had the wind knocked out of her. She had her new snapshot now, one she would never forget.

The question mark that had been trailing Sasha on the drive fell to the floor as the woman sat directly in front of Sasha and gently cupped her face in her hands. Her eyes turned misty, making the flecks of gold a deeper yellow.

For a while, neither woman spoke. Then Carmen exhaled and said to Sasha, "Look what God created." She touched Sasha's hair slowly, almost as if she were counting every single strand.

"God?" The high Sasha experienced when she wrapped her arms around her mother, for the first time she could remember, was unlike anything she'd found at the bottom of an empty bottle or the end of a glass pipe. This was real—lasting. There was no coming down from this feeling. All at once, Sasha knew she'd found the piece of her that she had been missing her entire life. Her missing link. They snapped together, arms intertwined. Sasha could not hold back her sobs. Her tears leaked as her heart opened.

A few minutes passed before either could break free from the other.

Carmen arched her back, raised her head and wiped her eyes. "Well, now. Let me get a look at you." The gold in her cat-like eyes melted. "So how long you been clean?"

"How did you…?"

"Honey, I've been in this place long enough to know a dope fiend, an ex-dope fiend, a soon-to-be dope fiend, and a wanna-be dope fiend. Hell, I was one myself." Carmen snickered and grabbed a packet of menthols from the side pocket of her jumpsuit, before handing the pack to Sasha.

Sasha put the cigarette to her mouth, lit it with the small lighter Carmen extended to her, and inhaled deeply. "Today marks my fifty-third day."

"Good job. Good job." She repeated the words as if Sasha were two and had just learned to use her potty seat for the first time.

"NA meetings?"

"Every Tuesday and Thursday night."

Silence followed, but it was not uncomfortable. Instead, it was a like a pause between breaths. Natural.

The visiting room was growing heavy and louder as more people came, always in a single file line, makeshift smiles on their faces. Pain and pleasure at the same time. Sasha watched the young lovers grow closer, looks of equal intensity in their eyes. Sasha wondered if the diamond-pierced young man was the reason the girl was living behind brick walls? *Isn't that always the case?*

Their breathing still in sync, Carmen said softly. "I wish I could have been there to spare you from all of that. A young girl needs her mother. I should have been there for you. Life would have turned out differently for both of us, you know, if I had just… just… Well, no sense in beating a dead horse."

"You never beat the horse with me."

"How many times can I apologize? I'm sorry, all right? I'm so damn sorry. I spend every waking day thinking about what I could have done differently, wishing that it never happened. But that's impossible. You don't get to go back and change time. The sad part is that it replays in my mind every day, like a movie stuck on the same reel. Oh, baby, I wish so much that we could go back to the no longer."

"The what?"

"Nothing. Just something I wrote once in a letter to RJ. Did you get the ones I wrote to you?"

"I never got no letters," Sasha said. Her recent etiquette and "proper talking" drive-by lessons flew out the window. Her eyes focused somewhere on an imaginary spot of happiness on the far concrete wall.

"Well, I sent them to Reverend Odom. Didn't he give them to you and RJ? I admit, it took me years before I could even face myself in the mirror long enough to write to you kids and… Well, I just had to work up my nerve."

"Please don't say the *good* reverend's name around me."

"Why, did he…?"

"So, did you fuck him?" Sasha lit another cigarette.

Carmen leaned away from Sasha as if to shield herself from the accusation thrown before her. Then she laughed and said, "Me and the reverend? Where would you get an idea like that?"

"He told me he had a thing for you."

Carmen straightened, her back at full attention. "I knew. I always knew. In a way, I toyed with that man. He might have been a man of God, but he was still a man, and all men's brains end at their buckle. I'd say a certain word and he'd blush. Never seen a black man turn three shades of red before. In my mind, it was fun and games."

"Reverend Odom wasn't playing though." Sasha exhaled slowly then stubbed her cigarette butt in the ashtray. She watched the last white puff of smoke escape into the air, and longed for something stronger.

"Anyway, I know you didn't come all this way to talk about old Reverend Odom. Tell me, you gotta man?"

"I did."

"What happened. Did he treat you right?"

"No. He beat me." There was a newfound clarity in Sasha's voice as she said this, leaving no room for a mistake to enter between the two of them.

"Damn. Here I am counseling these tricks in here about abuse, and I couldn't even help my own daughter. Hell, for that matter, I couldn't even help myself. But you can't go back now, can you?"

Sasha didn't answer. She looked at the windows covered in gray bars and wires, knowing fully well that there was no question here. No answers. And then she did something that surprised even her. "Mommy."

Sasha rested her head against Carmen's breast and sobbed. "Mommy. Mommy. Mommy."

Carmen rocked her slowly, caressed her back, and soothed her in the international way of all mothers, "Shhh."

"Everything will be okay."

"I'm here now."

Sasha held her mother tighter, submerged her nose into Carmen's mixture of musk and strongly-scented soap. She cried for that lost caterpillar of her childhood. She cried from the weight of it all. And with each tear she felt the heaviness lift, rise above the cage, and free itself. They stayed like that until the guard tapped Carmen on the shoulder, lightly at first, then harder. He murmured in a dry voice. "Visiting hours are up you two."

Carmen pushed Sasha away and gripped her daughter's shoulders tighter at the same time. "Now, you listen to me. I know it's too late to try and dish out advice to you now. But I tell my girls in my group meetings all the time: you gotta take back your life. Life is a gift that you not only deserve, but have the right to open every damn day, 'cause in reality, life don't owe you shit. Get the gift and don't let nobody, no man, take it from you. You hear me?"

All Sasha could do was nod. Then she smiled. "Are you sure you should be the one telling them that?" she asked. Carmen's eyes glistened.

"Here." In one swift motion, Carmen untied the yellow ribbon from her hair and handed it to Sasha. "It's yours, baby. I've had it since the day you came to visit me when you were a little girl. I know you probably don't remember. But I kept it for all these years. It's special to me, but I want you to have it now. Keep it and know that all for all those years you thought no one loved or cared for you, I did. And I always, always will."

"Thank you," Sasha whispered, stroking the still-silky material.

"All right, you two. Let's go." Dry Voice returned after making his rounds around the room.

Sasha watched as the couple finally pulled apart from each other. Then she noticed the television hanging in the corner above their heads. The local newscast was on, muted. Her mouth dropped open as a female news anchor stood right in front of her brother's house. Just like that, someone ran off with Sasha's gift again.

HONOR

Honor's family owned a second home on Captiva Island. They vacationed there every summer: one of three black families to actually own property on the island instead of just working at the resorts. It was a three-bedroom beach house that sat high atop matching white stilts. The waves lapped almost directly beneath the house's small front porch. There was no air conditioning, just a few ceiling fans with custom-made bamboo blades and shaded windows that tried to block the sun's rays during the day. At night, the ocean breeze crept inside to tickle her body while Honor lay awake listening to the seashore and the seagulls.

The house remained in the family for many years. Then one day, a hurricane ripped the island into pieces in seconds, carrying the house away in its fury of wind and rain. All its memories were gone: Shelling for hours on end with her sister. Swimming out into the depths of the gulf until her mother would scream out at the top of her lungs, *"Honor, you get back here this instant!"* Bon fires with freshly caught lobsters. Losing her virginity to Walter Hensley underneath the pier, the moon their only witness.

They never returned to the island after the storm.

But Honor was there now. She could hear the seagulls flying overhead and smell the ocean's waves. If she moved her feet just so, she could feel the seaweed tickling her toes. That is what she saw. What she felt. What she heard.

"Mrs. Ellis. Mrs. Ellis! I'm going to need some cooperation from you. Come on now, we've been at this for almost two hours. I know you've got to be hungry...at least thirsty. Just tell me what happened. Say one word, for Christ's sake, and you can have whatever you want. What happened to Day, Mrs. Ellis? DID YOU DROWN YOUR BABY?"

Seagulls. The sound of the waves grew louder. Honor dipped her hand into the water and smiled at the coolness of it all.

"Sam. Sam! Enough already! Can't you see this one's completely gone? Put her back in the holding cell until psych can get here in the morning," Good Cop said. He watched Honor draw circles on the tabletop with her fingertips, an unnerving smile plastered on her face.

He pushed Bad Cop away from the woman, unsure if it made a difference what they said in her presence right now.

"Nah, man, I ain't buying it. It's all an act. I done seen it too many times before. Can't handle becoming a mother so they play crazy, blame it on some post-partum depression bullshit. Not this time," Bad Cop said, incensed.

"Hey, man, I don't think this chick is faking it. I mean, look at her. Her head's spinnin' faster than a merry-go-round, and she's the only one ridin'."

"I still don't buy it."

"All I'm saying is, send her up to psych for a consult. Besides, you know who her husband is don't you? The father of the dead baby?"

"Naw, who is it?"

"The hotshot principal over at Urban Achievers. The one who's always in the paper?"

"No shit!"

"Yeah, so you know the media's gonna be all over this like flies to shit. We gotta be on top of our P's and Q's on this one. Hell, my neighbor's kid goes to that school. She was a straight flunky before she got to that school: drugs, screwing around, running away. Once she started there... Man, I swear it was like she changed almost overnight. They talk about that principal like he practically walks on water. I ain't sinkin' with this damn ship."

Bad Cop stared at Honor, a few feet away from where they stood in the corner. She was still drawing circles along the tabletop. *Damn!*

"Okay, maybe you're right. Let's have her evaluated. See what psych has to say about her. Meanwhile, we keep investigating and wait for the autopsy results."

Good Cop nodded. He, too, was staring down at Honor and noticed how truly oblivious she seemed to anything that was going on around her. She had stopped drawing imaginary circles with her fingers and was now staring down at her toes, wiggling them slowly and smiling. He was glad that his partner had come around because, either way, he knew they were about to dethrone Kansas City's very own Saint Principal. The water was getting higher and hotter by the second. If the principal didn't walk on water before, now would be the time to learn.

RANFORD

I wish all these people would get the fuck out of my house. RJ gripped his glass of scotch tight and willed it to bust wide open in his bare hand. He could crush the glass at any second, and watch the amber-colored liquor mix with his blood as it hit the floor. Maybe then, everybody would leave him be.

Oh, you poor man. You really shouldn't be alone at a time like this.

Anything you need, just let us know.

If there is anything we can do for you, please don't hesitate to call.

Such a travesty, everything that has happened.

And RJ's personal favorite: *I remember when my so-and-so passed away. I know what you're going through.*

How could anyone share in his living hell? How could they even begin to imagine a burial service with the tiniest of coffins? How could they understand having to wait by the phone for the coroner's report, to confirm what RJ had already seen with his own eyes? At night, could they pull him out from underneath his recurring nightmare? The one in which he woke up nearly suffocating from being smothered in dirt, his hands sore from trying to break free from the coffin? And what about this waking nightmare?

RJ sat down and closed his eyes, wanting everyone in his house out by the time he opened them on the count of three. It didn't work. When he opened his eyes, the mourners were still milling around, bearing food and wearing black. Such a dismal color.

"How you holding it together, big bro?" Sasha asked. She was standing above him in the ill-used, all-ivory living room.

"What? Oh, I'm holding it together."

Sasha reached down and rubbed his shoulder. Her touch was comforting. RJ stared at the transformation before him. How had she done it? Was it real? Is she for keeps? Even in his grief, RJ could see that Sasha was glowing. Her once acne-prone and scarred skin was damn near perfect. Her makeup was solid and her hair was on point. RJ had forgotten how pretty Sasha was. The drugs had made her ugly, inside and out. But now, the oyster had revealed a shiny pearl. She had put on a few pounds, in a good way, and now there was meat where there used to be nothing but skin and bones. Even her teeth were perfectly straight and white. RJ hadn't had time to ask her about what all had taken place to make her go straight. He just knew he was grateful, and shocked to find a day when he would need her more than she needed him. The table hadn't just turned. It had flipped over.

Had RJ had any semblance of faith, he would have considered it a blessing. But God was in short supply around these parts, so RJ just chalked it up to being something amazing that had taken place in his sister.

"What are you looking at?" Sasha asked. RJ saw that innocent little girl again. The one he once held in his arms and carried to Edwin's house.

"Um, nothing. I just can't get over how good you look."

"Well, thank you, big bro. I think I'm looking good these days too, if I do say so myself. And I just did. I'm learning to take it one day at a time. Every morning when I step out of bed, I give thanks to the one above. I pray that I will not do anything to set me back, and then I step out on faith. You should try it sometime, big bro."

"I'll pass."

"I hear you and I can't say I blame you with all this shit going on. I know it was hard for you to see Mom earlier. Just promise me you won't do nothing stupid, and you'll take it a day at a time?"

"When did you get so smart?" RJ asked.

"Hey, you weren't the only one born with brains in the family. You already know I got all the looks," Sasha laughed. To RJ, the sound was like rediscovering his favorite song on one of the dusty albums he stored in the attic. Familiar. Beloved.

RJ drained the last of his scotch and parted the curtains in front of him. The blast of sunlight accosted his eyes. Camera crews and reporters were still camped out on his front lawn. At least they'd had the decency to stay away from the funeral. Well, a few of the bastards were there. RJ saw them in the distance as he was being driven away in the limousine. What did they want from him, really? RJ would be damned if anyone was going to showcase his despair on a twenty-second sound bite. Twenty seconds was more than enough time for perfect strangers to cast judgment, to offer their opinions and false sympathies. RJ wasn't going out like a punk. He'd held his head high throughout this ordeal, never missing a day of work. He would remain the hero in his students' eyes, no matter what those sound bites said about him and his family.

Honor.

RJ could barely look at his wife during the funeral. It was the first time he had laid eyes on her since the drowning. Just knowing Honor was close sent his emotions swirling faster than mixing batter. Hate. Love. Betrayal. Lust. Longing. Loss. Emotions so strong that he wanted someone to come along and beat them out of him. Everything was so surreal and yet, there she was, just standing there. Hadn't he given her everything? Hadn't he been the best husband and father that a woman could ask for? Yes, there were other women, but none of them came close to knocking Honor off her pedestal. Not one. "Snapped." That was the term being tossed around like a twig when it came to Honor. It didn't make any sense to RJ.

RJ's emotions switched to automatic at the sight of his mother. What the hell was she doing there? What gave her the right to be anywhere near the proximity of his grief? He had not seen his mother in decades, yet there were no wrinkles or gray hair to reveal the passage of time. The same bouncy curls and saucy attitude that dripped with every step she made, even in the presence of the guards around her. She came close to her son and reached to touch him; RJ backed away as if prison were contagious.

"Hello, son. Please don't be mad at me for coming out today. I wanted so much to be here with you and Sasha. Hard to believe they allowed me to come, but they did. Just look at you: so handsome, so accomplished. I am proud of you, son. Your wife, she's beautiful. Go to her. She needs you now, more than ever. Sasha came to see me last week. I'm proud of her, too. Looking at you two well, it makes me realize that my life was not all in vain. I know what's done can't …"

RJ had heard enough, even though he'd barely listened to a word Carmen had spoken. "Whatever the hell you think you know…keep it to yourself. You have a lot of nerve, showing up here. Today, of all days! Get out of my face."

"Son, I can understand your anger."

RJ looked at her then, shook his head back and forth and slammed his eyelids shut.

"Well, just know I love you and that will never change."

How is it possible that both my mother and my wife would end up being jailbirds? It was a sick, twisted family reunion. The thought alone made RJ laugh sadly at himself as he looked back on the day's events.

"What's funny?" Sasha asked. RJ had forgotten his sister was standing in front of him.

"Nothing," he answered solemnly.

Sasha grabbed the glass from his hand. "Okay. It looks like someone has enough of the juice. I'm going to get you some tea instead. Hang on."

How long until this shindig is over?

Slowly, RJ left his post on the couch and walked through his house, looking around as if it were someone else's. In the kitchen, the counters were piled high with comfort food: fried chicken, catfish, spaghetti, ham, macaroni and cheese, greens, cornbread, buttered rolls, mashed potatoes, baked potatoes, strawberry pound cake, cheesecake, apple pie and various other desserts.

The smell of the mourners' buffet smothered the house and made it hard for RJ to breathe. He didn't know how many days it'd been since he'd eaten. What RJ did know was that he desperately needed another scotch.

RJ headed for the bar, but stopped when he noticed the Thompson camp outside on the deck beyond the piles of food. Vernon sat stiffly at the round patio table, his burly shoulders slumped and his hands glued to a glass of his own amber liquid. Olivia stood against the iron railing and stared into the trees, as if looking for answers, clues as to why she would standing there, this very moment her slender frame dressed in all black.

He didn't see Honor's sister. No doubt she was already on a plane headed back East to civility. RJ would be willing to bet that the two eldest of the family did not plan on staying awhile in Kansas City either. He guessed they'd be on the first plane out in the morning.

Neither one of them spoke to the other, looked at the other. Nor had they acknowledged RJ at the funeral or gone to Honor. RJ knew the deal: their daughter had tarnished their pristine image, stained it beyond recognition, and no amount of money would wipe it clean this time. News traveled fast in the South, even from the Midwest. They'd gladly leave their daughter and *her* mess behind them for the sake of their precious name.

RJ stared at them, finding it ironic the way he used to idolize Honor's parents and envy her for actually having a mother and father. Now he saw them for who they really were, two people who sat alone at an endless masquerade ball, permanent masks attached to their faces.

RJ's parents may have been out of the picture, but maybe that was better than having two people around who forced you to draw inside the lines your whole life because the final image was more important than the person who held the crayon and took the time to create it.

There was no place to hang drawings with marks outside the lines in a house of perfection.

Olivia turned, saw RJ watching them, and then, just as abruptly, turned her back to him. Damn if he'd let the old bag disrespect him in own house. He headed over to them.

A soft hand on his shoulder made RJ lose sight of his intentions. "RJ, I'm so sorry for your loss. I don't know what to say. I... I baked you a cake. A woman up front told me to take it back here with the others. It's a marble cake. Don't even know if you like marble. I wish there was..."

"Don't say another word." RJ flipped the cake and its glass container on the counter like a frisbee. He grabbed Regina's hand and led her behind the staircase into his office. He glanced outside the double doors to see if anyone was watching, then locked the door behind them.

"RJ, what are you—" RJ's lips were all over her voluptuous body before she could get another word out. Her mouth. Her face. Her hair. Her nipples that called to him from beneath the fabric of her black wrap-around dress. Her calves. Her thighs. Her toes. The v-shaped crevice between her legs. His search for more and more skin was relentless. RJ was hungry.

RJ threw Regina against the edge of his desk before she could reach out to touch him. He pushed her dress up above her ample waist, watched her backside wiggle a little in anticipation as he unzipped his pants. He pushed her matching black thong to the side and plunged in. Deep, wanting to swim, to lose himself, in the abyss of her wetness. Never mind that she was mostly dry, there was moisture to be found, and in the deep there was escape. RJ continued his search inside of her, banging her relentlessly against the desk, grabbing her now-exposed breasts as they hung over his basketball paperweight.

Regina began to moan. Loudly. He grabbed the lace belt that had held her dress together only moments before and stuffed it into her mouth, gagging her. He pulled at her hair roughly, until her neck snapped back and he could taste her mouth with his again. He grabbed her waist tighter and thrust harder until beads of perspiration spread across his lean body. It was all RJ could do not to cry out when he erupted inside of her, like an outdoor fountain set free after a long winter.

They remained like that, bent over the desk, until their labored breathing slowed to a quiet panting. Then RJ simply released himself, stood up and zipped his pants, and walked toward the door. His search was over.

"Get dressed and get the hell out of my house." *Bam!*

He headed for the bathroom and tried to find a sliver of sanity in his solitude. The knock on the door interrupted his attempts. *Can't I get some privacy in my own house?*

"RJ. It's me, Edwin."

"Uh, Edwin. How's it going, man? I'm sorry we haven't had a chance to talk since you've been here. It's just, well, it's kind of crazy around here lately, as you can see."

In all actuality, RJ had been avoiding Edwin. His presence, just being here with his wife and daughter, seemed like an extra helping of pain on misery's dish. The man who was like a brother to RJ had become a constant reminder of everything he'd lost, maybe things he'd never actually had in the first place.

Slowly, RJ walked out of the bathroom and faced Edwin.

"RJ. It's me, man. We family. You ain't had two seconds to spare some change with me ever since I got into town."

RJ stood eye-to-eye with Edwin, who had a little more girth around his middle and a few more grays. "Come on, brother, let's sit down and talk. Or how about I take you somewhere more quiet, where we can sit and just chill for a little bit? Catch up."

"Catch up? You want to…catch up. That's funny," RJ snickered at the thought.

"Come on, man. You know I didn't mean it like that. I just want us to talk. I'm here for you. I want you to know that."

"Thank you. I know you are, Edwin."

"So, let's talk, man. Let's sit…"

"Naw, man. Some other time. I've got a house full of people right now and nosey reporters snooping around my front door. Hell, my back door too."

Edwin's frown lines deepened and he paused before he spoke again. "The other night, when I was on my knees praying, I felt the spirit trying to tell me that something bad was going to happen to you. I started to get in my car and just drive to Kansas City then but God said, 'Wait.' Now I'm wondering if that was really God, or just me not wanting to be bothered. That haunts me, RJ. It really does. I went and saw Honor yesterday. I don't even think she knew who I was the whole time I was talking to her. They saying she may have to go before a jury. To think maybe I could have saved both of you from all this. But I have to believe that God works in mysterious ways. That His ways are not our ways."

"Look, Edwin, I really ain't trying to hear a sermon today. I just buried my son. I'm sure you, even the holiest of holy, can understand that."

Edwin stepped back from RJ then and turned away. His eyes turned moist.

"All right, then. I see some things don't change. I was going to wait until tomorrow to tell you this, but I'm taking Pop back home with us at the end of the week. I know we said it'd be a couple of more months, but we're ready for him and, frankly, I think he's ready to go. I appreciate everything you've done for him up to this point. I truly do."

You gonna take my father away from me now? RJ shook his head. Regina walked past them, eyeing RJ. He didn't notice.

"You do whatever you feel you gotta do."

RJ walked back into the bathroom and slammed the door shut. Then he let the water run at full blast from the faucet as he sat on the toilet and wept.

170

CYNDA

"Come on, Honor, you've got to give me something here! A grunt, a groan, maybe a hand signal. I know you're not a mute, because obviously you've had plenty to say to your little cellmate. Do you want to spend the rest of your life in prison? Is that what you truly want?"

Honor watched as her attorney's face turned about five shades of crimson. She listened as her voice rose an octave or two without even yelling. Her attorney was just that cool. Cynda Walters's very presence in the downtown holding facility had been bought with her parents' money. In one phone call, Vernon Thompson had not only hired Florida's most prestigious defense attorney, but he had also pulled some strings for her to practice *pro hac vice* in Missouri. When it came to his daughter and the reputation of their family, only the best would do.

Cynda was an average-sized spitfire of a woman, with long sun-bleached hair and a cracker Southern drawl that she could turn on or off at will. Like her size, she used everything to her advantage. People, the courts, other attorneys—they often underestimated her at first, but after more than twenty years practicing law, she had amassed a case record of wins and out-of-court settlements that left most prosecutors visibly shaking before the judges. Cynda breathed the law, and she never stepped outside of her house without being dressed from head to toe in starch business attire, unless she was going out for her daily four a.m. three-mile jogs along Bayshore Boulevard in Tampa. But no one noticed her then. At least, no one who Cynda considered worthy enough to care about.

When Vernon Thompson called in a favor, without hesitation she had gathered up the news clippings and broadcasts and caught a flight to Kansas City.

"Oh, and Cynda?" he had said gruffly.

"Yes, Judge Thompson?"

"This is my daughter. Do anything and everything you have to do to make sure this goes away."

"Yes...sir."

Very few people could make Cynda second-guess herself, and Vernon Thompson was one of them. Maybe it was because of the long-term affair they'd had many moons ago, or because Vernon's reputation superseded hers.

Right now, though, even she had to admit that she'd hit a wall with Honor Ellis. The woman refused to do anything that would aid her defense. It was like Honor wanted to be punished. But Cynda wasn't willing for her client to admit any guilt or wrongdoing. Every possible motive or piece of evidence in even the most damning of crimes could be manipulated to resemble something like innocence.

"Do you understand that the prosecuting attorney has filed felony charges against you, Honor? Do you? Do you realize that he is charging you with endangering the welfare of a child and involuntary manslaughter in the case of your son's drowning, and that you have already been denied bail?"

Honor said nothing. Instead, she sat at the table they shared in the glass-enclosed room with her hands folded tightly together, almost as if she were praying. The highlights in her hair were less visible now in the misshapen ponytail she had it pulled back in. She had lost weight, even more since Cynda had arrived in town less than two weeks ago, and there were defined circles underneath her large eyes. But Cynda liked the gaunt look. It would appeal better to the jury, if the case went to trial, and all indications were headed in that direction. Cynda would rather throw Vernon under a bus then go to trial. Pictures of a drowned infant would trump any of the defense's pleadings. Those images alone would become plastered into the jury's minds, no doubt causing them to lose sleep at night, maybe even inspire nightmares. So it was time to play the only ace Cynda had left.

"Honor, I took the liberty of pulling some strings, with your father's help of course, and I was able to subpoena your medical records," Cynda said, reaching into her oversized satchel. *Slam!* A brick of manila file folders hit the wooden table.

"Um, let's see here… Oh, a broken wrist, fractured tibia fibula, bruised ribs—at least twice that I can tell, and that's not even halfway into the files." Cynda pulled out another a small brown leather notebook.

"I spoke to some of your past coworkers at the insurance agency. Several of them described you as unhappy, severely anxious—oh, and my personal favorite: nice, pretty, but kinda mousy.'" Her Southern drawl was in full effect. "Let's see, you were also spotted several times by your coworkers hiding 'visible bruises' on your face and arms, even a 'busted lip' at one point. Both your parents and friends described as you as being 'isolated', not long after you married Ranford Ellis, Jr.

"Speaking of your pretty-boy husband, that man is some piece of work, isn't he? Making you stay at home and raise your child while he went out and nailed anything with a pulse. A pretty sad and lonely existence, if you ask me."

Silent tears began to stream down Honor's face and she placed her head down on the table, breaking into full-on sobs.

Houston we have lift off!

"But you couldn't say anything, could you? Why? Because pretty boy has an image to protect: a pillar of the black community, a risen saint come to help the low-income youth of the city. He's out winning community service awards, while he's kicking your ass at home. And who would believe you, even if you did tell someone? Not a soul. Now, whether you knew he was fooling around or not, in addition to the abuse? Well, only you can possibly know that. But something caused you to snap that day! You took his most prized possession away: a son that you didn't even want, according to the priest who saw you enter the Rockport Women's Center last April, and being dragged out by pretty boy only minutes afterward."

Cynda's last words caused Honor to jump from her seat and pace the sticky floor behind her.

"You're not crazy, Honor, and you never were. You were a battered woman pushed to the edge of sanity. You had nowhere to go. No one who you could turn to for help. SO YOU GOT BACK AT HIM THE ONLY WAY YOU KNEW HOW! By killing his son, the son you never wanted. Is that pretty much how it happened, Honor? Had you finally had enough of his shit?!"

"YES! YES! I robbed him of everything he stole from me! I did it! I did it!" Honor was standing in the far corner next to the room's only window, sobbing uncontrollably. Cynda walked over and put her arms around the back of her shoulders.

"That's it. Let it all out. Just let it go, Honor." Inside, Cynda was smiling. They had a defense now, and it was a damn good one.

Deer RJ,

I pray for you. It was so good to see you, son, but I never imagine it wuld be at my own grand baby's funeral. What is sadder? I see Honor and I look at my self 20 years ago. I smell the abuse on her. You beat that girl til she die inside. you beat her soul. Some times, I think it worser than laying on hands. The scars, they go but the words stay playing in yur ear like a bull horn. You ain't shit. You ain't go never be shit. You a slut. You a ho. You is fat. You is ugly. You bitch. No body else want you. I could look at that child face and tell you be saying them same words to Honor since the day you say, "I do." May be even be for.

I like to say I raise you better. But hell that ain't true. In a way, I blame my self for my grandson's death. Maybe if I wasn't locked up I culd have done some thing, any thing to stop you. I love you son. I always will, but it break my heart when I think bout how hard you work to make some thing of yur self, to be some thing, when you was nothing but shit in the inside. Son you in the cycle. The same one me and yur daddy was in.

I tell my girls in my RAGE class all the time bout the cycle. I tell you again. tenshion, beatin then lovey-dovey fuckin like rabbits. Aint' no midle. I always say each stage is like a big ole pot of hot water. Tenshion is when the anger is turn low. The pot just been put on the stove and ever thing is chill. But inside some thing stew.

Then come the beating. That pot of anger boils over. The abuser hurt the very 1 he love cause the anger gotta hold of him. The woman she like the steam on top of the pot. She want to go, but she can't. So what she do? She hide the scars from her soul. Then the pot of hot water began to cool down. The man ask his lady to for give him. "I never do it again, baby, I promise. Baby, baby, please!" His lady no she want to go but she start to fill pains. She make excuse for him, and she stay. All the while, she watch that pot, try to keep piece cause she afraid that any time, it gone blow again.

See RJ, her love so strong that she bilieve one day her man will change. She got hope. Her love is a dream. So she wait while he hate. Thats the circle and like most of my RAGE girls you was born into. That pot of anger only gets bigger as time go on. The beatings get worser til the only way out is a body bag. Hell, some time 2. I no. I live it. I tell this story so many times. This story mine to tell.

RJ break free! Get help! Find the power to be a beter man. Hasnt the anger all ready cause you enuff pain?

All my love,

Mommy.

CYNDA

It took less than two hours after Honor's admission for Cynda to schedule a full-fledged press conference on the steps of the Jackson County Courthouse. Every camera crew, anchorperson, and newspaper in Greater Kansas City was front and center.

"Thank you all for being here today. I called you here because new evidence in the Ellis case has come to light," Cynda said, purposely dialing her Southern drawl down to low so as not to sound like an intruder. Townspeople don't take well to strangers. Had she gone there, to her Southern roots, the throngs of reporters before her could easily turn into a Midwestern mob.

"What type of evidence?" an authoritative but high-pitched voice asked.

"My client, Honor Ellis, was a battered woman for many years. She suffered multiple fractures, broken bones, bruises, and scars, all at the hands of the man who proposed to cherish her the most, her husband, Ranford Ellis, Jr."

Cynda paused and waited for the audible gasp to pass over the crowd before she continued. "My client suffered from battered woman's syndrome at the time of the incident in question, and was in deep distress at the time of the drowning involving her son, whom she in no way meant to harm. She had simply been beaten beyond recognition on the inside. So much so that she was not in control of her faculties or actions when said incident took place."

"So, Ms. Waters, are you saying that this was no accident?"

Cynda smiled down at an anchorman whose face had fallen victim to too many plastic surgeries. She clenched her hands. *Relax, you got this.* "No, I am not saying that at all. The truth is, baby Day was the victim here. But he was not the only one. Honor Ellis was also a victim: of name-calling, attacks, and brutal beatings at the hands of her husband. Surely you can understand how years of abuse would suddenly cause a repeatedly injured woman to snap into a moment of blankness and loss of control?"

"Yes, but was the infant's death really a loss of control, or a carefully contrived action?" an over-pancaked Asian woman shouted out from behind a microphone that was almost as large as her head.

Time to hit 'em with the ole one-two punch. "My dear, what we have here is a case of victimization and post-traumatic stress disorder that clearly resulted in temporary insanity. Nothing more. Nothing less."

The crowd of reporters began to shout over each other, their words flying like one big blur in the afternoon air.

"Unfortunately, this is all the time that I have right now. But I will fight for Mrs. Ellis's rights in the hopes that it will shine a light on all battered women, especially those whose voices go unheard in the minority community. Good day, ladies and gentleman. I thank you for coming out today." Exit, stage right.

Cynda sat critiquing her earlier comments on the evening newscast, which had been broadcast on all of the local stations. She'd gotten the attention she wanted, but would it be enough? Maybe not. That's why she was in her downtown hotel room, sipping on her second miniature bottle of gin, poring over her files again, and going through her notes for any smidge of something that she might have missed before. In every case, there was always a way out. Only Honor wasn't interested in helping Cynda find an escape route. Cynda had really come to believe that Honor had been beaten beyond repair and it truly saddened her. There were times when Cynda could see sparks of Honor's former self: A semblance of beauty. A few spoken words of intelligence. One time, she even witnessed a smile so bright it could stop traffic. Those were the sparks Cynda wanted to see more of, just not in front of a jury. She needed Honor beaten. Did she kill her baby boy? Most likely. Was she a cold-blooded murderer? Not in the least.

Cynda had once watched Honor shoo a spider out of her cell, rather than step on it. The movement wasn't a contrived one either; Cynda would have picked up on it if it had been. Honor didn't want to end the spider's life, and she really didn't want to end her son's life. But if you trap anyone inside a raging inferno long enough, you'd be surprised at the lengths he or she would go to escape, even if that meant setting a bigger blaze in the process. Plus the pysch evaluation that had followed her arrest definitely proved that Honor was out of it at the time of the incident. In a way, she still was.

"Who let the dogs out? Who? Who? Who? Who? Who let the dogs out?"

Cynda's ringtone went off, startling her. She looked down at her cell phone and sighed before answering. "Hello, Judge Thompson."

"What's the status?"

"Well… There will definitely be a trial and it's been bumped up because the state is hankering for a speedy conviction. Jury selection starts the day after next."

"You'll be there?"

"Of course."

"No parents. No grandparents. And try to get as many of people of color on that jury as you possibly can."

Again Cynda said, "Of course."

"Let me know how it goes as soon as you get out of jury selection."

"I will do that, Vernon."

"Remember, Cynda, I'm paying you quite handsomely. So I better feel like I'm a fly on the courtroom wall throughout the whole process, you understand?"

"As soon as I know anything, I will tell you. You have my word."

"Good. Glad we have that understanding."

"Now, if there's nothing else, I really have to get back to…"

"Cynda, how's my daughter doing?"

The judge's question caught her off guard. Not once, in the weeks since she'd been in Kansas City, had Vernon asked about the wellbeing of his daughter. Did he want the truth, or a nondescript answer? Cynda decided on the latter.

"She's as well as is to be expected, hanging in there."

"Good, good. You know if I could, I'd be there to personally fry that bastard husband of hers myself. She should have drowned that son of a bitch." *Was taking one life better than the other?*

"I understand how you feel, Judge, and believe me, I'm doing everything in my power to keep her from going to prison."

"That's what I want to hear. Call me when you have news. No matter if I'm in chambers or not, have Violet put you through to me."

"I will do that, Vern… Judge." *Click!*

Cynda turned her cell phone off, wishing not to be disturbed for the remainder of the night. There was a ball of anxiety growing in the pit of her stomach, something like uncertainty. The feeling unnerved her. But she couldn't tell Vernon that, for once in her life, she was feeling uncertain, and that his youngest daughter could be facing some serious prison time.

RANFORD

Ranford had had a long day. A fight between two upperclassmen had taken place in the cafeteria during lunch, and he'd just been told that one of his best female students had received a full-ride scholarship to a larger private school across the state line. RJ was just about to reach for his private stash of scotch in the desk drawer when Byron Addison, board president of Urban Achievers Academy, stepped into his office without knocking.

"Hello, Dr. Ellis. How are you?"

"I'm all right, Byron. What's with all the formality?"

The rotund man appeared to be growing sweatier by the second. Sweat stains grew large underneath his cheap ivory shirt and he smelled like an ashtray. RJ didn't know Byron smoked.

"Um, this morning, the board held an emergency meeting."

"Without me?"

"Yes, without you. In light of the recent allegations that have come up in the press about you and with the upcoming trial and all, the board feels it would be in the best interest of the school if you took some time off for a while."

RJ stood. He turned up the sleeves of his pin-striped shirt. "Wait a minute, Bryon. Are you trying to tell me that I'm fired?"

"No, not exactly. The board feels it would be in the best interest of the school, and the students, if you took an extended leave of absence, with pay, of course. Pending the outcome of the trial, we would consider bringing you back on as principal."

"Cut all this board crap, Byron! I'm not the one on trial here! I am the victim. My son is dead and now you motherfuckas want to threaten to take my job away from me? Come on, Byron. It's me. You know as well as I do that I built this damn school. There would be no Urban Achievers Academy, a school that has gained national recognition, without me! You know this!"

"We appreciate everything you have done for this school, uh, RJ. But surely you can understand, that this type of publicity is not the type that we need, especially in light of the economy and budget cuts. Think of the students. Should they be the ones who are made to suffer because this place is now a media circus instead of an institution of cutting-edge curriculum? How can they possibly put their studies above everything else with all of these distractions?" Byron took a step over toward the closed blinds and lifted them to uncover reporters camped outside on the grass of the campus.

"You want me out, Byron?"

"That's not what I'm saying. Let's just wait until the dust settles and all of this blows over. Until that time, Vice Principal Brooks will act as interim principal."

"Are you serious? So how long you been planning this?"

"As I said, we only put it to a vote this morning. You will receive your full pay and benefits, and, should the situation continue to exist, a fairly equitable severance package."

"You motherfuckas! You think I'm just gonna sit back and let you take the school that I built away from me?" RJ was shouting, and he didn't care who heard him.

The board president backed against the door, turning the handle without looking back. "It's already been done, Dr. Ellis. Please take as much time as you need right now to gather your things. Security will escort you to your car. Take care of yourself."

RJ's drive back home passed by in a haze of anger and emptiness. Without the school, who was he? And if he didn't know, who the hell did?

RJ pulled into his driveway, looking past the teddy bears, cards, letters, balloons, and candles that served as a memorial of Baby Day. It had tripled in size since news first broke of the baby's drowning. Still, RJ couldn't bring himself to even look at the reminder. It was enough to realize that strangers were intruding on his property, invading his privacy, and he was powerless to stop them from coming. No one had earned the right to mourn with him. No one knew what type of hell he was living day in and out. RJ's grief was his, and his alone, to bear.

A silver Honda pulled into the left side of the driveway, the side that once was Honor's. "Shit," RJ muttered as he saw Edwin get out of the car and wave at him. He waved back, gritting his teeth. *What is it now?*

RJ fought the urge to push the button and close the garage. Edwin noticed the boxes in the backseat of RJ's car.

"RJ, what's going on?"

"I've been placed on an extended leave of absence pending the outcome of the trial," RJ held his briefcase in his hand, and snickered to himself when he realized that it no longer contained anything he needed. He chucked the briefcase into the backseat with the boxes.

"I'm sorry to hear that, RJ. Things will turn around, man."

"Will they? I'm starting to believe everything is only going to get worse." RJ closed the garage as soon as he spotted a reporter nearing the entrance to the garage. Edwin pretended not to notice. "That's where faith plays a big part. But I know you ain't trying to hear all that."

"So why did you come by, Edwin? I thought you'd be long gone by now."

"I can't leave. Pop's been waiting on you to come and say goodbye. But we've got to get back. The church needs us, so I told him he's got until tomorrow to say goodbye to you."

"So why didn't you just bring him by now? We could have squashed that. Where is he? Is he in the car? Hey, Reverend O, come on out!"

"He couldn't come today. He wasn't feeling too well. Plus, he feels you should come to him, and I can't say I blame him."

"So now you want to judge me to, Edwin?"

"Naw, man, it ain't nothing like that. We're brothers, man. Always. Do you remember that big fight we got into when we were kids on the corner in Wayne Miner?"

"You mean the one where I kicked your ass?"

"Funny, I recall it the other way around... But anyway, you remember when Pop made us clean the sanctuary afterward? Well, I realize now, he didn't do that as punishment. He did it so we would have some time to make things right between us, and you know what? It worked. That little bit of time together just may have saved our friendship. All Pop wants is to spend some time with you before he leaves for Chicago. He wants time to make things right between the two of you."

"All right. I'll stop by and see him tomorrow before you all take off. Not like I got anything better to do now anyway."

"Great. We'll be heading out a little before noon. Got an eight-hour drive ahead of us."

"I said I'll stop by. I'll be there." RJ needed a drink. Bad.

"Did you do those things, RJ? Did you beat up on Honor the way everyone is saying?"

"You got the nerve to come up in my house and ask me that? No, I never once hit my wife. I swear. You should know me better than that."

"Because if you did, we could get you some counseling. It would almost be a little understandable, given what happened between your father and mother. Have you even gone to visit your wife? Or are you just going to dismiss her too, like you did Carmen?"

"Edwin, I'm going to ask you politely, and only once, to get the hell up out my house."

"I'm just trying to talk, RJ. I'm concerned about you. We all are, and if you have issues that we need to address, I want to help you with them. God is here for you, RJ. I'm here."

"Didn't you fuckin' hear me? Edwin, leave, now!"

"Talk to me, RJ. This is me. If you just…"

RJ's hand went off like a time bomb and within seconds, RJ was on top of Edwin, pounding him repeatedly in the face with all his might. The blows were coming so fast that Edwin could barely shield himself from the onslaught.

"What do you know? You think you know me! You don't know shit! You come here, take the only father I've really ever known away from me…then…you accuse me of…"

RJ was becoming breathless. His lack of sleep and food took hold of him and he collapsed to the side of Edwin, sobbing out loud. Edwin sat up and pulled RJ up by his collar, so that they were face to face. Blood was seeping from Edwin's nose and mouth as he pulled RJ into a tight embrace and cried with him.

HONOR

They stared at her as if she were the main attraction at the freak show, the other women in the county jail. They threw things at her in the shower. Stole her food from her tray. Spit on her and touched her in her most private places when the guards weren't looking. She was a child killer. The worst of their kind, and they never let Honor forget it. Child killers had a special place in the jail's hierarchy, placed somewhere between the brown greasy gook that accumulated behind the stoves of the cafeteria's kitchen and the tampons that were constantly being pulled from the sewers, in spite of the "Please Do Not Dispose Of Feminine Products In The Toilet" signs next to every sink.

Then there were the letters that poured in by the dozens for her daily. Some of them opened like swords with words of seething and disgust. Others oozed like honey coated with sympathy and words of encouragement. This attention drew even more hatred from the other inmates.

But despite their best efforts, Honor could not be moved. She placed herself within her own internal isolation, with invisible walls that could not be penetrated.

She was staring ahead with that same glare of nothingness when one of the female guards unlocked the door to her cell.

"Let's go, Ellis. You got a visitor."

"Who is it?"

"Do I look like the butler around here, coming in here announcing shit? How the hell do I know? Now get off your ass and follow me."

Honor rose from her stained mattress. Her new cellmate giggled a little when Honor tripped over her outstretched foot, her head almost hitting one of the iron bars.

"Knock it off, Kelly," the guard said.

"Yes, ma'am."

Honor followed the burly guard into the visitor's room. Jeers from the prisoners greeted her every step of the way. Honor heard nothing.

The first thing she noticed about the older man sitting before her were his weather-beaten fingers. Then his genuine lopsided smile with the missing two teeth on the right side. Even then, it took a while for Honor to remember who he was. *Jesse.* The man who once drove her home, months ago when she was too scared to drive across the bridge.

A quizzical expression must have flashed across her face as she sat down across the table from him.

"Hello, Honor."

"Jesse, right?"

"Yes, Jesse. Laura, my wife... Well, she wanted to come too, but she hasn't been well lately. Doctors say she's got breast cancer."

"Oh, I'm sorry to hear that, Jesse." In truth, she was. It was the first time Honor had felt any emotion besides confusion since she'd come to this place.

"She is the one that said I should come here and see you. Not that I wouldn't have come along myself, eventually. We wanted you to know that we're sorry about everything that's happened."

"That's sweet, Jesse, but you didn't have to come all the way down here to tell me that."

"But I did. After we dropped you off that one day, Laura said that something just didn't seem right with you. It bothered her something awful for a long time after that. She said I should have reached out more to try and help you. She said the Lord told her something bad was going to happen. And sure enough, one day we were sitting there watching the TV and your face popped up on the morning news. We knew then that God had given her a premonition. But we ignored it and it ain't never sat right with us since then."

"Please, Jesse, don't think that. None of this is your doing. None of it."

"I brought you something."

"You did? What?"

From his lap, Jessie revealed a tattered red leather Bible. "I want you to have this and carry it with you always."

Honor swallowed. "Thank you, Jesse. I will treasure it and keep it near me. I promise."

"Good. Now place your hands on top of it."

"Excuse me?"

"Put your hand on top of the Bible."

When Honor didn't budge, Jesse reached out for her hand in one surprisingly swift motion. His hand was like sandpaper.

"What are you doing? Let go of me!"

"Repent. Repent. Repent from your sin, my child. Turn back from you evil ways. Tell Satan that he has no place inside you. Rebuke him!

"Let me go!" Honor drew back with a force so strong it knocked the chair over in the process. With widened eyes, she ran for the nearest exit. The guard stood on the other end of the room, a smile on her face.

"For the wages of sin are death…"

Honor ran back to her cell, letting the jeers override the sound of the crazy old man's voice. That night, she dreamed about the wages of sin.

RANFORD

RJ waited until he heard the sound of Regina's car tires screeching away before he jumped up from the bed in the guestroom and peeled the sheets back. A sympathy fuck, that's what she'd just given him, and RJ wasn't about to go out like no punk. He was done with tears and feeling sorry for himself. He had said his goodbyes to Reverend Odom and Edwin the day before and promised to visit them in Chicago as soon as he could.

"Sasha came to see me a few days ago," Reverend Odom had said out of the blue as RJ was headed for the door. He had no intention of staying for a long drawn-out fake family reunion.

"Oh, yeah," was all he had said.

"The Good Lord works miracles," Reverend Odom quipped. "I'm so proud of that girl."

Funny how you never said that about me. I was never a crack head either.

"RJ, I just want you to know that I love you. I love you, son."

Son. The word he'd been longing to hear for practically his whole life was being uttered as he chose to move thousands of miles away with his true biological son. RJ could not bring himself to respond. Instead, he walked away.

A quick shower, and RJ was changed into his shorts and T-shirt. He jogged four miles before his body gave out on him. He had to walk most of the way back home. Hunger punched him in the stomach and he returned to feast on whatever he could find in the kitchen. It was good to feel alive again.

His belly full from the snacks he'd eaten, RJ jumped up like old times to watch some television in the family room. Before he could reach for the remote, he noticed the honeymoon and wedding photos, the pictures that used to bring him such pride, atop the mantle.

He dragged the large trashcan from the kitchen and pitched all of the photos inside. Some of the frames landed with a thump, while the smaller frames crashed and shattered against each other. Then he went around the house pulling down every photo of the two of them together. Honor was put into the trash. She was garbage.

Tomorrow, he'd call the first real estate agent he could find and put the house on the market. Better to leave before this whole house of cards came tumbling down. He went on, dumping all of Honor's toiletries from the bathroom and throwing all of her clothes into one big pile in the center of the master bedroom they once shared, the one that he still refused to sleep in.

RJ was panting by the time he arrived in front of Day's nursery. The door to the nursery always stayed closed; so did the door to the upstairs guest bathroom. He opened it and stepped inside. The room was dark, so dark it mocked the bright sunny day outside. Not a sliver of sunlight shone threw a crack in the blinds or the curtains. RJ didn't want to turn the lights on. Instead he walked around, touching the cherry oak furniture he'd personally selected and smiling down at the basketball table lamp that matched the rest of the room's sports decor. *My son is dead. My son is dead and I can't do this. I'm not doing this! Why? Why? Why?*

There was only person he could ask. He turned from the room, shutting the door tightly closed behind him. Grabbing his keys, he sank into the leather interior of his car and took off in the direction of the Jackson County Jail.

HONOR

Honor froze as RJ walked into the visitors' room. Even in the safety of the iron bars, the many locks, and the excess of security guards loaded with live ammunition, she was still afraid of him. He walked toward her, smelling like a gym, and laid it on the table in front of them. Daring her to look down at it. To touch it. *It* had no place on the table. No right to be in plain sight in front of her.

"Go ahead, look down. Remember this? Our son's favorite stuffed toy. The one he slept with every night, even at nap time."

"Get that away from me," Honor's lip quivered.

"Look at it, bitch! Fine, I'll hold it up for you to see." A maze of bright neon colors—green, red, yellow and orange—set her eyes on fire, the turtle's bright colors the match. The only way Honor could survive anymore was to pretend that Day had never existed. That he was a lifelike caramel-colored doll that she had pretended was real for a while.

Honor stared at the girl who looked to be no older than a baby herself at the table next to them. She was crying. Her parents were comforting her with the only slight gestures that were allowed in the visitors' room. Then her eyes settled back on the man whose love had choked the sanity out of her.

"I saw the two of you, you know."

"What?" RJ dropped the stuffed toy onto the floor. A toddler that had been walking around swooped it up and ran away.

"Danny, give that back."

"No, it's okay," Honor answered. "He can keep it."

The girl, obviously new, said, "Thank you. Danny, what do you say to the nice woman?"

"Tank you." He pulled the string on the turtle, laughing as it shook.

RJ whispered, "What are you talking about?"

"You and the neighbor lady. I saw you. She told me you'd be there. Yet somehow I didn't believe her. After everything you put me through, in my mind… In my stupid mind, I refused to accept the fact that not only did you beat me down, but you cheated on me too. Even after everything I told you I'd been through with my father's numerous affairs, you still laid down with her. How many others were there, RJ? Huh?"

Now RJ was the one caught off guard. Hadn't he made sure that all of his indiscretions were carefully carried out with the thoroughness of a CIA agent? There was no way she could have caught him.

"What the hell are you talking about, Honor? You really are crazy. I never cheated on you. Ever. That's how deep my love was for you."

"She screamed out your name. Over and over and I just sat there. I. Just. Sat. There. Then I left. I closed the door behind me and I left." Tears were flowing down Honor's drawn cheeks.

The blue baby bootie. The one with the sailor ties. Regina. It all made sense now.

"What did you do, Honor? Oh, God, what did you do?"

"The night before, you had slapped me hard across my back for using the wrong diaper cream. You said it stunk. Do you remember that? You said that your son was too good to go around smelling like a medicine cabinet. He had a diaper rash. You never looked. Instead, you hit me. Then you threw the diaper cream at my face. You see this little nick above my eyebrow? That's where it landed. Do you remember that, RJ?"

"What did you do, Honor?"

"I stole from you just like you robbed me all these years. You robbed me of love, a marriage and pregnancy, motherhood. You took from me so I took from you."

"You crazy bitch. Do you know I can testify to everything you told me just now?"

"Go ahead. There is nothing more left of me to take. I doubt you will say anything though. How would it look if everyone knew the truth about who you really are? I never wanted to become a mother to your child. You knew that. How could I possibly love something that gave you so much joy?"

"You are gone. You are out there! I was giving you the benefit of the doubt at first. You know that? How could my wife intentionally kill our child? You killed an innocent baby. My son!"

"And you destroyed an innocent woman's life. The only difference is you didn't get a chance to kill me."

"You're sick, you know that? Sick! There's a special place in hell for folks like you."

Honor stared at RJ. "There is. Right beside you."

CYNDA

The line to The Rotisserie's counter was almost out the door when Cynda blew in for her morning cup of triple espresso. She counted her place in line. *One. Two. Three. Four. Five. Six. Damn!* She undid the top button on her tan suede suit jacket and smoothed her hands over the matching skirt. Cynda fidgeted in her sling backs as Number Three seemed to be taking forever trying to decide on whipped cream or not and which pastry she wanted. *Honey, lay off the pastries. Just get your damn cup and go.* It was times such as these that she cursed herself for being raised to have manners.

"*Who let the dogs out? Who? Who? Who? Who? Who let the dogs out?*"

I've got to change that fucking ring tone. She'd been saying that for four years.

"Vernon... Judge. How's it going?"

"Let's cut through the pleasantries. You still going for temporary insanity?"

"Yes, I am. I think, at this point, it's our best defense, probably our only defense."

"You know how many temporary insanity cases are actually won, especially in Missouri?"

"Yes, I'm aware of that. But it's a hunch I have to hang my hat on."

"So I'm just supposed to trust you with a hunch?"

"If you can't trust me, then you shouldn't have hired me." Cynda regretted it as soon as it spilled from her mouth. *Must have been my lack of morning coffee.* But wait a second: she didn't regret what she'd just said. Vernon had hired her because he knew she was the best at what she did. Now it was time to let loose the reigns and let her do what she did best.

"I'm sorry." *What? Did I just hear him right?* Was the Missouri fault line about to open right where she stood in this dump of a coffee shop?

"I'm just concerned is all. My daughter's future is at stake, and I will not let that punk of a man, or that sham of a marriage, jeopardize it."

"You do understand that your precious little girl killed her own son? Her baby son?"

"Yes, of course I understand that. You think I'm stupid? But I know that idiot of a PhD drove her to it. My Honor would never harm a fly."

"Or a spider."

"What?"

"Never mind. I think temporary insanity is still going to be our best defense. I've subpoenaed the husband. Tomorrow, once the jury sees for themselves what a jerk this RJ character really is, and hears about the personal hell she's been living in for all those years, they are bound to be sympathetic. And that sympathy is our ace in the hole."

Yes, finally she was second in line! "Well, you better damn make sure it is." *Click!*

The beatnik man before her shifted his feet back and forth for a few minutes, paused, then stammered. "I'll have a… uh… let me see."

Cynda knew a little bit about personal hell herself.

SASHA

Sasha gasped when she spotted Honor sitting alone at a picnic table outside the jail. Her sister-in-law's body had deteriorated into next to nothing. Her forehead seemed to be stamped *fragile* in very visible frown lines. Honor was facing the opposite direction, oblivious to the other inmates as they laughed and carried on like wayward children in the afternoon sun.

Did I look like that? Sasha shuddered to think that, indeed, she once had.

"Hello, Honor. How have you been since our last visit?" As if Sasha needed to ask.

Honor turned, looked at Sasha's House of Hope identification badge, and smiled—a little.

"Let's see... Your brother came to visit me. I finally had the nerve to tell him off after all these years. Oh, and everyone around here still treats me like I'm a rancid trash bag. Then, of course, there's still the daily hate mail I receive. Oh, and did I mention that my trial begins tomorrow? The fate of my life is going to lie in the hands of a few select total strangers."

"Anything else?"

"Yes, it's really a sad day when you are the only person that I have to talk to and look up to in this world."

There was a brief silence before the two ladies shared a rare laugh.

"I want you to know that House of Hope is behind you. In fact, the director, Ms. Jones, has written a three-page letter on your behalf."

"Great."

"Honor, this is your life we're talking about here. Do you realize that? I need you to leave this pity party you've been staying at and fight for yourself, 'cause at the end of the day, you are the only person that has to give a damn."

"My Day is gone. I can't bring him back. I try to think about that night. I think really hard, but I can't get past the running water... That's where everything draws a blank. I lay awake every night just trying to get past that running water and I can't. I can't see anything. It's just a black space...a giant hole where everything got sucked into...and I can't get it back. All I remember next is being taken away in handcuffs. Sure, I can talk a good game sometimes, like I knew what happened in the darkest part of my mind, but I don't. Who's going to defend that?"

"Look, Honor, we've all done things we're not proud of, maybe not to the extreme you have, but we have," Sasha said. A woman began inching closer to where they sat the picnic table. Her hair was plaited into tight cornrows and she was smiling and winking at Sasha, a cigarette dangling from her fingers. Sasha smiled back at her, then threw up her middle finger. The woman rolled her eyes and huffed off.

It had been awhile since Sasha had had any loving, but she wasn't anywhere close to admitting defeat and switching camps. All at once, she was thankful that Debbie had taken her to an adult toy store a few weeks ago and introduced her to masturbation. The memory alone made her smile.

"Debbie, I thought you were like all holy and sanctified. How you know about all this?" Sasha had said as they walked through the store, sizing up the array of vibrators and stilettos.

"Yes, I'm strong in my faith. But don't think Christians can't get their freak on too. There is no shame in the marriage bed. How do you think Jerry and I keep our marriage alive?" Debbie laughed. "Besides, I'm doing for this for you so you understand that you have options. You don't have to accept the first man that comes along, and you can find pleasure in being alone and taking care of yourself first for a change."

"I guess I never looked at it that way."

"I know you haven't. Plus, you starting to sound cranky all the time. Let's find you something to take that edge off."

They laughed, and left an hour later with a basketful of goodies for Sasha to sample.

Honor's next question jarred Sasha away from her pleasant memory.

"Do you ever miss it?" she asked.

"Miss what?"

"The drugs. Do you ever miss them? Sometimes, I wish I was an addict just so I can escape."

"I'd be lying if I told you that I didn't miss them…the drugs. I think about getting high every day, sometimes more than once. I'm always going to be an addict. That will never change. I've accepted the fact that it's a struggle I'm going to have to live with every day for the rest of my life. It scares me to death to think that just maybe, one day, the day is going to get the best of me and I'll be back at square one again. I have a good life now with people who love me, a nice little job, and I'm about to get my own place... Maybe even start saving for a car instead of borrowing the House's van all the time. I have a purpose for living that I didn't have before. I get up every day and I thank God that I'm in my right mind, and then I vow to save another woman from going to down the same path I took.

"I got high because it was the only thing I knew how to do to make it through. I've stole from folks. I have hurt a lot of folks. I have sold my body for what? A hit or two? And all the while He kept me, 'cause I shoulda been dead a long time ago. If it wasn't the drugs, it was going to be at the hands of Vance, or maybe a trick. The high, it ain't worth it to me no more, but it calls me back every day. I just gotta fight the urge, replace it with something else."

Sasha reached for a cigarette then, the heaviness of what she'd just said aloud weighing on her. When she inhaled, she noticed Honor fighting back tears.

"I don't have a reason to live anymore, Sasha. What kind of a mother can't remember whether or not she killed her own son? The autopsy says I did it. Public opinion says I did it. Hell, the whole world says I did it. But I can't remember. I can't even see his face."

"In time, it will come to you...everything that happened. Look, I love RJ dearly, but I know he beat the life from you a long time ago. We were both beaten beyond recognition, only yours was more in the inside. Oftentimes, that's worse. You stopped living long before that day. Even in my dazed state, I could see that. I just didn't want to admit it to myself. If I could see that, then I could see who and what my brother truly was: an educated, cleaned-up version of Vance. Who wants to open their eyes to see that shit? You have to find your reason for living. Nobody else can tell you what it is. My mother shot my father in cold blood. You let Day drown. I got high. All because of them blows given by the men who said they loved us. Those damn fists that left us more bruised on the inside then out. Nobody else can understand that, unless you've been through it. I never told you this, but watching you give birth to Day saved my life. I knew then that I needed to make some changes. So, just so you know, Day's short life was not in vain. He was, and will always be, my angel. Did I hate you at first for taking that angel away from this earth? Hell, yeah, I did! But then I realized that only someone who was truly hurting could have broken his wings."

Sasha stubbed out the last of her menthol with the heel of her brown flats, then she stood and outstretched her arms to Honor. "Come on, let's go back to your cell, I've got something for you."

"What is it?"

"Just get off your butt and come look."

There were no jeers as Sasha and Honor walked back to her cell. Something about seeing that House of Hope identification badge on Sasha's chest caused the other inmates to grow silent and wrestle their own demons.

When the guard opened Honor's cell, she was shocked to find four or five dresses lying neatly across her mattress. Honor touched the fabric of each of the dresses, most of them some shade of navy. It had been awhile since she'd worn anything besides an orange jumper. She'd forgotten what it was like to wear normal clothes.

Sasha said, "They're for the trial, courtesy of the house. We have shoes for you too, some makeup and costume jewelry. I guessed at your sizes so I hope everything fits. Well, go ahead... Try them on. Then we must do something about your hair, girl."

Hi Honor,

I find you! I want you to no these bars can't hold us back. We got a mesage to get out. No this leter is not bout my son or grandson. I greeve for them. My love for them is eternel, but I messed up with RJ. I mit that. He to far gone to ever see the errer of his ways. I culdn't save Day. But I can try and save you. I believe what they say on the news bout all the beatings you suffer at the hands of my son. There is no dobt in my mind it true. I no it the minute I see you at the funeral. A women can look into another women eyes and fill her pain. The pain only we no. I see it in Sasha's eyes to. All of us beaten in the name of love. Called ever thing but childs of God by the men we trust the most. Other women look at us, and say behind our back, "Why did you stay?" We no that being bled dry drains you, make you bilieve abuse is the only reality.

This bond we share.

A sad bond that only we no cause our men have shove us, push us, hold us down, kick us, chock us, slap us, bit us, punch us, lock us out our home and car, throw stuff at us, rape us, threaten us, cuss us, control us, harassed us, and make us think whore is our first name. We are the women with minds that spin while our body stay stuck.

A woman who love the rite way her hole life cant no what we have go thru. What cause us to fill like death is the 1 way out. Only when our men kill us do they fill. How can he kill her, they ask? All she try to do was walk away from him, they say. Such a shame, they say. They watch then, as our men go to jail over an anger they culdn't control. How can they no such a love?

I member when Randy first hit me, I was ashame, but part of me thought well if he hit me cause he jealous, then he must love me. How sad.

Folk want to sweep us under the rug with their brooms of jugment. They walk round us like they can't see the big pile of mess under there. Cases like yurs, Honor, it remind them that we here.

I no yur trial come up soon. When you go to court, I want you to go with yur head up. Let the angels walk in for you and keep you the hole way. Lawers have this sayin, what they say? Oh, these are crimes of pasion. But what do they really no bout crimes of the beaten and bruised?

I pray for you and love you from behind these prison bars. Always. The beaten brigade marches on.

With love,

Carmen Ellis.

195

CYNDA

Cynda followed a strict ritual before each trial. Two days before she would organize her files—opening statement, witness statements, and evidence—place them in her brown leather satchel, then put everything away in a closet where she couldn't see or touch it. The night before the trial she watched TV Land reruns until ten o'clock, then she would retire to bed. At three-thirty the next morning, she would change into her running clothes and jog her usual three miles, Stevie Wonder blasting in her ears from her iPod. Then she would eat a piece of dry toast, and keep it down until her nerves forced her to throw it back up.

She'd brush her teeth then and wash away the sour taste with a small glass of orange juice. Next, she'd lay one of her black suits on the bed with a matching camisole and thong. She'd take a long hot shower, blow dry her hair, put on minimal makeup—sheer lip gloss and eyeliner, so as not to look intrusive—and change into her clothes. Once all the tasks were complete, Cynda would look at herself and recite her favorite Robert Frost quote: "A jury consists of twelve persons chosen to decide who has the better lawyer."

Only then would Cynda allow herself to turn on the morning news and think about the case at hand. All of her cases made the morning news, and Honor Ellis's case was no exception. Already, it was the talk of *Good Morning USA*, *News Today*, and most of the cable news networks. Public opinion always intrigued her, the way people judged and commented on things they basically knew nothing about.

She'd shut off the television, button up her jacket, and head for her satchel in the closet.

"It's show time," she'd say to herself before closing the hotel room door behind her. It was a ritual she relished. Because, in the end, she'd never lost a trial.

HONOR

The camera crews pounced on Honor as soon as she arrived outside the Jackson County Courthouse. Their lights were blinding. Their words were overpowering. Honor wanted to shrink back into the car and go back to her cell. At least there, she'd be safe from this onslaught of prying eyes. *What do they want from me? Can't they see I have nothing else to give?*

She was saved as Cynda came out of nowhere and grabbed her by the elbow.

"Come on! Follow me!" she screamed over the reporters. Cynda life-flighted Honor inside the building. So tight was Cynda's grip on Honor's arm that they practically collided with RJ and his team of lawyers as they walked into the courtroom. RJ stared at her, his hazel eyes red-rimmed and puffy, darker even.

"Don't worry about him, Honor. He's no one. Nothing," Cynda pulled harder on her elbow. "Let's take our seats."

Honor was surprised to see her mother and sister sitting in the front row, just before the small swinging gate. *Why are they here?* Honor did nothing to acknowledge their presence. Neither did they. It was another proud family moment, worthy of the morbid scrapbook they mentally kept.

In a strange way, Honor was comforted by their appearance. At least they cared enough to support her, or maybe they were just being nosy and had to see for themselves the debauchery that had overtaken her life. The black sheep of the family had grown bigger, fatter, and blacker.

Honor took her seat next to Cynda. Sasha came from behind and touched her on her shoulder. Honor reached for her hand and placed her face over it, losing herself in the warmth of her touch for a minute. It was good to feel loved. Honor let go when Cynda pulled out a bunch of papers and manila folders from her satchel.

Enough time had passed for Honor to watch Cynda go through each file meticulously, arranging and rearranging them, before the back door of the courtroom opened. The jury filed inside and took their seats to the right of Honor. Honor began to shake. Her palms started to sweat and her breathing became constricted, like someone was tightening a belt around her throat. She had to fight the urge to bolt from the courtroom. The familiar panicky feelings returned.

"Hey, are you okay?" Cynda asked. "You don't look so hot."

"I'm alright."

"Here, drink a glass of water."

Cynda poured Honor a glass of water from the pitcher that was before them and handed it to her. Honor's hands shook and droplets fell onto the front of her dress as she sipped.

Sasha had chosen for her a modest navy polyester dress that fell close to her ankles. She wore two fake pearl earrings and a mock-gold necklace with another small faux pearl in the center. How different from the days when every piece of jewelry she wore had at least a five hundred dollar price tag. Honor's hair was shiny again, curled into an understated bob, thanks to the magic of Sasha's flat iron and joboa oil. On her face she wore nude lipstick. Nothing else. Honor could tell by the way Cynda was looking at her that she approved of her attire.

"All rise. The Honorable William D. Hayes presiding…"

That was all Honor heard as she stood, nearly knocking her glass of water onto Cynda's folders in the process. Luckily, Cynda caught the glass before the water did any major damage.

The judge reminded Honor of her father, although this judge was white and fresh-faced. Maybe it was just the power of the black robe and the title itself. She had grown up around the court system, watching her father climb the ladder from lawyer, to partner, to district attorney, to judge. She knew the law backward and forward because her father would often make Honor study the many law books in his personal library. He knew early on that one of his daughters was going to become a doctor, so that meant that the other was bound to become a lawyer.

The first strike against the black sheep.

Never had Honor imagined that she would be a part of the law she was forced to read about, and on the opposite side of the criminal spectrum. It was all sadly ironic.

"I'll hear opening arguments now."

Honor watched as a slender giant of a man rose from the bench beside them and turned to face the jury. His suit was cheap, even Honor could see that. His shoes worn, and what was left of his cinnamon-toned hair was wildly jerking to and fro with each over-exaggerated gesture he made with his large hands.

"Your Honor. Ladies and gentleman of the jury. The state will prove, beyond a shadow of a doubt, that Honor Ellis killed Day Brandon Ellis, her infant son, by intentionally drowning him in an infant tub of scalding hot water, as the autopsy reports will show. That Day Ellis not only drowned, but that he had second and third degree burns along most of his body, all at the hands of his mother. The very one who was supposed to protect him, take care of him, nurture him, and show him unabiding love. The state will prove that Day Ellis's death was not an accident and that his mother, Honor Ellis, was fully in her right mind at the time of his death. The prosecution rests for now."

"Christ, who uses the phrase, 'beyond the shadow of a doubt' anymore?' Where are we? In a bad wild west movie?" Cynda muttered just as she stood up and pulled her jacket further down her curvy hips.

"Your Honor. Ladies and gentlemen of the jury. Contrary to what the prosecution has alleged, my client, Honor Ellis, did not drown her son, Day Ellis intentionally. She did not purposely cause him to develop second and third degree burns all over his body. On the night in question, Honor Ellis simply snapped and lost control of her faculties, which led to the unfortunate drowning incident of her infant son. The defense will show that Honor was a woman who, for years, had been beaten and verbally abused on an almost daily basis, manipulated and controlled by her husband, Ranford Ellis, Jr., so much so that she became a ghost of a woman who could not even walk outside of her own front door. Police reports, medical records, testimonies, and witness statements will prove that Honor Ellis suffered severely from battered women's syndrome, post-partum depression, and post-traumatic stress disorder, and that she was not in her right mind at the time of the incident, or for several days after the occurrence. The defense rests for now, your honor."

"Call your first witness."

"The State would like to call to the stand David Collins, the arresting officer on the night of the drowning."

That was the last thing Honor heard before she returned to the beach house and listened to the waves gently lap and watched as they tickled her toes. Inside, she laughed as she left footprints in the sand.

CYNDA

It was a grueling three and a half days of testimonies and cross-examinations. During that time, Cynda had come to generally loathe the state's attorney, with his cheap suits and bad haircut. She had always viewed the prosecuting attorneys as equal colleagues, whose charge it was to argue for the other side. Worthy adversaries and sparring partners in the arena that was the law.

But this guy had gotten under her skin like a pesky tick that was sucking the blood from her being. Something about his frequent hand gestures and gross exaggerations. The way he seemed to gloat and flaunt the pictures of a dead baby around to the jury and judge. The way he faked having any emotional range beyond that of a shark.

If Cynda dared admit it to herself (and she never would) for the first time, she was scared. Nothing looked good for her client from day one. The jury was taking too long. The worst part was just when she thought it was over, the jury would ask to see another piece of evidence. Honor had transformed into a basket case again during the trial, and Cynda knew she could not risk putting her on the witness stand, for fear of what would come out of her mouth once she placed her hand across the Bible and swore to tell the truth.

On the fourth day, Cynda could admit that she was not her confident self. In her previous cases, waiting for the jury to deliberate was more a nuisance than anything because Cynda knew they always came back in her favor. Cynda had once convinced a jury that a man was innocent, even though the murder weapon was found with his prints all over it and DNA evidence was linked to the blood samples. When it came to juries, Cynda knew she could turn water into wine. She was drunk with the law. But now, she just didn't know. And not knowing was making her irritated.

That was her state of mind when she got the call on that fifth day. The jury had rendered a verdict. Trying hard not to let her voice betray her, Cynda calmly called her client and told her to be at the courthouse within the hour.

HONOR

"I remember now. What I said to RJ the day he came to see me in jail was true."

"What are you talking about, Honor?" Cynda asked. They sat in a small room adjacent to the jury proceedings. The room was barely big enough to hold a small table and three wooden chairs. A fourth chair with a missing front leg was in a corner, underneath a window so dingy that it made downtown Kansas City look like one hazy outline. Sasha sat next to Honor, holding her hand. Debra stood next to the women, counting her every breath.

"I remember what happened to Day," Honor said, staring out into the outline. Cynda rushed from her chair to try and stop her client from saying anything further. Somehow, she sensed that every word would be incriminating.

"Come on, Honor. You know you're not right in the right frame of mind to do this now. The trial, the verdict coming down, all the stress…"

"No, I know what happened to my baby," Honor said as tears streamed down onto her lap.

Now it was Sasha who jumped. "Honor, it's not important. Let's just get through the verdict."

Honor's voice was a notch above a whisper. "After I came back from hearing RJ sleep with our neighbor, I tried to pretend like it had never happened. I was stuck on routine, on making sure everything was on schedule. I knew that Day's bath time was behind schedule, which meant his bedtime would be pushed back, and what kind of mother would I be if I didn't get my baby to bed on time? I had also missed his evening feeding, so that surely proved that I was not a good mother.

"I didn't like Day…"

Cynda raised her voice. "Honor, that's enough!"

"It's true. I didn't like him. I never bonded with him the way a mother and child are supposed to bond. I tried. I did try. But every time I looked at his face, all I saw was RJ. That night, when I got him home and in the tub, I didn't intend to kill him. I didn't realize the water was so hot. I only knew that I was behind schedule. What would RJ say if he came home and he found that I had messed up on my daily routine? He had already completely dismissed my presence since Day came into this world. Yes, he had stopped beating me, mostly. But it was worse that he treated me like I didn't even exist anymore. So what would he do to me if his son was not dressed in his pj's and settled into his crib? Nine times out of ten, he'd run into the nursery and wake him up from his sleep anyway. But what would happen to me if RJ came home and found that Day was not where he was supposed to be? I hadn't even made dinner that night and there were no leftovers. Nothing I could throw together real quick before giving Day a bath. That was another thing too: I always had a plate ready for RJ. Didn't matter if he ate it or not.

"Sometimes, he would come home and tell me he'd already eaten after I'd tried so hard to make his favorite dishes. I was glad about that though, because that meant I knew exactly what to pack for his lunch the next day. RJ was wasteful, always eating from a brown paper bag, even when I bought him a lunch pale. 'Look,' I said, 'It'll keep your food cold longer and you'll have more room.' 'Take that shit back from wherever you got it,' he said. So I always prepared his lunch in the morning and put it into a brown paper bag. He was so wasteful."

Sasha spoke up then. "Honor, we know. We get it. My brother was a jerk, but you can't blame yourself for…"

"That night, I overfilled Day's infant tub. I let the water run too long. I didn't check the temperature. I undressed him. He was crying because he was hungry. But I didn't care. I placed him into the tub. He cried louder and squirmed more than usual. I couldn't find his baby wash. It wasn't anywhere near the tub. I thought I might have an extra bottle underneath the sink so I let go of Day and went looking for it.

"I had to dig behind some toilet paper and stuff, but sure enough I found a new bottle. That's when I came back to the tub and noticed Day's body was under water. Oh, he kicked and kicked for what seemed like awhile. But I stopped watching him. I sat on the side of the tub and I never looked over at him after that. I just sat there, knowing I was going to get in trouble for being off schedule."

A rush of relief came over Honor. It was the first time in weeks that she felt close to sane. She had a story to tell, and she had told it. It was out there in the air now, no longer confined inside of her. It was free. Telling it, though, had exhausted her, so she closed her eyes and slumped deeper into the hard wooden chair.

I let my son die.

Everyone in the room fell silent. Their eyes filled with tears as they sat in an incubator of mixed emotions.

"They're ready for you now." The door swung open as an older, pot-bellied guard stepped inside.

Honor stood first. "Look, whatever happens in there. I want to thank you gals for sticking by me. I know it hasn't been the easiest of choices. I've made my peace now, and I'm ready to accept my fate."

I am at peace. Honor walked alongside Cynda into the courtroom while Sasha and Debbie took their seats on the bench. RJ was there. Honor didn't dare glance in his direction. There were too many sad memories and regrets that way. Honor's family was not present.

"All rise."

Honor clung to the table for support, as the jury rose to their feet as well.

"Have you reached a verdict?"

"Yes, we have, your honor."

The court clerk retrieved a piece of paper from the first juror and walked it over to the judge, who read it and set it down next to his gavel.

"What say you?"

"We, the jury, find the defendant, Honor Ellis, guilty on the charge of endangering the welfare of a child. On the charge of involuntary manslaughter involving Day Ellis, we find the defendant, Honor Ellis, not guilty by reason of temporary insanity."

An emotional Cynda sank back into her seat. Honor could not move.

"Is this your final judgment?"

"Yes, your honor, it is."

"Okay, let it be placed on the record as such. Sentencing will be given in no less than two weeks, until which time, Honor Ellis will remain in custody at the Jackson County Courthouse."

"What does all this mean?" Honor finally asked Cynda.

"It means that Robert Frost was a bad motherfucker."

"Come on, Ellis, let's go." A quizzical expression remained on Honor's face as she was, once again, placed in handcuffs and led outside the courtroom.

EPILOGUE

RANFORD

"Sir, do you want the last of the boxes in the truck, or the car?"

"Tell you what, why don't place everything in the truck. No sense in me having to lug it around when I'm paying you all to do that for me."

"Gotcha. We'll move them onto the truck now."

RJ walked around his now-empty split-level house, looking chillingly casual in acid-washed jeans and a dark polo. The house no longer looked lived-in. He had hired a cleaning service to come in tomorrow and take care of anything that remained. All of the furniture and knick-knacks had been donated to the Metropolitan Ministries Retirement Community. RJ wanted nothing to remind him of his former life as he headed to Chicago and his new job as the assistant principal of a new charter school for boys.

He would be closer to Reverend Odom, and Edwin and his family. RJ had taken a substantial cut in pay when he accepted the job, but what was money to him now since everything else he had was gone? RJ needed a fresh start more than he needed designer suits and ties. He wanted desperately to break free of this house and the nightmares that kept him up at night.

Three months on the market, and no buyers. The realtor was frank with RJ and told him that, given the history, it wasn't guaranteed to move fast. "We have to let people forget what happened here, move on to something else. Then we'll start getting bites." Two open houses had netted next to no visitors, and those were the ones whose curiosity had been piqued just enough to want to go inside the circus-freak of a house.

New cards and candles still arrived in front of Day's curbside shrine every week. But RJ was no longer concerned. As part of his contract, he'd negotiated for his new school to pay the mortgage on the house until it sold.

Yes, a new start was exactly what RJ needed, away from the prying eyes and public scrutiny. *Here, come look at the man who drove his wife to the brink of insanity. The man who made her kill her only child.* The community had made him out to be a monster, and turned their attention away from the person who actually committed the crime. RJ was not the bad guy, despite this new morbid picture they painted of him. Well, fuck everybody. He was getting the hell out of dodge.

His thoughts drifted back to Honor, the way she looked in the courtroom the last time he saw her. RJ had to admit, she looked good. He had to fight the urge on at least two of those days to take her right there over the bench in the courtroom. After all, she was still his. At least for a while. RJ had filed for divorce after the verdict was rendered and, as soon as the papers were signed, there would be nothing left between them but bad blood.

Sasha had come to say her goodbyes a few days ago.

"So you really going, huh?"

"Yes, I am, little sis."

"RJ, are you ever going to get help, get counseling? I mean, you been through a lot and I think you put Honor through a lot. Maybe seeing somebody will help you get over everything."

"Huh, I'll think about it," RJ said, knowing full well he had no intention of laying on a couch and telling a stranger all of his business, in the hopes that it would "cure" all that ailed him. Better to deny his inner psychopath than admit that he had failed as a husband, and as a father.

"Well, promise me you'll take care of yourself."

"Only if you promise me that you'll do the same."

They shared a rare hug and kiss and RJ promised to call her often.

Then there was the issue of Regina: she was pregnant. And although she swore up and down that the baby she carried was RJ's, they both knew that the only way to be sure was through a paternity test. Part of RJ hoped the baby was his. It would almost be like a second chance. But he was unsure about having to spend the next eighteen years of his life dealing with Regina. So he'd leave that pregnant pause up in the air until after the paternity test.

RJ did one last walk-through. Without thinking, he found himself in the old nursery. Baseball mitts, bats, footballs, soccer balls, and basketballs still lined the walls of the room. If he inhaled real hard, RJ could swear he smelled the essence of baby lotion and soiled diapers in the room.

"There's my boy! How's my boy? Who's Daddy's boy?"

The sound of Day's laughter. His tiny squeals of delight as RJ gently tossed him into the air and held him tight.

In that instant, RJ hoped that the new owners would find the same joy in this room and that it would not end as abruptly as his had.

I am not a bad man. I am not a monster.

He heard his mother's voice. "See, RJ? I always told you niggas ain't shit."

I am not a bad man. I am not a monster.

RJ slammed the door shut behind him and leapt downstairs. The head mover waited at the bottom of the stairs for him, clipboard in hand.

"Ok, all I need you to do is go through this checklist to make sure we've gotten everything and then we'll be on our way."

"Great."

They walked from room to room, but when they got to the door of the nursery, RJ insisted that the door remain shut. He knew for certain there was nothing behind that door.

Finished, RJ watched the moving van take off. Then he closed the curtains and looked around once more. He opened his wallet to find his extra house key when he noticed the picture of Day. RJ smiled then, a pain-filled smile that hurt his jaws. RJ set the key on the counter next to the realtor's business cards and the house information sheet. He placed Day's picture next to the key. RJ did not look back when he shut the front door.

HONOR

Honor sat on the bus in handcuffs and shackles, headed for Fulton County. She had received the maximum sentence for her misdemeanor: one year in maximum security at the state-run psychiatric hospital. After that, she was to spend six months in a halfway house before undergoing further evaluations to see if she could fit back into normal society.

Only two other women rode with Honor. Both of them were blond, although Honor could tell that one was clearly a dye job. They seemed to be around Honor's age, in their mid- to late-thirties. Neither of them spoke. Then again, what was there to say to each other on a ride such as this? "Nice weather we're having, isn't it?" No, it wasn't that type of trip. Silence was better than opening up and releasing the skeletons in holed-up closets.

In her hands, Honor held the spiral-bound journal that Sasha had given her the day before she boarded the bus. On the cover was a bright yellow flower.

"I want you to write in it, every day if you can," Sasha said. "Write down what you're feeling. What you're doing. Your hopes. Your dreams. Whatever you want. Just keep writing. You'd be surprised at how much better you feel afterwards. It's like you're saying everything you wish you could say out loud to folks. But you can keep to yourself all those secrets you'd never share with anybody. At the House of Hope, every woman who comes in is given a journal and it's up to them whether they chose to share it with the group or not. I never shared mine. But I keep on writing. Try it, Honor, for me."

Honor said she would. Though, what did she have to write about? She had no hopes or dreams, no future goals. She simply existed.

Honor's thoughts drifted, once again, to the day before, when she had received the surprise of her life in a phone call from her mother.

"Honor, is that you? It's your mother."

"Yes, Mom, I'm here. I hear you."

"How are you? Are they treating you decent? Is there anything you need, that I should send you?"

"No, Mom, I have what I need and I'm doing as well as can be expected."

That is when she heard her mother begin to cry. Up until then, she had always thought of her mother as this impeccably dressed, emotionally void creature whose lipstick managed somehow to never smudge, even when she drank.

"Mom… Mom, don't cry. I'm alright."

"I'm so sorry I didn't listen to you when you told me about RJ. I was too scared my own damn self, so how could I help you? I should have let you come home and none of this would have ever happened."

"Mom, you can't blame yourself for my actions."

Her mother started to babble incoherently, something about not being strong and Daddy's affairs.

Then she said, "I was never the example that I could have been to you girls. I could have done better. If I had done better, left Vernon, you wouldn't be sitting up in jail right now and Netta wouldn't be gay."

"Netta's gay?"

"Never mind that. Just know I tried to do my best by you girls, but I was in denial. Know that I always wanted the best for my girls."

"I know you did, Mom."

"When you get out, you always have a home here, so don't even think about going anywhere else. Your father and I will send for you first thing. You hear me? First thing!"

"Thank you, Mom. I appreciate that."

"You're not crazy either. I don't care what folks are saying. You're my daughter and I know you. He pushed you to the brink, is all. My Lord, I should have been there. I should have…"

"Mom, I have to go now."

"Okay, promise you'll call me when you can. Promise me!"

"I will call you, Mom. I promise. Mom… I… love—"

With that, the phone went dead, but Honor said it anyway. " I love you, Mom."

Honor had not heard from RJ since the day he appeared in the visitors' room, and she didn't expect to hear from him. Whenever she thought of him, so many emotions came to the surface, the main two being anger and fear. She should have left RJ a long time ago, but Honor knew he would have found her if she had. He might have killed her. His love was a possessive one.

Even behind bars, Honor had awaken many a nights terrified that RJ was standing over her bed. Everything about him haunted her. Honestly, she didn't know if he'd try to find her again, if she ever got released. Maybe she was better off being a ward of the state. What right did she have to life, when she had allowed Day's to end? She stared out the window and watched the city stretch out into the distance. Nothing but farmland and trees lay ahead of her. If she stared long and hard enough, maybe somewhere out there beyond the trees she'd be able to find that mother's love and instinct she had never known or been able to give. Maybe, in the distance, her suffering would end.

It was then that Honor felt something slight touch her shoulder, a tap that sent shivers through her body. But she was not afraid. The touch was a comforting one and she leaned in closer to the warm sensation. Honor looked up into the clouds and smiled. A touch this sweet could only come from heaven.

SASHA

Three customers were left in World Boutique, although it was five minutes past closing time. Sasha cursed under her breath and hurried to flip the "CLOSED" sign so that no other snobbish Midtown women could come in and demand special treatment because privilege was their constant state of mind.

Sasha was beyond tired. The last few weeks had zapped her energy, and even though Ms. Caswell had insisted Sasha take some time off, she had refused. Now, though, Sasha wished she'd reconsidered her offer. Between work, Honor's trial, NA meetings, and her volunteer time at the House of Hope, Sasha was having a hard time keeping it all together. The slightest decision or inconvenience seemed to overwhelm her at times. *Why couldn't I have just stuck to being a crack head? I was good at that.*

Ms. Caswell was talking about promoting Sasha to an assistant manager trainee, a position that would come with more money and medical benefits, but more headaches too.

Sasha needed a cigarette bad, and the fact that these uppity heifers were still in the shop trying on clothes and going through racks was driving her to the absolute brink.

"Can I help you ladies with anything?"

"Tell me, how much is this?"

One of the ladies held up a fuscia-colored halter dress. Sasha walked closer.

"Exactly what it says on the tag, ma'am. Two hundred and thirty-six dollars."

"Well, wouldn't it be reduced? I got it from the thirty-percent off rack."

"No, ma'am, all sale items are clearly marked with a red tag, and that dress is not marked."

"I'm not paying full price for that dress. I've been a customer here for years and I swear the prices keep going up each time I walk into this store."

Sasha held her tongue. "I'm sorry you feel that way, ma'am."

One of the other women appeared from the dressing room, totally topless. "Tell me, does this dress come in a size six? They must be sized differently because I always, always wear a size four."

Or maybe your old ass is just getting bigger. "Let me check on that for you."

The ladies left the shop armed with their shopping bags no less than thirty minutes later, and Sasha began the task of closing up and cleaning the shop for the morning saleslady. After the money was counted and placed carefully in the safe, she dusted, vacuumed, and straightened the racks and display cases. Then she turned on the alarm and began to walk the few blocks to her apartment. *My own apartment!* A slow beam spread across her face. Never in her life would she have imagined a place just for her, with no loud noises or partying or drug binges that could last for days. It was hers and hers alone. Well, in truth, the apartment in the middle of the converted three-story house was Ms. Caswell's. She had bought it and only rented it out to former residents of House of Hope until they were able to get something a little more substantial, if they wanted. The newly remodeled apartment came furnished, even down to the forks and knives, and she kept the rent at five hundred dollars a month, which was a lot cheaper than even the worst dump in Midtown.

Sasha was proud to call her new place home. The trees rustled in the night air as Sasha continued along the sidewalk. Although she had never been to the ocean before, she imagined that the sound of the trees was much like the waves whipping against the shore. Sasha shut her eyes for a minute, wanting to become closer to the sounds, wanting to listen as God spoke to her.

She climbed the stairs to the porch and turned the key. Immediately, she noticed the front door to her apartment was open slightly. She stepped inside and flicked the light switch. Vance was sitting on her couch, watching a crime drama on the television, a bag of corn chips in his hand, his dusty tennis shoes on top of her coffee table. Sasha closed the door behind her.

"Hey there, stranger."

"What are you doing here?" Sasha asked.

"Well, that's a dumb ass question. I came to see my baby."

"How did you find me, Vance?"

"That's it? That's all I get after you just up and left me? Where's my hug, woman? Where's the love?"

Sasha had to admit, Vance did look good sitting there in South Pole gear. His hair perfectly faded. His body clean and smelling like a man. Seeing him there, like this, took her back to her teenage years, when he was her world. She wondered if he was doping still and, if not, where he'd gotten the money to appear clean.

"By the way, I saw all your little toys in the nightstand. Cute, but you won't be needing them anymore. I'm back home now."

"Vance, how did you find out where I live?"

"Don't worry about it, girl. Vance has ways. You my woman; I'm always gonna find you. Got yourself all dolled up now, looking good. Looking real good. Teeth all nice. Hair lookin' fly. Ummm…ummm…sexy. My sexy woman. Come on over here and lay one on me. I know you missed me. Yes, sir," Vance laughed. "Daddy's home."

"Vance, this is not…"

"And I know you really missed this." From his pants pocket, Vance pulled a plastic bag filled with tiny white rocks. "Yes, sir, got these for my baby. I knew you'd be feening for some about now. It don't take long, does it?" He laughed again. He held the bag up in mid-air. Sasha watched as it swung back and forth beneath his grip. The rocks began to call to her. *Sasha. Sasha. Sasha. You know you want us. You know you do! We're right here in front of you. Take a hit! Just one last time. One time ain't gone hurt a thing. Come to us!*

"Look at your slobbering over them already. I got you, baby. I know what you need. I know what you want before you even ask. Now come on so we can get this party started right!"

"Hold up a minute. Let me go in the bedroom and change out these work clothes," Sasha said.

Vance began to set up shop and Sasha hurried into her bedroom and closed the door behind her. She paced the floor and wrung her hands tightly together, knowing that now would be as good as time as any to call her NA sponsor. But what harm would one hit honestly do? *I can just get one little taste, that's all. One taste.* Vance must have lit up because Sasha could smell the familiar smoke coming from underneath the door. And just like that, it didn't smell so good to her anymore.

"Baby! Baby! What's taking you so long? Bring your fine ass on out here to Daddy. Let Daddy spank it for you, cause you know you've been a bad girl. But I'ma let all that slide. You know why? Cause you my baby. All we got is each other. That's all we've ever had. What the…"

Sasha opened the door, a loaded shotgun in her hand aimed directly at Vance's head.

"Bitch, have you lost your damn mind?!" Vance jumped up from his spot on the plaid couch. Corn chips and tiny white rocks flew everywhere.

"Vance, I'm only going to say this once. I'ma need you to get your shit and get the hell up out my house, lock the door behind you, and don't even think about coming back."

"Bitch, you think I'm scared of you? You ain't gone shoot me. Bitch, you don't even know how to use no real gun, let alone a rifle. What, you think you got some balls now? Gone point a gun at me! Who the hell you think you are?"

"I'ma count to ten and you better get your crack head ass out my house, and take your shit too. Do you know what it took for me to get clean? The shit I done been through to get here, and you think I'm just gonna let your ass come in here and fuck it all up in one day? You the one done lost your damn mind. All the shit… Shit, the hell you put me through. Selling me to other dudes. I was sixteen, motherfucka! You did that shit to me! You did! Now get out!"

"Wait, now baby, just listen…"

"One. Two. Three. Four."

"Bitch, you ain't gone shoot me. Who you foolin', huh?" Vance said, as he picked up his wares and headed toward the door.

Sasha released the safety and aimed. *Click. Click.*

"You wanna try me? Or did you forget? I am my mother's daughter."

RESOURCES

The National Domestic Violence Hotline:
1-800-799-SAFE (7233)

National Online Resource Center on Violence Against Women:
www.VAWnet.org

Women of Color Network:
http://womenofcolornetwork.org/

National Coalition Against Domestic Violence:
http://www.ncadv.org/

National Network to End Domestic Violence:
http://www.nnedv.org/

ACKNOWLEDGMENTS

This book is a product of my tears, the outpouring of joy that I feel in my heart each day, and the gratitude that I have for those who have shared in this journey called life with me. First and foremost, I thank God, my divine source of inspiration and creativity. Where would I be without you? To my children, Danielle and Christopher, who suffered through many "sandwich" nights while Mama wasn't around to prepare dinner: I thank you for your patience. To my editor, Mallory Ragon: thank you for lending your hand to this effort. I truly appreciate all of your hard work. To Bonnye Brown: there are not enough ways and words to thank you. You're an incredible artist and you inspire me. To my parents, Vicki and Carlous Abner: your support is worth more than a million dollars in the bank. To Sharif Wilson: man, you know you bad. The moon is your only option. Lastly, to every woman or man who is suffering, or has suffered, from the words or fists of others—this book is for you. This is not your last chapter.